Praise for
THE GHOSTS OF
TUPELO LANDING

★ "This sequel shines thanks to
Turnage's deft, lyrical language."
—*Kirkus Reviews*, starred review

★ "The perspicacious Mo LoBeau is at it again!
Humor and action abound."
—*School Library Journal*, starred review

★ "Turnage's ability to create convincing characters and
her colorful use of language combine to make this a
fresh, droll, rewarding trip to Tupelo Landing."
—*Booklist*, starred review

★ "The budding detective has clearly taken to heart
something her foster mother always emphasizes:
'All the world's a stage, sugar, so hop on up there.'"
—*Publishers Weekly*, starred review

★ "We certainly hope there is more to come
from the Desperado Detectives."
— *BCCB*, starred review

A Junior Library Guild Selection
A SIBA Okra Pick for best Southern-flavored literature
A *Bookpage* Most Anticipated Children's and Teen Book of 2014

"A good detective starts with the obvious and works toward the strange."

"You're making that up," he whispered.

"It could still be true," I said. "Somebody's messing with us," I added, walking to the bottom of the stairs: two solid stairs, three missing steps, eight solid stairs. "Hello?" The dust on the stairs lay thick and untouched.

Someone skipped along the upstairs hall. "That's a definite girl," Dale whispered. "A boy would rather die than skip like that." He whipped around to stare at me, his blue eyes wide. "Did I say die? That's just a figure of speech. I didn't mean anything."

A laugh floated down the stairs.

"Run," Dale said.

I grabbed his arm, spinning him in a circle. "Hold your ground. If we run, it will be all over school. It's probably Attila, trying to show us up."

"I don't think so," he said, pointing to the open door. Outside, Attila sailed across the inn's lawn, making a beeline for the auction tent.

Another laugh floated down the stairs. Queen Elizabeth threw back her head and howled wild as a wolf in moonlight. I looked down at Queen Elizabeth. She looked up at me.

We both looked at the open door.

Dale was halfway across the yard, elbows and knees pumping like the devil's hounds were nipping at his heels.

OTHER BOOKS YOU MAY ENJOY

The Ghosts of Tupelo Landing

by Sheila Turnage

PUFFIN BOOKS
An Imprint of Penguin Group (USA)

PUFFIN BOOKS
Published by the Penguin Group
Penguin Group (USA) LLC
375 Hudson Street
New York, New York 10014

USA • Canada • UK • Ireland • Australia
New Zealand • India • South Africa • China

penguin.com
A Penguin Random House Company

First published in the United States of America by Kathy Dawson Books,
an imprint of Penguin Group (LLC), 2014
Published by Puffin Books, an imprint of Penguin Young Readers Group, 2015

THE LIBRARY OF CONGRESS HAS CATALOGED THE KATHY DAWSON BOOKS EDITION AS FOLLOWS:
Turnage, Sheila.
The ghosts of Tupelo Landing / by Sheila Turnage.
p. cm.
Summary: "When Miss Lana accidentally buys a haunted inn at the Tupelo Landing
town auction, Desperado Detectives—aka Mo LoBeau and her best friend Dale—opens
up a paranormal division to solve the ghost's identity before the town's big 250th
anniversary bash" —Provided by publisher.
ISBN 978-0-8037-3671-9 (hardcover)
[1. Mystery and detective stories. 2. Hotels—Fiction. 3. Haunted places—Fiction.
4. Ghosts—Fiction. 5. Community life—North Carolina—Fiction.
6. Identity—Fiction. 7. Foundlings—Fiction. 8. North Carolina—Fiction.]
I. Title.
PZ7.T8488Gho 2014
[Fic]—dc23 2013019376

Puffin Books ISBN 978-0-14-242571-8

Printed in the United States of America

Designed by Jasmin Rubero

1 3 5 7 9 10 8 6 4 2

For Rodney

Contents

Main entry

driveway

cemetery

the inn

meadow

Red's
house

springhouse

store

Judas
Trail

footpath

Fool's
Bridge

dance
pavilion

Tupelo Landing

Chapter 1
A Master of Disguise

Desperado Detective Agency's second big case snuck up on Dale and me at the end of summer, dressed in the happy-go-lucky colors and excitement of an auction.

"Mystery is a master of disguise," Miss Lana always says, and this one proved her point. It pitched a red-and-white striped tent in a meadow by the ancient Tupelo Inn, on the edge of town, and plastered the countryside with notices of its arrival:

AUCTION, WEDNESDAY AUGUST 24—
THE OLD TUPELO INN!!
1880 inn & medicinal springs
Closed October 22, 1938
READ ALL FINE PRINT
Buddha Jackson, Auctioneer

The mystery Dale and I came face-to-face with there would wake up ghosts and shake up history.

Not that I—Miss Moses LoBeau, rising sixth grader and cofounder of Desperado Detective Agency—was thinking Mystery that Wednesday morning as I shoveled crushed ice into the café's water glasses. I scanned the breakfast crowd and the 7UP clock on the wall. 6:45 a.m.

Where on earth was Dale? He should have been here a half hour ago.

Dale Earnhardt Johnson III, my best friend and co-sleuth, lives just outside town. Ever since his daddy went back to jail, he's been sleeping ragged and long. So has his dog, Queen Elizabeth II.

"Order up!" the Colonel called over the café hubbub.

"Got it," Miss Lana cried, spinning past in her pale yellow 1950s sundress and glossy Ava Gardner wig. Miss Lana, a former rising star of the Charleston community theater, adores Old Hollywood and has the wigs to prove it. "Tuck your shirttail in, sugar," she murmured to me. "With the auction crowd blasting toward us, we'll be standing room only within the hour. We want to look our best center stage." She whirled away, her white sandals whispering against the tiles.

Miss Lana and the Colonel are my family of choice and I am theirs. We operate the café together. They like me to look good in a crowd.

I tucked in my shirt and grabbed some silverware for my friend Sally Amanda Jones, a fellow rising sixth grader. Salamander pushed her red Piggly Wiggly sunglasses up on top of her head. Sal's daddy stocks shelves at the Pig and her mama sews. They aren't money, but there's not a sharper dresser in Tupelo Landing. "Pancakes, please. And . . . is Dale here?" she asked, her gray eyes hopeful as she peered toward the kitchen.

Sal loves Dale like midnight loves stars. So far, he hasn't noticed.

I broke the news easy: "Dale's in pre-arrival mode, but I'll check his ETA for you," I told her, and sped away.

"Batter Up on table four," I called as I passed the kitchen door.

The Colonel peeked out at me. He keeps his gray hair military short, but his brown eyes glow warm and friendly.

"Pancakes, sir," I explained. "New code."

He winked and the door swished shut behind him.

I grabbed the café phone and dialed. Dale picked up on the third ring. "H'llo," he mumbled. "Why is it?"

Why is it?

Unlike me, Dale doesn't wake up good. "Because," I replied. "They're auctioning the Tupelo Inn today and if you don't get over here, you'll miss our ride."

"Mo," he replied, and hung up. Dale's not an inline thinker.

I gave Sal a thumbs-up as a white minivan wheeled into our gravel parking lot. The Azalea Women, aka the Uptown Garden Club, tumbled out and scattered like pigeons. They chatted their way to the café door, and threaded through the crowd.

"I'll be glad to see that old inn go," one said as they bumped two red Formica tables together near the juke-box.

"I hear murder closed it down," another added.

The café went quiet.

Murder?

Grandmother Miss Lacy Thornton, who sat at the counter serenely nibbling her toast, whipped around to stare at the Azalea Women. The toes of her navy pumps just grazed the floor. Grandmother Miss Lacy's short, like me. We aren't related by blood; she took me as her honorary granddaughter in first grade. She's the oldest *nice* person in Tupelo Landing. Also the richest.

"Rumor-mongering," she murmured. "How sad."

"Yes ma'am, it's tragic," I said, and waved at the Azalea Women. "Have a seat. I'll be right with you," I called, slipping a clue pad into my pocket.

Few people know it, but waitressing is like deep cover—with tips.

I ferried a tray of ice water to their table. "Did you mention a murder?" I asked, dealing the glasses around. "Because Desperado Detective Agency is now accepting new clients. Misdemeanors and felonies are our pleasure. Murder's our specialty. How may we help?"

It was borderline true.

Dale and me opened Desperado Detective Agency at the beginning of the summer and solved our first murder in June. Since then we'd had just two cases, both of a Lost Pet nature. First Hannah Greene's dog Mort, who we found running with a bad crowd at the trailer park. Then Sal's goldfish Big Frank, who'd gone dust-to-dust behind Sal's aquarium. Dale broke the news: "It looks like suicide," he'd told her, his voice grim.

A second high-profile murder would be good for business.

The Azalea Women looked away from Grandmother Miss Lacy's icy stare and studied their silverware.

I tried a different tack. "Today's low-carb iced beverage comes to you compliments of me," I said. I draped a paper napkin over my arm. "My name is Mo LoBeau, with the accent on the end. I'll be taking care of you ladies today."

"You don't need to introduce yourself, Mo," one of them said. "We've known you since the day you washed into town."

"True," I replied. "But I like to keep things professional to encourage tips—which, by the way, I'm saving for college. A possible orphan has to plan ahead. Today," I continued, "we got a breakfast menagerie, which is French for sausage and egg casserole with cheese. This comes with hot biscuits au molasses for five dollars. For anyone trying to skinny down, I can substitute you a wheat toast with sugar free. What can I start you with?"

"Coffee and skinny," they chorused.

"An excellent choice. And your murder selection?"

This time the lead Azalea Woman stared straight at Grandmother Miss Lacy. "I won't go into details," she sniffed, "but I hear Red Baker's involved."

Crud. Another Red Baker rumor. Grandmother Miss Lacy shook her head.

"Believe you me," the Azalea Woman continued, her voice going stiletto, "whatever happened out at that old inn—if anything did—is Red Baker's fault. Or his people's before him."

I slapped my clue pad closed. A total dead end.

Red Baker, who lives outside town, mostly keeps to himself. The Colonel says he's second generation moonshine and 100 percent trouble. Mr. Red, who visits the café once in a blue moon, has never been mean to me. But it's a town rule that if anything goes wrong, he's behind it. Him or else Dale's daddy, Mr. Macon, if he's out on bail—which, at the moment, he ain't.

"Mark my words," the Azalea Woman said, her eyeglasses swinging on their chain, "Red Baker's people have always been bad news. And the apple doesn't fall far from the tree."

"Mine did," I reminded her. "I been searching for my family tree since the day I was born. All I know so far is it's somewhere Upstream." I headed for the kitchen. "I'll get your order in right away."

Minutes later, the café was hopping. "Let's chill things down, sugar," Miss Lana said, sashaying toward the air conditioner. Miss Lana's built tall and slender. I'm built more like a roller derby queen, but that could change at any minute.

Puberty happens.

While Miss Lana cranked the temp down, I turned the overhead fan to a quicker swipe. The auction notice on the bulletin board fluttered in the breeze. "Miss Lana," I said, "are we catering the auction? Because tips should be good once everybody gets whipped into a mindless frenzy, which the Colonel says is inevitable."

She smiled. Her Hollywood-style makeup gave her eyes a smoky, mysterious look. "Catering is a lovely idea. But no, you and I will travel incognito as part of the general public today. We'll leave after the breakfast rush," she added. "Miss Thornton's offered us a ride."

Miss Lana doesn't drive as a public courtesy.

"Batter Up," the Colonel barked, coming in from the kitchen. I grabbed Sal's pancakes as the café door swung open.

"Greetings, fellow citizens," Mayor Little sang, letting the door bang shut behind him. He smoothed his ice-blue tie over his round belly and took in Miss Lana's dark wig, sundress, and white sandals. "Ava Gardner, 1958," he guessed. He cocked his head. "Oh my, and Frank Sinatra on the jukebox. How romantic."

His tasseled loafers tick-tick-ticked across the tile floor. "Beautiful day for an auction," he said, slipping onto his regular stool. "Buddha gave me the VIP tour yesterday. The entire property is deliciously dilapidated, thoroughly antiquish. Nothing's changed since the day the inn closed. You can't put a price on that kind of charm, my friends. Not until the bidding starts, anyway," he added. He winked at the Azalea Women, who ignored him.

The Colonel splashed coffee in the mayor's cup. "What idiot would buy that dump?" the Colonel growled.

"Not me," Tinks Williams said, slapping his John Deere cap against his leg as he strolled in. "Roof leaks like a sieve last I heard."

The mayor tucked his napkin in his collar. "I'm picturing condos, golf courses . . . My friends, Fate smiles on Tupelo Landing today."

The Colonel snorted, did a quick about-face, and marched into the kitchen.

"Was it something I said?" Mayor Little asked, his neat eyebrows drifting up.

"Not exactly," I said, stepping onto the Pepsi crate I keep behind the counter for extra height. "It's just that the Colonel says Fate is bipolar and ought to be on medications. May I take your order?"

"The special," he said as Dale rocketed into view on his faded red bike, his mongrel dog Queen Elizabeth II loping behind. He performed a flying dismount at the edge of the parking lot and slung his bike into a patch of shade.

"Hey," he said, blasting through the door. His sandals squeaked to a halt and he ran his fingers through his blond hair. The men in Dale's family have scandalous good hair.

Sal knocked her pancake syrup over.

"Morning, Dale," Mayor Little said. "Solved any murders today?"

"No, sir," he replied, waving at Sal and me. "But it's early."

Like I say, Dale and me solved Mr. Jesse's murder at the beginning of the summer. We went famous for about a week until the gravity of habit pulled our lives back into regular orbit. Small towns have rules. One is, you got to stay who you are no matter how many murders you solve. That's why I'm back to being regular Mo LoBeau—the girl Luck washed into town the day she was born. And why Dale's back to being just plain Dale, the son of level-headed Miss Rose and the recently incarcerated Macon Johnson.

"Specials, you two?" Miss Lana offered, swishing by.

Dale vaulted onto a stool. Dale is athletic. I ain't. "Thanks, Miss Lana," he said. "Mama says will you please put it on her tab." Miss Lana smiled and slid us a basket of biscuits. Her and Miss Rose are best friends. There ain't no tab between them.

Fifteen minutes later, the café was standing room only—just as Miss Lana had predicted. Dale and me, who'd barely had time to brush the crumbs off our chins, flew around the café, carrying waters and taking orders. Miss Lana floated between phone, customers, and cash register, graceful as a dandelion seed on the wind.

I'd just cleared a table when Priscilla Retzyl, my teacher, swept in. A coffee cup shattered on the other side of the café. "No! My new shorts!" Dale cried. Even a whisper of teacher rattles him. Dale grabbed one of Miss Lana's aprons, and hustled to take another order.

As I turned, Anna Celeste Simpson—blond hair, brown eyes, perfect smile—stiff-armed me to grab a window table.

I am to Anna Celeste as Sherlock Holmes is to Moriarty: Enemies for life.

"Hey, *Attila*," I said.

"Mo-*ron*," she murmured. "Mother and I will have the Garden Omelets and tomato juice. Good morning, Miss Retzyl," she simpered, cutting her eyes toward our teacher. "I can't *wait* for school to start tomorrow."

School. Tomorrow.

The words thudded into my heart like dull wooden stakes.

"Make our omelets to go," Attila's sour-faced mother said, skinnying into the chair across from Attila. "I'm eager to scout the inn's antiques." She squinted at Attila. "Elbows, dear."

Attila took her elbows off the table.

I sighed. Take-out mostly means no tips. For me, tips matter. I currently got $7.26 to my name, plus a Canada dime somebody dumped in the tip jar.

"You look tired, Mo," Attila said, smiling to flaunt new braces. "Did your family vacation this summer? Mother and I loved Montreal."

Montreal? In *Canada?* I reached in my pocket, to my Canada dime.

I hate Anna Celeste Simpson.

"You want me to put an Official Rush on this order?

It only costs a dollar more per plate and that includes your tip," I offered.

"No," Attila said, flouncing her hair.

I scribbled her order: *2 Gardens. Take your time.*

As I worked my way back to the counter, Dale stuffed a biscuit in his apron pocket and headed for Queen Elizabeth II, who lay snuffling beneath a shrub. Queen Elizabeth's allergic to Miss Lana's rosemary plant. Also the big-haired twins.

I slid a special to Mayor Little, who smiled at Grandmother Miss Lacy. "Miss Thornton, do you remember the old inn's medicinal springs?"

"The springs? Goodness yes," Grandmother Miss Lacy said. "Those springs cured hundreds of people. Not everyone who came, of course. Which reminds me: Will the old cemetery be auctioned with the inn?"

The hair on the back of my neck stood up. *The old cemetery?*

The café clattered to silence.

"*Cemetery* is such an unwelcoming word," the mayor chided. "I prefer to think of it as a gated community for the dearly departed. Landscaping, ironwork, statuary . . ."

The screech of tires on pavement gobbled up the rest of his words.

The café whipped toward the window as a bright red

sports car skidded across the parking lot, spewing an arc of sand.

"Hey," Dale shouted, stepping in front of Queen Elizabeth. "Watch it!"

The car doors flew open. A dark-haired man and a blond woman jumped out, the woman shouting and the man jabbing his finger toward her face.

"Oh my," Miss Lana murmured as a boy—a younger, thinner version of the man—unfolded himself from the car. He wiped his palms on his shiny black slacks, looked from the man to the woman, and then at Dale.

Dale's flowered apron fluttered in the breeze.

The boy grabbed the man's arm and pointed. The trio turned to Dale like a pack of jackals. Dale's hand twitched toward the apron, but I knew he'd die before he took it off now. The man's laugh cracked like a whip.

Bullies.

My temper sprang straight to my mouth. "Hey you," I yelled, charging into the sunshine. "Crawl back in that clown car and get out of here."

Dale gasped.

"Not real clowns," I whispered. Dale has a terror of clowns. Also of ghosts.

The café door opened behind me, and the Colonel's hand fell gently on my shoulder. The man studied the Colonel and whispered in the woman's ear. The couple jumped in the car and fishtailed across the parking lot.

"Wait!" the boy shouted. He chased the car for a few awkward steps. "Stop!" His arms fell to his sides as the car disappeared around the curve.

"Despicable," the Colonel muttered. "Never leave a comrade on the battlefield, Soldier."

"No sir," I said. "I won't."

"Me either," Dale said.

The Colonel glanced at Dale. "You're out of uniform, son."

Dale ripped the apron off and held it behind his back. "New shorts," he explained. That's what Dale bought with his summer job money: school clothes. That and a pawnshop guitar. Dale is musical. I ain't.

The boy from the car turned and walked toward us, barely whistling.

From a distance, I didn't like him. Up close, I liked him less. Black hair, thin face, mole under his left eye. Scuffed black shoes, cheap clothes put together to look like money. He walked up lanky as a coyote, his thin shoulders sloping a modicum to the left.

"At ease, you two," the Colonel said as the boy scuffled to a halt.

The boy's eyes drifted from the Colonel, to me, to Dale. "Crenshaw," he said, trying to make his voice low. "Harm Crenshaw." Like he was Bond, James Bond.

Give me a break.

"The Third," Dale replied. "Dale Earnhardt Johnson the Third. And this is LoBeau, Mo LoBeau. And . . ."

"The Colonel," I said before Dale could get tangled up.

Crenshaw, Harm Crenshaw nodded, not quite meeting our eyes. "I need a ride to the auction," he said, shoving his hands deep in his pockets. "Anybody going that way?"

Chapter 2
Crenshaw, Harm Crenshaw

An hour later Dale and me settled in the backseat of Grandmother Miss Lacy's old Buick. "I don't see why *he* has to ride with us," Dale said, watching Harm Crenshaw swagger across the parking lot.

"Grandmother Miss Lacy's generous about giving rides," I said. "It cuts both ways." The dark-haired boy opened Dale's door and peered in. "Queen Elizabeth gets queasy without a window seat," I told him. "You sit in the middle."

Harm Crenshaw crawled over Queen Elizabeth and Dale and collapsed into the space between us, reeking of cheap aftershave. I rolled my window down. "You aren't old enough to shave," I said. He stared straight ahead, his knobby knees nearly bumping his chin.

Grandmother Miss Lacy slipped behind the wheel and adjusted the rearview mirror. "You look familiar, Harm," she said as Miss Lana clambered into the front seat with her white parasol. "Have we met?"

"Nope. I'm here for the auction and then back to Greensboro fast as I can go."

"Don't 'nope' her," Dale said, pulling Queen Elizabeth into his lap. "It ain't polite."

Harm shifted, his pants legs rising to reveal pale, bony ankles and no socks. "Somebody told me the inn they're selling is haunted," he said. "It's got to be a lie. Who'd want to spend eternity *here?*"

I glared at him, but Dale gulped. "Haunted?"

"Don't be ridiculous," Grandmother Miss Lacy said. "I've lived here eighty years. If there were a ghost story connected to that inn, I assure you I'd know it."

We rode in silence past the Piggly Wiggly, past the old brick school, to the sign at town's edge: Tupelo Landing, population 148. Someone had scrawled a 7 over the 8. Harm Crenshaw raised an eyebrow. "Murder," I explained. "Dale and me solved it."

"Sure you did," he muttered.

"Press kit," Dale whispered.

I reached into my olive drab messenger bag and rummaged through the clue pads and hand-lettered business cards for our laminated newspaper clip. I passed it to him.

LOCAL KIDS HELP SOLVE MURDER

Miss Mo LoBeau and Dale Earnhardt Johnson III, rising sixth graders, have helped solve a murder, authorities say. In the process they also helped put Dale's father behind bars and jump-started the memory of Mo's guardian, the Colonel—a café owner who's had total amnesia for over a decade.

"To make a long story short, I remembered I'm an attorney and that I used to be engaged to Lana," the Colonel told this reporter. "Realizing I'm an attorney has been a blow, but Mo and Dale did a great job with their first case and I'm proud of them. Now order something or get out."

Mo and Dale, who founded Desperado Detective Agency in June, are accepting new cases. Call the café for details.

Harm Crenshaw handed it back without a word. *Jerk.*

"What are you buying today, Miss Lana?" I asked, to break the silence.

"An umbrella stand," she said. "A bit of Tupelo history."

"Boring," Harm Crenshaw said beneath his breath.

I elbowed him—hard.

"And I'm only here for the excitement," Grandmother Miss Lacy said.

We crept across Fool's Bridge, past the old store with its ancient bubble-headed gas pumps, through acres of spent tobacco and drying corn. "Here's my old short-cut," Grandmother Miss Lacy said, easing the Buick onto a faint path. "Father used to come this way in the Duesenberg."

Dale jumped like Queen Elizabeth spotting a squirrel. "A *Duesenberg*?" He looked over at me. "Duesenbergs were super-expensive roadsters made in Germany," he said. Dale's people know cars.

"Made in Indiana, actually," Harm said as we bounced into a clearing. "Jeez," he gasped before Dale could reply. "Who lives *there*?"

The unpainted farm house listed on brick piers like a squared-off old woman rising on a bad knee. Queen Elizabeth jumped up, her tail wagging as she peered at a pack of bone-thin beagles in a rickety pen. "I believe that's Red Baker's place," Miss Lana said as the Buick eased forward. "Why?"

Harm shouldered Queen Elizabeth aside to stare out the window. "*Whose* place? Does he even have electricity?" Good question. There wasn't an electric line in sight.

"Red Baker," I said. "The moonshiner. The Azalea Women say—"

"Mo LoBeau," Grandmother Miss Lacy said, "I will not have you spreading rumors." She slammed on brakes, sending Queen Elizabeth tumbling to the floor, and whipped around to stare at Harm. "Do you know Red Baker, young man?"

"Me? How would I know somebody like that?" The wind shifted and he grimaced. "Doesn't he ever clean out that dog pen? It stinks."

She gave him an inscrutable old-person stare as Dale hoisted a kicking Queen Elizabeth back in his lap. "Will wonders never cease," she murmured to Miss Lana, and turned back to her driving.

"Old people," Dale whispered. "Go figure."

Miss Lacy eased the Buick through Red Baker's dirt yard, into a grassy meadow of cars and trucks. Dale pointed to a red sports car as we tumbled from the Buick. "Over there," he said.

Harm stalked off without even a good-bye.

This time I said it out loud: "Jerk."

I did my Upstream Mother scan of the crowd—a check for possible relatives.

"See anybody that looks like you?" Dale asked.

I squinted. The grounds swarmed with strangers and townsfolk. The Azalea Women trooped toward the red-and-white auction tent. Sal, in her red sunglasses, sailed behind them. Miss Retzyl sat beneath the tent while Attila, who'd perched beside her, was chatting her so-called heart out.

I shook my head. "But there's Lavender!" I cried, and my morning went golden.

Dale's big brother, Lavender, stood in the shade of a maple, his tanned arms crossed, talking to one of the big-haired twins—either Crissy or Missy, I couldn't tell which. Have I mentioned I will one day marry Lavender? Lavender, who's nineteen, laughs whenever I ask him—which is not the same as saying no.

"Lavender," I bellowed, rocking up on my toes and waving. A grin split his face as I sprinted toward him. "Hey," I said, skidding to a sophisticated halt. "I see you run aground on a twin."

"Crissy," he said, "you remember Mo LoBeau and my little brother Dale, don't you?"

"Sure, I remember," she said, sipping a Diet 7UP. "I met them at the Speedway the night you wrecked your racecar. Met him too." She nodded toward a nearby picnic table. "He was driving the car that spun you into the wall."

"*He* did that?" I said, zeroing in on the driver of the red sports car.

"Flick Crenshaw," Lavender said. "He drives the 45 car." Flick looked about Lavender's age. Beyond that, they were alike as yes and no.

Lavender has eyes blue as October's sky and hair like

just-mown wheat. He's wiry and tall, and flows like a lullaby. Dark-haired Flick Crenshaw looked coiled and compact, an explosion set to happen. Flick smirked at us, scooped the blond woman close, and whispered in her ear. She barked out a laugh.

"Ignore them," Lavender said. "Cars bump, Mo. It's part of racing."

"Almost killing somebody ain't."

He shrugged. "Flick's one of those guys you pass in life. You steer around him if you can. If you can't, you don't let him slow you down more than you have to."

"Right," I said, making a mental note to hate Flick for eternity.

Crissy narrowed her eyes. "Wonder what Flick's doing here," she said. "You think he's buying the inn?"

"Nah," Lavender said. "If he has money he's driving it or wearing it. But I hear Red Baker's interested. His property backs up against this one. And he has money."

"He got most of Daddy's," Dale said. "That's what Mama says."

"Let's go talk to people," Crissy said, like Dale and me weren't people. She slipped her hand into Lavender's, but he didn't budge. I followed his gaze to Harm, who elbowed through the crowd with three drinks. Flick grabbed two, handed one to the blond, and punched Harm's shoulder. Harm swiveled with the blow, hiding a wince.

"That's Flick's little brother," Lavender said, glancing at Dale. "I'd stay away from him if I was you. He'll be trouble soon as he figures out how." Dale nodded.

"I'd love to stay and chat with you, Crissy," I said, "but I and Dale are here on detective business. Come on, Dale," I said. "Let's check out the inn."

"Now?" Dale gulped. "After what Harm said about a ghost?"

Lavender gave him a wink. "Go on, little brother. There's no such thing as ghosts," he said as Crissy tugged him away from us.

"Bye, Lavender," I called. "Good luck with those head lice." Crissy dropped his hand. Lavender grinned at me and followed her into the crowd.

I peered at the tent where auctioneer Buddha Jackson warmed up the crowd. "Everybody got a number?" Buddha asked, whipping the microphone cord behind him like a rock star. "Bidding's easiest with a number. We'll auction a little furniture, then the inn with whatever's left inside."

"I only want an umbrella stand," Miss Lana shouted. She'd slipped into her 1960s sunglasses—the round ones with the white rims—and closed her parasol.

Buddha pointed at her. "Yes ma'am, Miss Lana. I'll be looking for you. Now let's talk about what conveys. That means what goes with the inn itself. Those of you bidding on the inn, listen up. I think you'll find this amusing." He continued as Miss Lana and Grandmother Miss Lacy Thornton meandered toward the refreshment wagon.

I turned to Dale. "As Tupelo Landing's most successful detectives, we really ought to scope out the inn. Investigating means bragging rights in sixth grade. And Lavender says it's safe," I reminded him.

To Dale, Lavender's word is gospel. He gave a faint nod.

"Race you," I said before he could change his mind. We sprinted for the wooded path leading to the inn, Queen Elizabeth at our heels.

"There it is," I said as the path opened onto a ragged lawn. The ancient two-story inn may have been a beauty in her day. But today, with her windows boarded up and her front porch sagging, she looked forlorn and helpless on her knee-deep carpet of weeds. The steps listed. Rust streaked the tin roof. Shaggy cedars crowded the drive.

"Okay, we've seen it," Dale said, stepping over a No Trespassing sign someone had pried from its post. "Let's go."

"Don't be a baby," I told him as a quick *pop-pop-pop* rolled from the thicket. My heart jumped. "Who's there?" I demanded.

The thicket rustled. A white-haired man with a sharp fox face peered between the branches. Queen Elizabeth growled, her hackles rising, and Dale grabbed her collar.

Red Baker stepped onto the path.

Most days, Mr. Red looks like a bundle of throw-away clothes. Today he wore shoes fresh from the box, creased chinos, a blinding white shirt, and a red bow tie. "Hey," I said, and his pale eyes flickered over me like lizard eyes over a fly.

Mr. Red looked Dale up and down. "You're Macon Johnson's boy," he said, his voice splintery as just-sawn pine. "I hear he's doing time in Raleigh for a murder he didn't commit."

"You almost heard right," Dale said, very smooth. Dale's family's jail prone. To him, jail time is as normal as clean socks. "Daddy's over in county lock-up on reduced charges. We're hoping for a plea bargain or a smart attorney."

That "we" would be Dale and Queen Elizabeth—not Dale's mama, Miss Rose, who hocked her diamond in June. Miss Rose ain't studying Dale's daddy. Neither am I. Not after the things he's done.

"You bidding today, Mr. Red?" I asked. "I hear you want to buy the inn."

"You're nosy," he said. He didn't say it mean; he said it straight out.

"Occupational hazard," I said. "Detective," I added, in case he hadn't heard. He cracked his knuckles. That explained the popping sound. Nervous joints.

He licked his thin lips. "You headed for the inn? There's nothing in there but run-down, wore out, and fell through. And it's haunted thicker than the devil's parlor. I'd turn around if I was you."

"Haunted? Thicker than the . . . the devil's parlor?" Dale stammered. "I didn't know he had one." He turned to me, his blue eyes worried. "Have you ever heard of that?" he whispered. "A parlor at . . . the bad place?" Dale is Baptist. He doesn't worry about much in life, but he worries about the devil afterwards.

Mr. Red stared at him. "You two best head for folks that make footprints." He peered up the path and cracked his knuckles again. "Who's that?"

A boy strolled around the bend, barely whistling.

"Harm Crenshaw," Dale said. "From Greensboro. You want to meet him? I've been working on my social skills. I can introduce you." He cupped his hands around his mouth. "Hey Harm, come meet Mr. Red Baker," he called.

Harm froze. He and Mr. Red stared at each other like wild animals. Harm spun and marched the other way as Mr. Red faded back into the forest.

"Weird," Dale murmured.

"True. But we got enough weird in our lives without worrying about theirs. Come on. We haven't got much time," I said, and plowed through the weeds to the inn's creaky steps. The wind blew, setting three splintery old rocking chairs rocking.

"And what did Mr. Red mean when he said we should head for folks that make footprints?" Dale asked as we crossed the front porch.

"He meant to scare you."

"Right," he said. "I'm pretty sure it worked."

I pushed the heavy front door and it moaned open, scraping an arc across the dusty floor. I followed Queen Elizabeth into the gloom, and waited for my eyes to adjust. A tin ceiling soared high above us. A snaggle-toothed mahogany staircase climbed along one cracked plaster wall. To our right, the huge dining room stood a-jumble in crippled tables and upturned chairs. Its chandelier wore a bride's veil of spiderwebs and dust.

Queen Elizabeth darted away, her nose zigzagging across a carpet worn so thin, I could see the plank skeleton underneath. "This way," I whispered, heading into a parlor of sheet-covered settees and chairs.

"Hey! A piano," Dale said, relaxing. Like I said, Dale's musical. He strained to open the keyboard. The hinges' rusty squeal echoed around the room. Dale spread his hands over the uneven, yellowed keys and the piano's tinny voice plinked through the dusty silence.

The front door banged against the wall behind us and we jumped.

"For heaven's sake," a woman said, "I don't care what that hideous old man says, that is *not* a ghost playing the piano." A pin-skinny woman minced into the room trailed by a pudgy man. She surveyed us like we came with the furniture. "See? Just kids."

I surveyed her right back: thin face, spiky black hair, jittery eyes. Sleeveless black sweater, skinny pants, black stilettos. She crossed her bone-thin arms and jutted her hip forward like a high-fashion wharf rat. "She ain't from around here," Dale whispered.

Dale has a flair for the obvious.

The woman squinted at the pressed tin ceiling, clacked to a window, and peered between the boards. "At least it's waterfront. I'll pay two hundred ten thousand. Not a penny more. Let's register," she told the pudgy man. "You kids stay away from that piano. It's mine," she added, and headed out the door.

"Rat Face," I muttered. I would have said more, but Miss Lana don't allow cursing. She does allow the creative use of animal names.

"*She's* buying this place? Because she'd be a terrible

neighbor," Dale said, looking nervous. "Unless she sings alto, which Mama says if you can sing alto, that means a lot to people." Dale's mama directs the church choir.

"Don't worry," I said, "she'd only buy this place to tear it down. But she *would* make a rotten neighbor. Miss Lana would hate her. Grandmother Miss Lacy would too."

Upstairs, glass crashed to the floor. Queen Elizabeth yelped and darted behind me. "Who's there?" I shouted, trying to rub the goose bumps off my arms. I caught a whiff of rosemary, and Queen Elizabeth sneezed.

A laugh floated down the stairway, secret and low. My heart jumped. So did Dale. "Steady, Dale," I said, my voice shaking. "Don't leap to conclusions. A good detective starts with the obvious and works toward the strange."

"You're making that up," he whispered.

"It could still be true," I said. "Somebody's messing with us," I added, walking to the bottom of the stairs: two solid stairs, three missing steps, eight solid stairs. "Hello?" The dust on the stairs lay thick and untouched.

Someone skipped along the upstairs hall. "That's a definite girl," Dale whispered. "A boy would rather die than skip like that." He whipped around to stare at me, his blue eyes wide. "Did I say die? That's just a figure of speech. I didn't mean anything."

A laugh floated down the stairs.

"Run," Dale said.

I grabbed his arm, spinning him in a circle. "Hold your ground. If we run, it will be all over school. It's probably Attila, trying to show us up."

"I don't think so," he said, pointing to the open door. Outside, Attila sailed across the inn's lawn, making a beeline for the auction tent.

Another laugh floated down the stairs. Queen Elizabeth threw back her head and howled wild as a wolf in moonlight. I looked down at Queen Elizabeth. She looked up at me.

We both looked at the open door.

Dale was halfway across the yard, elbows and knees pumping like the devil's hounds were nipping at his heels.

Chapter 3
Going, Going, Gone

Moments later Dale and I skidded into our seats beneath the auction tent. "I was *not* scared," Dale said again. "I just hate being late is all."

"Stop panting and look professional," I said, wincing at the catch in my side. Onstage, Buddha Jackson wiggled out of his shiny suit jacket and pointed to a battered desk and chair. "Lot number six," he shouted, and launched into a wild chant. "Who will give me two hundred dollars, two two two two, who will give me two hundred dollars?" Silence. "A hundred and fifty? One fifty one fifty one fifty?" We stared at him blank as stones. "All right, Tupelo Landing. Make me an offer."

"Twenty-five dollars," Attila's mother said. Attila sat beside her, calm as pond scum. It sure wasn't her in the inn. Then who?

"I have twenty-five, who will give me thirty? There," Buddha said, pointing to the Azalea Women. "I have thirty over here, who will give me fifty?" The flow of the chant, the pulse of the bid. The auction swept over me like a dizzy tide.

"Hey," Dale said, breaking the spell. "There's Thes." I looked across the crowd. Red-headed Thessalonians and his dad, Reverend Thompson, had miraculously found seats behind the Azalea Women. "Thes!" Dale hissed, waving. "Over here!"

"I got fifty dollars over here!" Buddha shouted, pointing at Dale.

"No!" Dale clamped his hands over his mouth and his blue eyes filled with tears. "I was just saying hey," he wailed between his fingers.

"Who will give me a hundred?" Buddha boomed.

"Please," Dale whispered. "Somebody bid. I'll sing in church every Sunday 'til Judgment Day." He grabbed my arm. "Mo," he said. "Bid."

I jerked my arm free.

"Going once," Buddha cried, pointing in our direction.

"Hide," I said, and threaded my way to the Azalea Women, who sat neat as a choir on the third row. "That's an out-of-towner bidding against you," I said. "She says keep your money for azaleas because yours are the tackiest she's ever seen." The Azalea Women gasped. Three hands shot into the air.

"A hundred in the third row!" Buddha crowed as I raced for the exit.

"Come on, Dale," I said, dragging him toward sunlight.

Dale had turned a throw-up shade of green. He leaned forward, putting his hands on his knees. "I ain't never going into an auction tent again, not even if somebody's life depends on it," he panted. "Well, maybe if Mama's life depended on it, I would," he said. "Or Lavender's." He looked up at me. "They're family. Of course, we're best friends. That's almost family."

"Take deep breaths," I told him.

I looked up. Harm Crenshaw slouched against a tree, a crooked smirk on his pale face. Of course. It must have been him in the inn. He had opportunity: We'd seen him on the path. And motive: He's a proven jerk.

"Dale, can you stand up?" I asked. "People are staring." Harm cradled his arms like he was rocking a baby, and kissed the air. "Come on, Dale," I said, glaring at Harm. "Let's get something to drink."

Two Pepsis later, Dale's color found his face. Buddha's voice wafted from the tent to the refreshment cart. "Sold to number 72—Miss Lana, you got your umbrella stand!"

Miss Lana exited the tent, lugging her trophy.

We ran to her as Rat Face scuttled by. "If you ask me, they should sell all this junk in one lot," Rat Face told Miss Lana. "But, when you go to a hick auction, this is what you get. Hicks."

Miss Lana's eyebrows rose unnaturally high on her forehead. Dale and me took a big step back.

"And what's that auctioneer's name?" Rat Face continued. "*Buddha* Jackson? Can you believe it?"

"If I'm not mistaken, Buddha's a family name," Miss Lana said in a voice shaved from ice. It was quasi-true. *Bubba* is a family name. Buddha's mama is dyslexic.

Rat Face narrowed her eyes. "Nice spot for condos, though. I'll wait," she said, and scurried away.

"Dreadful woman," Miss Lana said, watching her burrow back into the crowd. "Mo, would you and Dale put our umbrella stand in the Buick? Hurry, sugar. We have what we came for, but you don't want to miss the main event."

We made it back just in time. As we edged to the front of the tent, Dale took off his belt and handed it to me. "If I bid, strangle me," he whispered. "Mama will understand."

"Here we go," Buddha Jackson said, rubbing his hands together. "The inn with the furniture that's left, plus the medicinal springs, the pavilion, and all the fine print. Who will give me a half-million dollars?" Nobody breathed. "Four hundred thousand?" We sat still as tombstones. "Make me an offer," he said.

Mr. Red Baker scratched his sandpaper face. "Twenty thousand dollars," he rasped as Flick Crenshaw stepped up beside him.

"Forty thousand," Rat Face replied, studying her finger-nails.

"Who will give me fifty?" Buddha sang. Mr. Red cracked his knuckles and nodded. "Fifty thousand says Mr. Red," Buddha said. "Now who will give me—"

"Sixty," Rat Face said, her voice like a steel trap.

"Seventy."

"A hundred thousand."

The crowd murmured like pines in a breeze. "A hundred twenty," Mr. Red said.

"One hundred fifty thousand," Rat Face called.

"Mr. Baker?" Buddha said. "It's up to you." Mr. Red shook his head. "Going once," Buddha said, pointing to Rat Face. "Going twice."

"A hundred and sixty thousand dollars," a familiar voice sang out from the back of the tent. The crowd swiveled. A white parasol popped open.

"No!" I tore across the tent. "Miss Lana," I cried, grabbing her parasol and popping it closed. "We don't have that kind of money!"

"I will *not* have that horrible woman for a neighbor," she said.

"And we won't have her replacing our history with condos," Grandmother Miss Lacy said, seething.

"One hundred eighty thousand dollars," Rat Face said, crisp as a poisoned apple.

Dale lurched to a stop beside me. "Stop, Miss Lana. That inn's haunted sure as I'm breathing."

"Pish," she replied. She looked at Grandmother Miss Lacy, who nodded. "Don't worry, my dears, we'll re-sell the inn to somebody nice," she said. The worry melted from Dale's face, just like that. "Two hundred thousand dollars," Miss Lana cried.

Rat Face jumped up, her thin face twitching. "Two hundred ten."

"Miss Lana, that's her top bid," Dale said. "We heard her say so in the inn." He reached in his pocket. "I got a five. It's yours if you want it. And Mo has a life savings of seven dollars and twenty-six cents," he said. "Plus a Canada dime."

"My little hero," she said, patting his face.

"We bid twelve dollars and twenty-six cents more than she does," Miss Lana screeched, pointing at Rat Face. "Plus a Canada dime."

"Sold to number 72," Buddha Jackson shouted. "Miss Lana, you just bought yourself a historic inn—with a bona fide ghost in the fine print!"

Chapter 4
Ghost in the Fine Print

"What?" Miss Lana cried as the crowd burst into applause.

She bowed gracefully, twice, and then rushed Buddha's stage.

"Congrats, ladies," Buddha said, rolling a speaker to the edge of the stage as the crowd jostled away, talking and laughing. "You got a real bargain."

"Yes," she said, twirling her parasol. "But for a moment I thought you said we have an actual *ghost* in the fine print. Imagine!"

Buddha nodded toward a stack of papers. "That's right," he said, and her smile wilted. "The law says you got to list ghosts strong enough to affect the property value. Same as a leaky roof, which you also got. This place has changed hands several times over the years, and your ghost got listed along the way. As you may recall, I talked about the fine print—including the ghost—before we got started. Sign here."

Miss Lana shot a look at Rat Face, who now stood chatting with Flick Crenshaw. *"Strong enough to affect the property value?* But as soon as she's gone, we intend to re-sell the inn to someone *nice*."

"There's no such thing as ghosts," Grandmother Miss Lacy said firmly, handing Buddha her pen. "Here you are, dear. Just X that bit out."

"Sorry," he said, winding a cord. "I could lose my license."

Miss Lana snapped her parasol closed and slammed it against a speaker. A bad sign. "For heaven's sake," she said through clenched teeth, "who in her right mind would buy a ghost?"

I clamped my hand over Dale's mouth. "Rhetorical," I whispered. Dale's a sucker for rhetorical questions, especially Miss Lana's.

I slipped a clue pad from my pocket. "The name of the alleged ghost?"

Buddha shrugged. "Fine print doesn't say. Maybe you can figure it out." He nudged the papers toward Miss Lana. "No refunds."

I slapped my clue pad closed. "Dale and I will be in our mobile crime unit if you need us," I said, very professional. Dale's blue eyes flew open. "The Buick," I whispered. I marched into the crowd, chin up and eyes straight ahead the way the Colonel taught me.

Sal, in her red Piggly Wiggly sunglasses, waved at Dale. He gave her an absent smile as Attila ambushed us by her mama's Cadillac. "Interesting buy, Mo-ron," she said. "But I suppose a ghost friend would be nice for you. Someone like your long-lost mother—not quite here, not quite there."

"Leave my Upstream Mother out of this, Attila."

She looked across the crowd and did a double take. "Who's that?" she asked, her voice shifting gears.

I followed her gaze. Harm Crenshaw skulked by the refreshment wagon. "Anna," Attila's mother said, mincing up. "We don't mingle with the unsavory. Hurry, dear. You'll be late for Voice."

Attila's the only kid in rising sixth grade who takes Voice. It doesn't help her all that much. She hopped in the car, her eyes still on Harm Crenshaw. The Cadillac oozed through the crowd.

"Did she just call us unsavory?" Dale asked, his voice sharp. "Because that's rude." He lowered his voice. "What does it mean, exactly?"

"It means we reek. Look," I said. Flick Crenshaw had cornered Harm against a picnic table. As Flick talked, Harm's face went thunderous as an August storm. "Looks interesting," I said, darting through the crowd. We rocked to a halt behind a large, sweet-smelling woman in a flowered dress. I peeped around her sausage-like arm as Flick thumped his finger against Harm's chest.

"You'll do what I say," Flick growled.

"But *why?*" Harm demanded, his voice cracking. "It's not fair."

"Because I said so. Because I make the money. Because you're cramping my style."

"What style?" Harm muttered as Flick turned and pushed through the crowd. He climbed in his red sports car and roared away. Harm's eyes met mine and he blushed. "What are you gawking at, Ghost Girl?"

Ghost Girl. Great.

"Not much," I said, looking him up and down.

With that, I stalked through the crowd and climbed into the Buick. Dale helped Queen Elizabeth onto the seat between us as Miss Lana stormed up. She swung into the passenger's seat, breathing ragged as torn construction paper, and slammed the door. "As God is my witness, I never meant to buy a ghost," she said.

Grandmother Miss Lacy slipped behind the wheel. "We didn't buy a ghost, we bought an *inn,*" she corrected. "That ridiculous ghost story doesn't make a whit of difference except that we planned to re-sell the inn and now we possibly . . . can't."

Miss Lana adjusted her wig. "Everyone breathe," she gasped. "We simply need a Plan B." Miss Lana thrives on Plan Bs. So do I. In fact, my entire life is one big fat Plan B.

"The inn's still a lovely purchase. The fact that there's a pedigreed poltergeist dwelling within is, well . . ."

I pictured myself walking into sixth grade the next day. "A paranormal disaster," I said.

Dale shot me a Sympathy Look and rummaged in his snack pocket. "Accidental ghost purchase. Your social life is certified roadkill," he said. "Peanuts, anyone?"

Miss Lana held out her hand.

"Very well," she said as he shook peanuts into her palm. "We've hit uncharted rapids on the river of life. Don't panic, don't stand up in the boat. And not a word of this to the Colonel until our Plan B is in place."

The Colonel!

I grinned. "Miss Lana," I said, "I know the Colonel hates to admit it, but he *is* an attorney. If anybody can get you out of fine print, it's him."

"Of course," she said, her face brightening. "How could I have forgotten?"

"Rhetorical?" Dale whispered, and I nodded.

"The Colonel will straighten this out in a jiffy," she said. "We just need to broach the subject artfully."

"And quickly," Grandmother Miss Lacy said, cranking the Buick. "The entire town will head to the café to see how he takes our news." We fishtailed across the meadow and headed for town.

₊₊*₊*

Moments later Dale held the door as we filed into the empty café like a lineup of nervous suspects. Like Lavender, Dale has manners. This is thanks to Miss Rose—not his daddy. "Hey, Colonel," I said.

He peeked up from the coffeemaker. "Hello, Soldier. Your report?"

"The auction was exciting," I said. Which was true.

Miss Lana smiled. "Auctions are so electrifying."

Suspicion shot across his rugged face. "What did you buy?"

Dale jumped like somebody bit him, and Grandmother Miss Lacy peeled away to pour a glass of water. "An umbrella stand," Miss Lana replied. "It's in the Buick."

The Colonel relaxed. "Good. I thought we might offer tuna salad sandwiches for lunch today, with your Practically Organic Soup."

"Perfect," she said, sailing toward the kitchen. "I'll get the blue plates. They're so soothing. And while I'm thinking about it, I bought the inn. Would you like the sandwiches on white or whole wheat?"

"What?" the Colonel asked, wheeling to face her.

Poor Colonel. "She said white or whole wheat," I said.

"Lana? You bought that ramshackle hotel? Have you lost your mind? It's over a hundred years old. The roof leaks, the windows are busted, the wiring's shot. And who would stay there? Nobody comes to Tupelo Landing. Not on purpose, anyway."

She shrugged. "Life takes unexpected turns, *mon cher.*" Miss Lana likes to pretend she's French. She says it helps her metabolize stress.

"How much?" the Colonel demanded, his brown eyes wide.

"Two hundred ten thousand dollars. And change."

"A bargain, since she has a partner," Grandmother Miss Lacy added. "Me."

The Colonel sank into a chair, the vein on his forehead bulging. He took three deep breaths and I knew he was counting to twenty, which is what he tells me to do when counting to ten won't cover it.

The café door flew open. Mayor Little and the Azalea Women strolled in laughing.

"You people are a gold-plated hoot," Mayor Little said, beaming at us. "Congratulations. Historic inn, springhouse, pavilion. I can't wait to see what you do with the ghost!"

"Ghost?" the Colonel barked.

"The Colonel doesn't believe in ghosts," I said. "Neither do Miss Lana and Grandmother Miss Lacy."

The Azalea Women turned to the Colonel, their eyes glinting. He studied the parking lot as four cars and a pickup pulled in, spilling auction-goers toward our door.

Then he picked up a cloth and attacked a nonexistent spot on the counter. His lips weren't moving, but I knew he was still counting.

"I'll admit a historic inn is a risk," he finally said, giving the mayor a gray-lipped smile. To me, Miss Lana looked worried. "But Lana and Miss Thornton are astute businesswomen. I trust their instinct. As for the ghost story . . ." He swallowed hard. "We're regarding it as a public relations boon."

Miss Lana smiled. "That's right," she said. "People will come from the ends of the earth to visit our faux ghost. I'll handle the PR myself." As she drifted toward the kitchen, I slipped my arm around the Colonel's thin waist.

The Colonel is a genius. He's also a sure bet in a fight.

That night, I settled into bed and plucked *The Piggly Wiggly Chronicles,* Volume 6 off my bedside table. I started *The Chronicles* in kindergarten. Volume 1 features drawings of Attila Celeste covered in mud. Later volumes hold the clues to my life story and letters to the Upstream Mother who lost me in a flood the day I was born.

I used to think she would find me. Now I know she won't. I write anyway, mostly to focus my thoughts.

Dear Upstream Mother,

How are you?

Today, Miss Lana accidentally bought a haunted inn.

After our lunch rush, Miss Lana, the Colonel, and Grandmother Miss Lacy drove over to scout the place. The Colonel came home pale. Miss Lana and Grandmother Miss Lacy returned stiff and fake-cheerful, like plastic daisies at Christmastime.

We all hoped the Colonel could get Miss Lana out of the contract, but he can't. He says Buddha Jackson may appear to have the brains of a rutabaga, but his contract has less wiggle room than a straitjacket.

Tomorrow's the first day of school. The ghost news is all over town. My life can't get no worse than this.

Mo

Chapter 5
My Life Gets Worse

"Welcome to sixth grade," Miss Retzyl said the next morning, the sun from the windows gleaming off her neat white blouse and blue skirt.

"Thank you," I said very regal as ghost murmurs rippled across the room.

I bypassed the empty seat in the first row and slung myself into my usual desk next to Dale's. There were nineteen of us if you count the Exum boys, who I hoped were only visiting. "Who's the empty seat for?" I asked. "Because we're all here, plus some."

The Exums, on the back row, sat straight and still, one with brown hair and one with blond. They both wore pit bull faces, plaid shirts, jeans, and no necks. The Exums go to Creekside Baptist, with Dale. I know them from Bible school, where they've been voted Most Likely to Go to Hell three years running.

"Miss Retzyl, most of us been together since first grade," I said. "There's no point in adding Exums."

Dark-haired Jake Exum raised his hand. "I'm Jake

Exum," he said. "This is my brother Jimmy. Until now we been homeschooled."

"Mama expelled us," Jimmy added.

Miss Retzyl twitched like a squirrel but recovered fast. "Welcome, boys," she said, tucking a strand of auburn hair behind her ear. "In fact, welcome to all of you. We're going to have a wonderful time this year." That would be in comparison to last year, when we had her for fifth grade thanks to the Curse of the Combined Grades. "This year we're studying fractions, history, analogies, sentence construction, science . . . Anna, would you pass out the science books?" Attila jumped like a puppet possessed. "Any announcements before we get started?" Miss Retzyl asked.

"Miss Lana bought a ghost," Atilla said, gathering an armload of books.

The class snickered. I went for a diversionary tactic, which the Colonel says makes a good defense. "Thank you for that intro, Anna," I said, very smooth. "And let me be the first to congratulate you on those braces. Miss Retzyl, Dale and me got an announcement: We got our names in the newspaper this summer for solving a murder."

"We were in the paper in a good way," Dale added. "Not under *Recent Arrests*." Like I say, Dale's family's jail prone. *Recent Arrests* is practically his family newsletter.

Attila pulled a ragged science book from the bottom

of the stack and plunked it on my desk. "Actually, Miss Lana bought a *certified* ghost. Which is worse," she said.

"I also got a *What I Did on My Summer Vacation* paper in here somewhere," I lied, rummaging through my messenger bag. "It highlights the details of our recent cases. If you feel like extra crediting me, go ahead. I'll get it to you at the end of class."

Dale grabbed pencil and paper, and went into a quick scrawl:

WHAT I DID ON MY SUMMER VACATION
By Dale
What Mo Said.

He folded the paper and raised his hand. "I got that too," he said.

"Wonderful. I'll read them at home," she said. "Other announcements? No? Well, I have good news."

Good news from a teacher. Dale and I exchanged looks. Danger. We slid low in our desks.

"We have an unusual opportunity to do something important for our community, and we have an important guest to introduce that opportunity. Class, please help me welcome Mayor Little."

Our door swung open and Mayor Little bustled in, waving and beaming. "Good morning, future voters," he said, tossing his hat on Miss Retzyl's desk. "Thanks for inviting me here today."

Dale raised his hand. "We didn't invite you," he said.

"Thanks, Dale," the mayor said, smoothing his tie. "You have a wonderful way with the truth. The whole town appreciates what you and Mo did for us last summer."

Attila dropped the last book on Jake Exum's desk. "I don't," she said. "I also don't appreciate Miss Lana buying a ghost, which makes the entire town look stupid."

He rubbed his chubby hands together. "Thanks for that thought, Anna. Now, who knows what year it is?"

I raised my hand.

"Wonderful," he said. "Mo?"

"Miss Lana's not here to defend herself, so let's leave her out of this," I said, glaring at Attila.

Mayor Little looked uncertainly at Miss Retzyl, who stepped up beside him. "Class, let's hold our thoughts until the end of the mayor's presentation."

He shot her a grateful look. "All right," he said. "This is an important year for Tupelo Landing. Why?"

Thes raised his hand, but the mayor looked the other way.

"Because," the mayor continued, "this year marks our community's 250th anniversary. A milestone. And I am delighted to have led us to this dramatic moment in time. And where do you fit in?"

"Rhetorical," I whispered, and Dale nodded.

"I'm pleased to announce that you, the sixth grade, will have the honor of writing a history of our community based on your interviews with our town elders."

Dale folded forward, his forehead thumping against his desk. "Old people," he moaned. "There's nothing harder than old people."

"I share your excitement," the mayor replied. "I understand there's extra credit for the student interviewing the oldest person. And best of all, we'll make your papers into a book as part of our celebration. Miss Retzyl will handle the details."

Attila raised her hand. "How long do the papers have to be?"

"Three pages," Miss Retzyl said. "We'll start choosing subjects today."

Attila raised her hand again.

Miss Retzyl closed her eyes. "Before anyone asks, the papers will be half your history grade for first semester."

Attila lowered her hand.

"Your family is a good resource."

Dale stopped breathing. Dale and me both run short on elders. Mine live somewhere Upstream. His are mostly Up the River.

"We'll take Grandmother Miss Lacy," I whispered, and he exhaled.

Attila raised her hand. "Dibs on Miss Lacy Thornton."

"Hey!" I shouted. "She's *my* grandmother! I'm taking her!"

"Oh, she is not your grandmother," she sniped. "You only call her that because you don't know who your family is, plus she's richer than God."

"Take that back," I said.

"I asked her at the auction, and she said yes."

At the auction? She gave Mayor Little a smile that would put a bee in a sugar coma. "No fair, the mayor tipped her off," I said as Mayor Little grabbed his hat.

"Well, I'm glad this went so well," he said. "Ta-ta for now, future voters. And by the way, I'm sure Mother would give someone an interview. She's a real pip."

"Thank you, Mayor Little," Miss Retzyl said. "Class, please let me know by the end of the day who you'll ask for an interview."

That afternoon I sat watching the clock's hands jerk toward the final bell. Dale, who was practicing his ninja invisibility skills, sat so still, it was hard to be sure he was breathing. Miss Retzyl started taking names for interview subjects.

"Thes?" she asked.

"I got Great-Uncle Leroy," Thes said, his voice dull. "He served in a war."

"Wonderful," she said, marking her book. "A war hero.

Anna Celeste?" Attila sits in front of Dale. Dale stopped breathing altogether. His lips turned blue.

Atilla flounced her hair. "Like I said, I'm interviewing Miss Lacy Thornton, the oldest nice person in town. Automatic extra credit."

"Thief," I whispered.

"Thank you, Anna Celeste," Miss Retzyl said. "Mo? Did you say something?"

"Three minutes," Dale whispered, staring at the clock. "Stall."

I nodded. "Yes, ma'am. It's about you and Detective Joe Starr, which on behalf of the entire class I'd like to congratulate you on your rumored upcoming nuptials, which we're hoping you've set a date." The Exums applauded. "I also want to mention Dale does a killer 'Have-a-Maria,' which goes over good at weddings."

"That's '*Ave* Maria,'" she said.

"Exactly. Naturally, I'm available for emergency bridesmaid if needed," I added.

In truth, she could do better than Detective Joe Starr—Desperado Detective Agency's main competition. But Starr, who's from Winston-Salem, has somehow charmed Miss Retzyl and hangs around now much of the time.

Jimmy Exum raised his hand. "I got a suit. I can tote

rings," he said. The class gasped. The Exum boys are like crows when it comes to glittery objects.

"We can talk rings later," I said. "The main thing is, right now we'd all like to get your date down so we don't miss the Big Event."

Sal beamed and opened her weekly planner.

Miss Retzyl, who secretly likes me, narrowed her brown eyes. "Detective Starr and I haven't set a date, Mo. Let's get back to the interviews. I'd like to know—"

The classroom door swung open. A lanky boy slouched against the door frame: thin face, tan shirt, black pants, scuffed shoes.

Crenshaw, Harm Crenshaw. What is he doing here?

Miss Retzyl smiled. "You must be Harmond. I have a desk right here for you," she said, pointing to the front row.

He sauntered into the room. "It's Harm. Harm Crenshaw. Brother of racecar driver Flick Crenshaw. I'll be here a couple weeks and then I'm getting back to my real life in Greensboro." He swung into the empty seat and turned to smirk at me. "Hey Ghost Girl. Seen any haints?"

Attila tittered, and his eyes flashed over her.

"Harm, Mo was just telling us about her interview for her history paper."

"Dale and me are working together," I said, willing the bell to ring.

"That's fine," she said. "You'll need six pages rather than three."

Attila smiled at Harm, pointed at me, and rolled her eyes.

Heat walked up the back of my neck. "Dale and me are interviewing somebody older than Grandmother Miss Lacy," I said.

"Dale and *I*," Miss Retzyl said. "Mayor Little's mother is the oldest person in town."

I shivered. Mayor Little's mother is black-cat mean.

"No," Dale whispered. "Not her."

"It would mean extra credit," Miss Retzyl reminded me.

"Yes," Dale whispered. "Take her."

Extra credit looms large with Dale, who specializes in the Recess Arts. On the other hand, Mrs. Little curdles milk by smiling at it. "Thank you, Miss Retzyl, but Dale and me got somebody even older," I said, trying to think of someone.

Attila flashed her braces. "There isn't anyone older, Mo-ron."

Harm Crenshaw corkscrewed in his seat, his dark eyes laughing. "Mo-ron," he mouthed.

My temper popped like bacon on a hot skillet. "There

is too somebody older." I glared at him. "Dale and me are interviewing a ghost."

The problem with having a temper is you find out what you're going to say at the exact same minute everybody else does.

The class gasped.

"No," Dale moaned.

Like the Colonel says, sometimes the only way out is forward. "A ghost means extra credit," I said as the bell rang. "There ain't nobody older than dead."

Chapter 6
Pre-Flunked

"I am not interviewing a ghost. I want out," Dale said, hopping off his bike and dropping it by his mama's front steps. "Hey Liz," he murmured as Queen Elizabeth trotted over to greet him.

I leaned my bike against the porch. A scarecrow in a blue-plaid bathrobe watched over Miss Rose's sprawling fall garden: pumpkins, collards, cabbage, gourds. "Isn't that the robe you gave your daddy last Christmas?" I asked, squinting across the garden. Dale has a way with scarecrows.

"Don't use the Colonel's diversion tactics on me," he said. "This is sixth grade, Mo. We got to get *real* interviews. With quotes and footnotes. It's on the handout."

There was a handout? And Dale took one?

"And I'm scared of ghosts," he said. He picked up a stick and hurled it across the yard. Queen Elizabeth tilted her head, her pink tongue spilling out the side of her mouth. "Get it, girl," he said. "Fetch!" Queen Elizabeth sat. She's a self-starter unless she sees a squirrel, in which case she can't be held responsible. "A ghost," Dale said, his voice bitter. "I just hope Miss Retzyl hasn't called Mama to pre-flunk us."

Pre-flunk us? My blood ran cold. "You're making that up."

"It's like being preapproved for a credit card you ain't never gonna get," he said. "Get on the pre-flunk list and you never get off." Dale's people ain't good with credit cards. Neither are mine, but that's because the Colonel doesn't allow them, not because they don't allow us.

Dale took the steps two at a time. "Mama," he called, letting the front door slam behind us. "I'm home. I brought Mo."

Miss Rose stuck her head out of the kitchen. "Hey, you two. How did it go?"

Dale slung his backpack on the settee and headed toward her. "That depends," he said. "Did Miss Retzyl call?"

"No," she said, looking puzzled.

"I guess it went okay then," he said. "Do we have orange juice?" Miss Rose nodded toward the refrigerator—an old, round-shouldered Frigidaire.

"Hey Miss Rose," I said. "You're looking nice." It was true. She wore faded blue corduroys and a blouse with the soft stripes washed near off of it. She held a tape measure. A yellow pencil jutted from behind her ear.

Miss Rose used to be smack-down gorgeous before Dale's daddy latched on to her. That's what people say. She's still pretty, but a tired shade of pretty: green eyes, bold chin, a sway that's almost like dancing. She's got music in her bones, Miss Lana says. Same as Dale.

Dale kicked the Frigidaire's door closed. "I might as well tell you, Mama," he said, pouring the juice and handing me a glass. "Sixth grade looks hard. I may be a repeat attender."

"Don't tell me your new ninja skills aren't paying off," she said, and I caught a hint of her dimples. "What's that paper you've been studying?"

"Breathwork and Focus—Go Invisible the Ninja Way," he said. "Sal and Skeeter found it on the Internet for me." Skeeter—a seventh-grade legal whiz—got high-speed in July. High-speed's rare in Tupelo Landing unless you live on First Street, which has cable. "My ninja skills are maybe working some," he continued. "I didn't disappear today, but I didn't get called on, either."

"Then what makes you think you'll repeat sixth grade?"

Dale tells Miss Rose everything sooner or later. My Detective's Instinct cried out for later. "Dale and me got assigned a history paper," I said. "Dale's antsy, is all."

"I hate to be nosy," I added, bending the conversation in a safer direction, "but why are you holding Lavender's tape measure?"

She laughed. "How do you know it's Lavender's?"

"I'm practically his assistant," I explained. "I know Lavender's tools by heart."

She stretched the tape across her faded countertop. "Lavender's installing a dishwasher for me," she said. "I'm deciding how I'd like my kitchen to flow." Miss Rose is one of the last in Greater Tupelo Landing to get a dishwasher. Dale's daddy used to say if he had a dishwasher, he wouldn't need a wife. That's before Miss Rose kicked him out.

"Good. A dishwasher beats Dale's daddy any day," I said. The words went rancid the instant they hit the air.

Miss Rose didn't look up from her tape measure, but a shadow darted across her face. "Macon is my ex-husband," she said, smoothing the sharp from her voice. "Not Dale's ex-father."

"Sorry," I mumbled, and Dale nodded.

She smiled at Dale. "That reminds me, Lavender says he'll take you over there Sunday if you want to visit your daddy." *Over there* means the county jail.

"Lavender's driving? I'll go," I offered.

"Maybe later," Dale muttered.

Dale's always claimed two speeds for forgiving: fast or never. Lately I suspect he's developing a new gear just for his daddy. One that grinds slow. Real slow.

"So what's this I hear about history?" Miss Rose asked, turning to her measuring.

"Ghost," Dale blurted. I winced.

She stopped scribbling. "What?"

"Mo volunteered us to interview a ghost for history. I'm going to fail sixth grade. I hope you aren't disappointed." Silence settled over us like plaster dust. Miss Rose tilted her chin and let her glasses slide down the bridge of her nose.

I gave her my best smile. "A ghost means extra credit, plus Miss Lana can use our interview for her public relations campaign, for the inn. It's win-win."

She blinked at me rapid-fire, like an alien brain-mapping a new life form. "There's no such thing as ghosts, Mo," she said. "I'm sure Miss Retzyl will let you choose a new subject."

"It's too late," I told her.

She picked up her tape. "It's never too late to make a better decision, Mo. Dale, why don't you show Mo what you've learned on your guitar?"

"Come on, Mo," he said. "I can already play a song."

"That went better than expected," he said, sinking into his beanbag chair.

I walked over to his terrarium, where his newt, Sir Isaac Newton, stirred beneath a leaf. By Newton's terrarium sat a paperback, *Manners Girls Like.* Lately, Dale thinks about dates. I will never go out on a date until I am old enough to go with Lavender, which gives me seven years to plan my wardrobe.

"Social skills," Dale explained, watching me thumb through the book. "I need some in case a girl ever likes me." In case? If Sal likes Dale one degree more, she'll evaporate. "We got to think of somebody else to interview, Mo."

I walked to his bookshelf, playing for time. I scanned the titles: *I'm Okay, You're a Dog. Hound: A Spirit Journey. Get Rich with an Earthworm Ranch!* "You're missing the beauty of my plan," I said. "If we interview a ghost, we'll go famous." I let the word *famous* sit like bait on still water. I jiggled the line: "You enjoy famous."

He slipped me a sideways look. "Some," he admitted.

"If we *don't* land an interview with a ghost," I continued, "we'll fake one in ghostly voices. Easy A."

He shook his head. "Mama doesn't like me to cheat." He picked up his guitar and strummed. "I wish Miss Lacy Thornton would dump Attila so we could interview her. *That* would be an easy A." He snorted. "Attila probably didn't even ask her. She was probably bluffing."

Bluffing? I hadn't thought of that.

The Colonel says great leaders compromise. "How about this: If Attila's bluffing and Grandmother Miss

Lacy says yes to our interview, we'll grab her. If she says no, we'll stick with the ghost—if you don't mind risking fame."

"Deal," he said, laying his guitar aside. "Let's roll."

A few minutes later we dropped our bikes in a spatter of red dogwood leaves by Grandmother Miss Lacy's steps. "Who's that?" Dale asked as a silver BMW roared away from the curb.

"Rat Face, from the auction," I murmured. "What's she doing here?"

"Hello, dears," Grandmother Miss Lacy called. She sat in her porch swing, picking out pecans calm as Sunday. Grandmother Miss Lacy lives in the grandest house in town: two stories, with a wide front porch. Its clapboards wear dark green paint and its tall shutters wear black. Grandmother Miss Lacy keeps it decked out in flowers.

"What was Rat Face doing over here?" I asked.

"Don't worry, it's nothing a phone call won't fix. What are you two up to?"

Dale perched on the rail. "We're practicing our social skills," he said. He opened his pack, pulled out *Manners Girls Like,* and shyly tilted it toward her. "After my Anna Celeste disaster, I decided to brush up."

Groundwork for our interview request. Brilliant. "You may not realize it," I said, "but Anna Celeste liked Dale for a few days this summer and then dumped him like a truckload of bad meat. She about broke his heart."

He nodded. "That's why I've taken up the guitar."

"A wonderful channel for heartbreak," she said. "How's sixth grade?"

I studied her powdered face. "That depends," I said. "On you." I took a deep breath. "Grandmother Miss Lacy, we want to interview you for history, only Anna Celeste claims she already asked. I hate to say anything bad about her but we feel like she's Devil Spawn and we're pretty sure she's lying. We dropped by to ask, may we please have the honor of an interview?"

She gave the swing a little push. "Oh, dear. She asked me at the auction. I'm sorry, dears, but I didn't realize I'd be such a popular commodity." She cracked a pecan. "I believe Myrt Little might be available, though."

"The mayor's mother? But she's mean as a snake," Dale said. "Unless she's your best friend," he added, very smooth. "In which case she could be secretly nice."

"Oh, I doubt that," she said. "Come in. I have some cookies for you. And don't worry, you'll stumble across a suitable old person somewhere."

As she disappeared down the paneled hall, Dale and I wandered into her parlor. "Wow," he said. "I didn't know she lived in a museum." I followed him across the flowery wine-colored carpet, past the settee, to a round marble-top table. He picked up a photo in a silver frame. In it a slim, dark-haired woman leaned against a long pale car.

"That's the Duesenberg." He wandered to the fireplace, where black-and-white photos lined the mantelpiece. "Nice," he said as Grandmother Miss Lacy breezed in.

"Thank you, Dale." She put a plate of chocolate chip cookies on the marble-top table. "I find black-and-white film captures emotion so much better than color. The only exception would be school photos," she added, glancing at her Mo LoBeau Collection.

Dale perched on her settee and gulped cookies like a seal gulps fish. I nibbled, like Grandmother Miss Lacy. Miss Lana says that's how you learn manners. By watching people who've got them and doing what they do. She says that way you move like a bird in a flock, banking across the sky, adjusting so smooth, nobody notices you.

The Colonel says that's a good way to get shot.

"You know, dear," Grandmother Miss Lacy said, "since Dale's taking up the guitar, you might want an art form too." She went to her bookshelf, took down a small black box, and handed it to me. Its stippled sides felt cool in my hands.

Dale leaned forward. "What is it?"

"My old camera," she said.

I turned it in my hands. Two silver-rimmed portholes stared at me. I ran my finger across a series of levers and knobs on the front and top of the camera. "Where do the batteries go?"

"No batteries, dear." She flipped up a little window on the top of the box. "You look in here, focus here, and press the shutter," she said. "Light does the rest."

"It's solar," Dale breathed. "Cool."

"I thought you might document the inn's changes. They'll be dramatic. Historic."

"Historic?" Dale said, perking up.

"We could display the photos in the inn's lobby," she said.

"Sounds like extra credit," Dale said, looking at me.

I grinned. "Maybe I can even photograph the ghost."

Grandmother Miss Lacy laughed. "There's no such thing, Mo, but do give it your best shot. That's photography humor—best shot. And please tell Lana I'll see her at supper," she said, rising. "I'll bring the camera over and give you a few pointers."

"Yes, ma'am."

We ran down the steps and grabbed our bikes. "That went great," I said, picturing my photos on the inn's wall.

Dale swung onto his bike. "Not really. We're still stuck interviewing a ghost."

Chapter 7
Deadlines

The next afternoon—Friday—Miss Retzyl took out her grade book. "Let's nail down your interview subjects," she said, and scanned her book. "I'll need a potential interview subject from everyone today; otherwise you drop a grade. Mo? I encourage you and Dale to rethink your selection. I'm requiring taped interviews."

Sal raised her hand. "Plus they could lose their souls."

Dale went pale.

"Thank you, Miss Retzyl, but Dale and me plan to interview our ghost on a full moon to be arranged. We'll need the project deadlines as soon as possible, in case we need to consult outside experts," I added, very professional. "I understand they teach ghost hunting at the community college."

"Did she say *dead*lines?" Harm asked, and Attila tittered like a wind-up toy.

"Harm, that's enough," Miss Retzyl said. "Dale?"

Dale sighed. "I'm with Mo," he said, his voice limp as

an old sock. "We'll get modern historic photos. Maybe of the ghost too."

I nodded. Brilliant. All it would take is a sheet in a window.

"Grandmother Miss Lacy's loaning us her solar camera," I explained. "An automatic footnote. I had my first photography lesson last night."

The class buzzed.

"Photographs? A wonderful idea," Miss Retzyl said. "And of course you know I'll recognize your voices if you try to fake an interview with a ghost."

My stomach swallowed itself alive. "Fake an interview? We'd never dream of it."

Dale put his head on his desk.

"I'll also expect background interviews," she said. "With the living. Last chance, you two. Change your minds?" Harm and Attila smirked.

"We never back out on a case," I said. "Desperado Detective Agency's Paranormal Division is open for business."

She marked her book. "Very well. Sal? What do you have in mind?" Sal's the smallest girl in rising sixth grade—a full half inch shorter than Dale. She fluffed the Strategic Ruffles camouflaging her lipstick-shaped physique. "I'll interview Grandmama Betty, Retro Fashionista. Her mother specialized in semi-tailoring deluxe Sears garments—which were the bee's knees in the '30s." She smiled at Dale, her eyes bright. He didn't even try to lift his head.

"Excellent. Harmond," Miss Retzyl said, "whom will you interview?"

Whom. She said it like it made sense.

Harm shifted his lean body. "Skip me. I won't be in the boondocks that long."

Miss Retzyl's pen clattered against her book.

The class gulped.

"I mean, I won't be in Tupelo Landing that long, Miss Retzyl," he finally said. "Besides, I don't know anybody here. I can't get an interview."

Attila raised her hand. "You have to know *somebody*. Where do you live?" she asked. "Not that I care," she added. "It's just that some of us wonder."

"Yeah," I said. "Guess whom." I smiled at Miss Retzyl, hoping for a compliment on *whom*. Nothing.

"Where I live is my business," Harm said, his voice cracking. He took a breath, packing calm around his anger the way Miss Lana packs tissue paper around her mother's crystal. "I'll give you an answer next week, Miss Retzyl," he said as the bell rang.

Our stampede for the door muffled her reply.

Dale and I walked across the playground, to our

bikes. The afternoon heat lay against the earth, swollen and still. "Why doesn't Harm want anybody to know where he lives?" I asked.

He shrugged. "Maybe he's in the witness protection program. Or maybe he doesn't want Attila zipping after him like a bloodhound. You want to come over and watch me practice my guitar?"

The school door banged opened and Harm swaggered out. Attila loitered near the edge of the playground, cradling her books in a sophisticated high school way. She zinged him her best smile. He looked her way, swung onto his bike, and headed toward Fool's Bridge and the inn.

I smiled at her and waved.

"Come on," Dale said. "I'll let you feed Newton."

Newton eats dead bugs. "I'd love to, but Newton's gaining weight and I'd hate to put too much strain on his knees. Miss Lana says added pounds mean added sorrow later in life." I watched Harm pedal away. "Where's he going? He headed the other way yesterday—toward the Piggly Wiggly."

"Who cares?" Dale yawned.

"Okay, I'll feed Newton, but let's swing by the inn first," I said. "We need *before* photos."

He grinned. "You want to follow Harm Crenshaw," he said, hopping on his bike. "I'm curious too."

Five minutes later, Dale skidded to a stop on the black-top. We stared up and down the empty highway. "Harm Crenshaw doesn't have invisibility skills, does he?"

The sweat trickled down my spine and wicked along the waistband of my shorts. "No. Just long legs and a fast bike. Maybe he hid," I said, scanning the drying corn-fields along the road. "Come on," I said, heading for the inn's drive. "Let's get some photos."

We stopped in the last curve of the cedar-lined drive. I held the old camera against my belly and lined up my first shot of the inn. *Click.* Dale pointed to an upstairs window. "Who's that?"

"Where?"

"In the corner room. Somebody's watching us."

The wavy old window glass glinted as a gust of wind shook the cedars, and the clouds shifted overhead. "The sun, maybe," I told him, but even in the afternoon heat a shiver tiptoed up my spine.

"Maybe it's the girl from auction day. I hate to say ghost," he whispered.

"Auction day? That was Harm Crenshaw."

"You're guessing," he said as we crept toward the inn.

"I'm deducing," I said. "Clue number one: We'd already caught him following us once—on the path with Mr. Red. Number two: Harm wasn't in the auction tent when we got back. Clue three: Lavender said it himself—Harm's trouble."

I peered at the upstairs window. "In fact," I said, heading for the steps, "if anybody's in that window now, I'm betting it's Harm Crenshaw."

A gust of wind sent a swirl of leaves tumbling down the porch. An old rocking chair creaked. *Click.* I pushed the front door open, strolled to the foot of the staircase, and lined up a photo: two stairs, three steps missing, eight good stairs to the top. "Thirteen steps," Dale muttered. "That's bad."

"Detectives ain't superstitious," I told him. *Click.* "Hello?" I called, aiming my camera at the top of the stairs. "Harm?"

Nothing.

"Be careful, Dale," I said, starting up the stairs. "Keep to the edges." When I reached the missing steps, I balanced on the runners. "Hello?" Still nothing. I looked down the long hall. "Which room, Dale?"

He pointed to a closed door.

"If it's Harm, we got him cornered," I whispered.

"If it's a ghost, it's got *us* cornered," he said, his voice bleak.

I tiptoed to the door and turned the knob. The door squeaked open on a room lined with bookshelves. "A library," I said. I walked to the window and pushed back a rotting curtain. "An old one," I added as dusty light flooded the room. *Click.*

Dale rounded an ancient leather sofa. He brushed a shelf, sending a book tumbling to the ragged carpet. I scooped it up and blew the dust off. "Geometry," I murmured, opening it. Faded brown ink flowed across the end paper.

"Cursive," Dale whispered, and I nodded. Miss Retzyl's a fan of cursive writing. I tilted the book to the window's light.

I hate math. N.B.—August 28, 1937.

Inky fingerprints stained the bottom of the page.

Dale ambled to the window. "I must have been seeing things," he said, peering behind the curtain. "There's nobody up here but us." He padded to a cabinet with double doors at its base. "What's in here?" he asked, squatting down.

He tugged. The doors didn't budge. He shifted his weight, and yanked hard. Harder. The doors flew open. Dale rolled backward, a ragged wave of mice scurrying across the rug. "Rats!" he screamed, swatting at his feet.

I grabbed the back of his shirt and dragged him toward the door. "Run!" We thundered down the stairs, hurling ourselves over the missing steps and landing at the bottom of the staircase, panting.

"Mice," Dale said, looking sheepish. "Maybe babies."

I tried to catch my breath. "Miss Lana says everything's relative," I told him, shoving the geometry book into my messenger bag. "They looked relatively huge to me," I lied. Dale scuffed to the old piano and opened the keyboard. Music settles Dale the way rain settles dust.

"'Heart and Soul'?" he invited, scooting the piano bench out. "Heart and Soul" is the only performance piece I got. Miss Rose tried to show me more, but when it comes to music, I'm a good listener. I put the camera on top of the piano, slipped onto the bench, and placed my fingers in the go position.

He sang as we played. "Heart and soul . . ."

Upstairs, a door slammed. Footsteps pounded to the top of the stairs.

"That's not mice!" Dale said, jumping up and spinning to face the stairs.

"Harm Crenshaw?" I bellowed. "Cut it out!"

A girl laughed and a wave of cold fell over us like a curtain of ice. "That ain't Harm," Dale whispered. Footsteps flew down the empty staircase like a ragged drumroll, hitting every step dead center—all thirteen of them.

They turned and clattered straight for us.

"Run," I cried, grabbing my camera. We scrambled to the door and yanked it open. I spun to the piano. *Click.*

The keyboard slammed closed, sending an unearthly collision of sound rolling through the inn as Dale pounded across the porch.

"I'm Mo and that's Dale and we need an interview!" I screamed, tossing our business card on the floor.

And I ran for my life.

Chapter 8
Blueprints and Party Plans

At the top of the driveway's curve, Dale skidded his bike to a halt. "That was *not* Harm Crenshaw," he said. "That ghost is real as we are. Maybe realer."

"Right." I looked up at the gray cloudbanks rushing overhead. "We better get home. It's going to storm."

"Mo," Dale whispered, clutching my arm. "Over there." A flash of silver melted into the trees as thunder rumbled across the sky.

Harm Crenshaw? *Again?* It couldn't have been, not this time.

I looked over my shoulder, at the inn—at a girl in the window—and my heart sputtered. I blinked and the window stared back empty. My mouth went desert dry. "Race you to the café," I said as raindrops pattered across the drive. "The Colonel and Miss Lana will know what to do."

Moments later we dropped our bikes in the café parking lot by a white minivan: Azalea Women. "Don't breathe a word of this until we get the Colonel and Miss

Lana alone," I warned. "Ghost news will zip through town lightning-fast. Maybe faster."

"Right," he panted as I opened the café door. "Not a word."

We stepped inside. "Ghost," he said.

Miss Lana and Grandmother Miss Lacy looked up from giant blueprints they'd spread over a corner table. Two Azalea Women by the window stopped drinking tea in mid-sip. Violin music wafted from the jukebox. The air smelled warm and yeasty.

"Sorry," he whispered. Sometimes I could kill Dale.

"He means ghost in the fine print," I said, very quick. "Old news," I added for the Azalea Women. "Don't bother telling it. It's all over town."

The Azalea Women slipped back into conversation.

The Colonel says loose lips sink ships. Dale's could sink a fleet.

"Buon giorno," Miss Lana said, smiling.

"Back at you," Dale said, and leaned toward me. "French?" he whispered.

"Italian," I replied, pointing to the Leaning Tower of Pisa salt and pepper shakers center stage of the red-and-white checked tablecloths.

The Colonel runs the café like a military operation— all polish and precision. Miss Lana prefers a theme. You know who's in charge the instant you walk through the door. "Come in," Miss Lana said, smiling. "We're creating a new spinach lasagna tonight. We'd love to have your opinion, Dale. You're such a connoisseur."

"Connoisseur," I whispered. "French for know-it-all."

He headed for the phone, his sandals slapping against the floor. It was a comforting, real-world sound. "I'll ask Mama if I can stay," he said, grabbing the phone. "She'll probably want me to, with a storm rolling in." He stepped over something behind the counter. "Hey Lavender. What you doing under there?"

Lavender? Here?

I darted through the tables and slid to a halt, my plaid sneakers squeaking against the tiles. "Good afternoon," I said, hooking my elbow on the counter, very sophisticated. "What a pleasant surprise."

He looked up, flat on his back, his shoes braced against the baseboard. "Hey yourself, Mo LoBeau," he said. He tugged hard at something under the counter, straining until his arm muscles bulged and his face went red.

Even beet red, Lavender's fly-apart gorgeous.

"That should do it, Miss Lana." He stood up and dropped a pipe wrench in his battered red tool box. "If that fitting gives you more trouble, just call."

When Miss Lana wants something fixed, she mostly calls Lavender. She says it's less trouble than strangling the Colonel. Plus she likes to contribute to Lavender's car fund. "Tell Mama hey for me," he told Dale.

As Dale dialed, the door swung open. Sal and twelve-year-old Skeeter MacMillan, Tupelo Landing's attorney-in-training, blasted in on a gust of wind. "Afternoon," Miss Lana said, heading for the milkshake machine. "The usual?"

"Yes please." Sal pushed her red sunglasses on top of her head and led the way to a table as Miss Lana scooped ice cream into a metal cup.

Skeeter ticked opened her briefcase. "Is the Colonel in? I'd like his opinion on a legal matter."

Miss Lana popped the metal cup in place. "He's in the kitchen. But if it's a legal matter, I hope you'll wait," she said as the Azalea Women looked up.

Miss Lana hit the milkshake machine's *whir* button.

"The Colonel would rather eat maggots than talk law," I told Skeeter, using the machine's whir for cover. "His amnesia only lifted a few weeks ago. He's still sensitive."

Skeeter closed her briefcase as the whir died and Dale hung up the phone. In the silence, I could just hear Grandmother Miss Lacy humming a familiar song.

The hair on my arms rose up like ghosts as I recognized the tune. "Heart and Soul"—the song Dale and me just played at the inn.

Dale leaned close to me, his eyes glued to Grandmother Miss Lacy. "That song," he whispered. He gulped. "I hope she ain't been repossessed."

Her melody morphed into another tune. "You mean possessed," I whispered. "Let's investigate."

He shook his head. "I want to talk to Salamander."

Right. I headed for Grandmother Miss Lacy. "Hey, I never heard you hum to yourself," I said, settling beside her. "How do you pick your tunes?"

"Oh! Was I humming?" she asked, running her finger over the blueprints. "Forgive me, dear; when you live alone, you find unusual comforts. Take a look at these blueprints, Mo. They're fascinating." At the window table, the Azalea Women gathered their rain gear and headed for the cash register, leaving a twenty-five-cent tip.

I leaned over the blueprints. Salt shakers at each corner kept them from curling like scrolls. "Where'd you get them?" I asked as Lavender sauntered over.

"Found them in the courthouse," he said. "Allow me. Here's the inn, and the main drive. Here's the shortcut by Red Baker's place. But look at this," he said. "A path from the inn to the old store—a path I've never seen before."

"That's the old Judas Trail," she said. "Nobody's used it since the inn closed. I doubt you can even find it anymore."

Dale gulped. "The *Judas* Trail? No wonder nobody

uses it, with a name like that." He smiled at Miss Lana as she passed the shakes around. "Mama says thanks for inviting me to supper and may I please spend the night. Her headache's back."

Miss Rose gets headaches ever since Dale's daddy went to jail again. Not because he's in jail, but because she's divorcing his sorry self. Miss Lana says even good changes can be stressful. "Of course you can stay," she said.

Excellent, I thought. We'll deliver our ghost news after supper.

"Hey Dale," Sal said, taking a package from her satchel. "Your order's in."

Skeeter and Sal started their new business—Skeeter-Bay—the day Skeeter went high-speed. They'll order anything that's legal if you pay cash up front plus twenty percent.

Sal blushed as Dale sat beside her. "*Instant Guitar: Three Chords to Fame and Fortune* with a bonus section: *Songwriting 101.* It looks like a great book, Dale." She tilted her head, her gray eyes soft. "I just know you're going to be a star."

"Thanks," he said modestly. Dale kills me.

Lavender pulled up a chair by mine—a gold-star moment in a so-far hideous day. "Where's the medicinal springs?" I asked, studying the blueprints. Lavender, who's between cars, usually smells like motor oil. Today he smelled faintly of sawdust and pine.

"In the old springhouse," he said, pointing to a drawing of a small building with numbers clustered on the floor. "Each spring cured a different ill—or not," he added, tapping a prickle of tiny crosses in the woods.

"The old cemetery," Grandmother Miss Lacy said, and a chill skated across my skin. "It's on a pretty little rise, as I recall. Thousands came here hoping to be healed by the springs. But you're right: Some of them do rest in that cemetery."

And maybe some of them don't rest at all, I thought.

"Check out the date," Lavender said. "Norton Blake renovated the inn in 1938," he said, "which means the wiring's too old to be safe. We'll have to rewire it."

"Sounds expensive," Miss Lana said, her voice tight. She'd already bled her bank account dry to buy her half of the inn. "With the cost of the painting . . ."

"Don't worry," Grandmother Miss Lacy told her. "We'll be fine."

Like I say, Grandmother Miss Lacy's the richest person in town.

"There's good news too," Lavender continued. "The floors are heart pine, and the windows antique glass. The inn needs a lot of elbow grease and paint, but she'll be a work of art when she's done."

The Colonel marched in from the kitchen with a box of cups. "Lavender's agreed to supervise the day-to-day construction on the inn if I head the project," he told Miss Lana and Grandmother Miss Lacy. "We can start hiring tomorrow—if it suits you."

Lavender? At the inn? Every day?

"Suits me," I said. "Dale and me got a ton of research to do out there. And I'll immortalize you in film."

At the next table, Sal stripped the paper off her straw. "I'm glad you stuck with your ghost research, Dale. That's brave. I just hope you don't go zombie," she added, holding her arms out and rocking back and forth in her seat.

"Zombie?" Dale said, his voice quaking. "Can that happen?"

"We ain't worried," I told Sal, and Lavender grinned. Lavender's grin makes me feel like I can do anything except maybe fractions. "Dale and me already presented our card to the disembodied in question."

Dale choked on his milkshake. "We did?"

"Impressive," Sal murmured.

The café door swung open. Queen Elizabeth shot between the mayor's tasseled loafers, scuttled across the floor, and sprawled at Dale's feet, panting. "Darnedest thing I've ever seen, the way that dog can find you," Lavender said as Sal reached down to smooth Liz's ears.

"She's psycho," Dale explained, and Sal snatched her hand back.

"He means psychic," I told her.

Mayor Little smoothed his tie over his round belly. "Happy Friday afternoon, fellow citizens," he said. He sniffed and took in the tablecloths. "Rome?"

"Sì," I replied as the Colonel measured fresh coffee into the coffeemaker. "The spinach lasagna ain't ready but I can make you a PB&J Italiano. It comes hand-squished flat on the plate or fluffy, with a sprig of parsley on the side."

He tossed his rain hat on the counter. "Gratci Mo, but I'm here on business." He beamed at us. "Have I mentioned the town's 250th anniversary party?"

Miss Lana lit up like neon. She loves parties like Lavender loves the scream of tires. "We'll host it here, won't we, Colonel?"

The Colonel sighed. "Probably."

"Thanks, you two," the mayor said, "but I'm thinking full-blown gala. Music, food, out-of-towners. Maybe even the governor. I was wondering about the inn. We have a little jingle in the town coffers . . ."

"Jingle?" Sal said, looking up from her milkshake. Sal possesses a warp-speed calculator for a brain. She slipped a pencil sharpener from her book bag.

"Not a fortune," the mayor warned. "More like a little

mad money in my sock drawer. I'm thinking November first-ish."

"The inn closed October 22, 1938," I told him. "It's on the auction flyer."

"Perfect." He beamed. "October 22 it is."

"Of *this* year?" Lavender said. "Impossible. We have to rewire, patch, paint. There's no way we can be ready in time."

"Production bonus," Sal said. "If Lavender finishes on time, he gets cash for his car fund." She fluffed a ruffle. "A tight schedule means extra stress and possible therapy costs. And overtime means extra taxes. Lavender needs a thousand dollars and no penalty in the unlikely event that he fails."

Lavender blinked. His blue chambray shirt makes his eyes look even bluer—something he pretends not to know. "A thousand dollars? Are you serious?"

"Done," the mayor sighed.

"I'll draw up the agreement after I finish my homework," Skeeter said. She flashed the Colonel a look. "Unless you want to, sir."

The Colonel hesitated. For a split second, I thought he would say yes. "Thank you, Skeeter, but no. Carry on." He headed for the kitchen.

Sal smiled at Lavender. "We didn't discuss our fee, but we have a hair dryer smoking up our office space."

Skeeter's law office is in the storage room of her mama's hair salon. Sal's accounting firm occupies a corner desk. "If you could fix it . . ."

Lavender nodded. "Done again."

"We'll need entertainment," Miss Lana said.

"I'm developing DJ skills to defray future law school expenses," Skeeter said. "I'll *pro bono* you as a public service. I think my expenses are tax deductible?" she asked Sal, who nodded. Nobody knows for sure if Sal actually files taxes. Dale and me suspect she fills out the forms for fun, same as Miss Lana does Sudoku.

"Wonderful. I hope you'll spin some beach music classics," the mayor added, slithering his loafers across the floor and shaking his hips.

"Shoot me," Dale muttered.

The mayor twirled, his jacket flying open. "What was that, Dale?"

"I said I'll sing," Dale said. "And play my guitar if I learn it good enough. If anybody wants me to."

"I do," Sal said.

"Then it's settled," Miss Lana said. "This is just what we need to help us focus."

"She's right," Dale told his brother. "Stress focuses you right up until it sucks your brain dry. Standardized testing taught me that."

Mayor Little paused at the door. The wind grabbed

the sycamore, sending autumn's first golden leaves to the parking lot. "No pressure, Lavender," he said. "But the whole town's counting on you."

"Right," Lavender groused as the door banged shut. "We've got to replace windows, patch the roof, redo the kitchen . . ."

"And evict a ghost," I said.

Everybody laughed except Dale and me.

Chapter 9
A Plan of Attack

"We'll tell the Colonel and Miss Lana about the ghost straight out and professional," I told Dale that evening. Me, Dale, and Queen Elizabeth had kicked back in my flat, which some folks mistake for a closed-in side porch with a bathroom stuck on the end. Miss Lana and the Colonel had settled in the living room.

Our home, which takes up the back half of the café building, overlooks Miss Lana's gardens and the creek. The café, in the front half of the building, overlooks the parking lot and highway. Like me, the Colonel and Miss Lana each have their own living spaces. Miss Lana's suite lies across the living room from my flat. The Colonel keeps his quarters, near the kitchen, spit and polish neat.

I crossed to my Salvation Army desk and opened my top drawer. It sticks.

"Ghost news is like Band-Aid removal," I said. I jammed my hand all the way to the back and grabbed a crumpled clue pad, just in case. "It's best to do it quick." I peeked into the living room. Miss Lana sat in her rocker, reading *Historic Hollywood* magazine. The Colonel sat at a card table, leafing through a law book.

"Are they kissing?" Dale whispered. "Because I don't want to see that."

"No," I said. "And they never will."

I hated to admit it, but since the return of the Colonel's memory, the possibility of romance had occurred to me too. And maybe to him. Last week he brought Miss Lana a scraggly handful of goldenrod, a pale root dangling from the stem. "Sorry," he'd said, "I'm rusty." She'd looked like Skeeter's little sister just bit her. Then she'd laughed and put it in a pale blue Mason jar, root and all.

I mentioned it to her that night, in her suite, as she brushed out her Jean Harlow wig. "I don't mean to sound negative, but the Colonel bringing you flowers gives me the dry heaves. Can you make him stop?"

"He's just remembering our long-ago engagement, sugar," she said. "It's history, but as his amnesia lifts, his truth expands. That shifts my truth a little. And yours too, apparently."

Sometimes Miss Lana talks like a fog bank. I do the best I can.

"This new truth doesn't suit me," I'd said.

She shook Jean Harlow. "The truth is like spandex, sugar. It may not look like a good fit at first, but if you ease into it and wiggle around, it winds up fitting like your skin. Hand me that comb," she'd said. "Jean's snarled."

Now I looked at Dale. "If they can handle spandex, I'm pretty sure they can handle a ghost. Remember," I told him. "Act professional."

We slipped into the living room, Queen Elizabeth ticking along behind, and settled on Miss Lana's old curlicue settee.

She looked up from her magazine. "Paws," she said. Queen Elizabeth hopped off the settee and stretched out at Dale's feet.

"Good evening," I said, very professional. The Colonel looked up from his law book. "Nice weather if you're a duck," I continued, "but Thes says the rain will clear out by morning."

"Excellent," he said, and smiled.

Miss Lana turned a page in her magazine. "Homework all done?"

"It's Friday," I reminded her. "We prefer our homework to age over the weekend, making it tender. We're here on business. It's about the inn."

She closed her magazine. "Wonderful. I've been considering your interview. A brilliant idea! Such creative children. Ghost stories can be very lucrative." The lamplight made her hair glow coppery. "We'll need a sweet ghost. A poster ghost, really, something amusing for guests. Have you composed your interview questions?"

"The questions aren't due for weeks," I said. "The thing is, Miss Lana . . ."

"I'd gladly give them a look-see when you're ready," she said, and winked. "Or help you get started." The Colonel cleared his throat. "Not that we'd cheat," she added. "But since I'll build my PR campaign on your interview, we want a good foundation. We might even bring in a ghost investigator. My treat."

The Colonel snorted.

"Thanks," I said. "I'm glad you're excited, because we got a Situation."

"Snacks?" Dale asked, jumping up. Dale is a stress eater.

The Colonel turned a page. "Pantry," he said without looking over. "Second shelf." Dale padded past Miss Lana's suite, into the kitchen.

"Dale and me bumped into the entity in question this afternoon," I continued. "She comes across kind of . . . cold. More like the Anti–Poster Ghost."

Dale ambled back with a bag of coconut macaroons and settled beside me.

Miss Lana blinked slowly. "What could I possibly do with a cold ghost?"

"Rhetorical," I whispered to Dale. Too late.

"You could try a catch and release, but you'd need a live trap," he said.

A *live* trap?

The Colonel looked up from his book.

"That's what Lavender does when possums come after Mama's chickens at night," Dale continued. "Of course," he added, "we'd have to consider bait."

A hush fell over the room.

The Colonel closed his book. "You actually believe there's a ghost in the inn? Why? Did you see something?"

"Not exactly," I said. "Unless you count the piano slamming shut on its own."

"I'd count that," Dale said. "And I *did* see a girl in a window, but she'd evaporated by the time we got there. Unless she was a shadow."

"But we *heard* her," I added, keeping my eyes on the Colonel. "She ran down the stairs—including the ones that aren't there. And she laughed."

"Alternative explanations?" he said. The Colonel's big

on alternative explanations. It's one of the things I like about him.

"The first time we heard her, I thought it might've been Harm Crenshaw," I said. "But today it couldn't have been."

"Well," Dale said, helping himself to another cookie, "we did see a silver flash at the edge of the meadow. And Harm's bike *is* silver."

"It couldn't have been him," I said again. "The footsteps ran straight at us. And those footsteps were empty. And it got cold—a funny cold, one without edges."

"Like a bite without teeth," Dale added.

Miss Lana and the Colonel exchanged looks. The Colonel tapped his long fingers against his law book. "I'll look into it first thing in the morning, Soldier. You have my word. Thank you for your report."

I relaxed. The Colonel's word is gold.

"Maybe Dale and me can look with you, sir," I said, and Dale choked, sending a soft spray of crumbs across the settee. "Tomorrow's Saturday, and this *is* our case," I said, staring at Dale. "And half our history grade."

"I guess so," he mumbled.

"We just need a good plan of attack."

The Colonel nodded. "I'd appreciate the reinforcements. Why don't you two come over after you help with the breakfast rush?" He rose. "Cot or couch, son?"

"Couch," Dale said, heading for the linen closet. Dale stays here so much lately, Miss Lana gave him his own sheets.

I snatched Miss Lana's Rainbow Row pillows from the couch and tossed them into a chair. Ghost Patrol with the Colonel.

We'd have our ghost sorted out in no time.

Chapter 10
Ghost Patrol
with the Colonel

The next morning, Dale and me pedaled for the inn. "Let's take the shortcut by Red Baker's," I said, coasting across Fool's Bridge and into the countryside.

"No," he said, looking at Queen Elizabeth, who loped behind us.

Before he could explain, the cornfield beside me exploded in a flash of silver. I slammed on brakes, skidding sideways as Dale slid to a halt alongside.

"Looking for me?" Harm asked, balancing his bike with his toes. "I know you been following me. Thought I'd help you out."

"We have not been following you," I lied.

"Well, we did try," Dale admitted. Dale will go truthful faster than anybody I know. I like that about him, but it can cripple an investigation. He looked at Harm's bike. "Fast ride."

"Smart rider," Harm replied, smiling. He wasn't entirely

bad when he smiled. "Where you headed? Tell me and I'll go slow so you can keep up."

"To the inn," Dale said. "The Colonel's put us on—"

"On photography duty," I said before Dale could say *Ghost Patrol.*

"Right. I hear he's hiring," Harm said. "Him and Lavender. It's all over town."

"Maybe," I said. "What you doing in Red Baker's cornfield?"

"Waiting for you. I'm hoping you'll put in a good word for me with the Colonel," he said. "I can build most anything. I took shop in Greensboro."

Me? Put in a good word for *him?*

Dale whistled between his teeth. "Shop. Nice. I do a good scarecrow, but that's about it," he said. "I made one for Mama and I got a freelance one not too far from here. I'm self-taught. We don't have shop until high school."

"Right," Harm said, not even bothering to smile. "Think about it, Ghoul Girl," he said. "You'd be doing the Colonel a good turn." He shoved off, heading for town.

Dale leaned down to scratch Liz's ears. "He's got some nerve, asking you to do him a favor and calling you names in the same breath."

"Race you," I replied, and blasted off down the road.

As we rocketed up to the inn, Lavender's mechanic, Sam, stood on the porch talking to Tinks Williams. "Morning, sunshine," Sam said, giving me a lopsided grin. "The Colonel's inside. Me and Tinks just signed on."

"Great." I grabbed my camera and lined them up. *Click*. "Hey Dale, stand over there," I said. "I'll immortalize you."

Dale bounced up on the porch and leaned against a fancy post, Liz by his side. "Give me a second, this ain't automatic," I reminded him. I held the camera against my belly and peered into the window on top.

Dale grinned.

"Don't smile," I told him. "Think DVD cover. And hold still."

He crossed his arms and leaned against the post, setting off a shower of paint flakes. "Attitude, Liz," he said. She slouched as Dale blazed a look into the camera.

"Perfect." *Click*.

"Hey, there's Mama," Dale said as Miss Rose rumbled across the yard in a pickup, a horse trailer bouncing behind. Dale rushed to open the trailer. His ill-tempered mule, Cleopatra, stomped out braying and rolling her eyes. "Isn't she a beauty?" he said.

Miss Lana says beauty's in the eye of the beholder. Cleo proves it. Long soot-black ears, sullen black-rimmed eyes in a maple-colored face, legs too stubby for her body. Miss Rose grabbed Cleo's bridle. *Click.*

"The Colonel invited Cleo to eat this grass down," Dale said, "which is lucky for us. Our pasture needs a rest." I nodded, but if I knew the Colonel, luck didn't write that invitation.

The inn's front door creaked open. Lavender in a tool belt. *Click.*

"Hey Mama," Lavender said. "Come in, I'll show you around. Mo, there's some shots in here that will blow you away." Lavender in a tool belt had already blown me away. Now I just needed the Colonel to handle our ghost.

The Colonel had his battle plan. We searched the downstairs room by room. First the vestibule, with its check-in desk. Then the dining room, small back rooms, and dungeon of a kitchen. "All clear," the Colonel sang.

Finally the parlor, with its piano.

Dale hadn't looked square at the piano since we got there. "We were playing 'Heart and Soul' last time, sir," I said. "Maybe we should play it again."

He nodded and grabbed a picnic basket. "Carry on. I'll set up Lana's picnic."

"Miss Lana's picnic and not his," Dale whispered. "That's good." It was true. Miss Lana packs a picnic like it could be your last meal. The Colonel leans toward beef jerky and water.

"Come on, Dale," I said. He slipped onto the bench and opened the keyboard. "You might want to move away from the stairs," I told the Colonel. "She's fast."

"Ten-four, Soldier." He carried the basket to the desk, and lifted out a white tablecloth and a silver candlestick.

Dale rolled an easy river of sound through the inn and I placed my hands in the go position. "Now," he whispered. He sang as I plinked out the melody. "Heart and soul . . ."

I looked over my shoulder, at the staircase. "Keep singing," I whispered. We played the song top to bottom three times. Nothing, nothing, nothing.

Being stood up by a ghost hurts, mostly because there's no way to get even.

"Perhaps your ghost is upstairs. We'll check after lunch," the Colonel said. He shook open his cloth napkin. "Lana's picnic is served."

A half hour later he polished off the last of Miss Lana's chicken salad, licked his fingertips, and smiled. "Ready, Desperados?" he asked, looking at the stairs.

"I'd better go check on Cleo," Dale replied, grabbing a handful of Oreos.

"Cleo's fine," I told him, putting the lid on Miss Lana's

Practically Organic Bread-and-Butter Pickles. "We're ready, sir."

The Colonel stacked our plates in the basket and blew out the candles. Dale looked at the stairs. "I got a question before we go up, sir. In case I don't make it back down."

"We'll make it down," the Colonel replied. "But shoot."

"It's about Daddy."

I grabbed the tablecloth and bunched it up to hold in the crumbs.

I knew Dale would ask about Mr. Macon sooner or later. On one hand, it made perfect sense: Mr. Macon and the Colonel used to be friends, so you'd think the Colonel, who's turned out to be an attorney, might help Mr. Macon now. On the other hand, it didn't make a lick of sense, as Mr. Macon was in jail for helping kidnap the Colonel and Miss Lana, and for giving Miss Rose a black eye.

If you ask me, jail suits him fine. Nobody hurts my people and walks free—not if I can help it.

"Daddy needs a good lawyer," Dale said. "I know most people say you're crazy, but I figure you're still better than most."

"Thank you," the Colonel replied, and dropped his napkin in the picnic basket. "Dale, I can't represent

Macon, if that's what you're thinking." Dale bobbed his head, same as he does when he learns he flunked a test. "In fact," the Colonel said, "I'll probably be called as a witness against him." His brown eyes searched Dale's face. "You and Mo might be called too."

Us? Testify? I'd never thought of that.

"We're ready, sir," I said, and Dale twisted his napkin.

"I'm not," Dale said.

The Colonel studied him. "Macon's in jail because of what he did, Dale. Not because of what you did."

"That's what Mama says," Dale told him, twisting his napkin tighter. The Colonel took it from his hands and tossed it into the basket. "I just figured you ain't all that reliable as a witness because of your amnesia. So maybe they'd let you be an attorney instead." He gazed into the Colonel's eyes.

The Colonel grinned. "Good point. One that's sure to come up at trial. I can't defend Macon," he added. "But I'll make sure he gets a good attorney."

Dale smiled and offered his hand. "Thank you."

The Colonel shook his hand and clapped his shoulder. "I believe Lavender's put boards over those missing steps," he said. "Let's track your ghost."

I grabbed my camera and looked at the stairs. My chicken salad sandwich flapped its wings. "Age before beauty, sir," I said.

"Thank you, my dear," he replied, and headed up the steps.

The wide upstairs hallway, with its faintly stained wainscot and faded wallpaper, split two sets of rooms. An old steamer trunk stood halfway down the hall. I lined up a shot of its worn leather handle. *Click.*

The Colonel tried guestroom #1. Saggy brass bed, a rocking chair, a tilted washbasin. *Click.* "Nobody here," he said, peering in an open chifforobe.

We headed down the hall, opening door after door. #2, #3, #4. Nobody, nobody, nobody. #5, #6, #7. *Click, click, click.* "Last room," he announced.

The library door creaked open. A mouse scurried from the cabinet, and Queen Elizabeth bounded after it. "No, Liz," Dale shouted. "Spit it out!"

"Lana will love this room," the Colonel said, and plucked a ragged book from the shelf. He leaned against the window frame, opened the book, and held it flat on his palm. *Click.* A paper slipped from his book and swooped to the floor.

"A photo!" I said, picking it up.

Two girls in old-timey dresses peered at us from the photo. A blur of a boy reached for a third girl. The camera had caught only her heel and ragged skirt-tail as she ran away. "Who's this?" I asked, turning the photo over, hoping for a footnote. Nothing.

"Miss Thornton might know," the Colonel said, and Queen Elizabeth sneezed. "We're out of rooms," he added, his patient brown eyes watching mine.

"Colonel, I know I heard somebody run down those stairs," I said, pocketing the photo. "And the keyboard slammed shut and the place chilled meat-locker cold."

"I know it too," Dale said.

The Colonel crossed his arms over his thin chest. "Whatever you saw is no longer in evidence," he said. "I'm not sure what else we can do."

Downstairs, the front door opened and closed. Lavender called up to us. "Colonel? The mayor's here."

The Colonel scowled. "I'd rather go toe-to-toe with your ghost," he muttered. "I haven't had time to explore the grounds," he said. "Could you two investigate?" He reached in his pocket. "You're welcome to my compass."

The Colonel never leaves home without his compass.

"Thank you, sir," I said. "But we'll stick to the paths."

Downstairs, the Colonel headed for the mayor and I made a beeline for Lavender, who was sanding the old reservation desk.

"No key," he said, tugging at a small drawer. "I'd hate to call a locksmith." He smiled. "How'd Ghost Patrol go?"

"Bad," I admitted. "Just like our surveillance of Harm Crenshaw."

The door swung open. "Speak of the devil," Dale said.

"That's some hello." Harm walked over to Lavender and stuck out his hand. "Crenshaw," he said. "Harm Crenshaw. Mo tells me you're hiring."

I glared at him. "I did not."

"I'm good with tools. I'm strong. And I'm not afraid of ghosts. How about it?"

Lavender smiled, but the friendly didn't make it to his eyes. "Lavender Johnson," he said, giving Harm's hand a quick shake.

"You know my brother, Flick," Harm said—like that would be a good thing. "I'm only in this two-bit town until Flick gets me set up in Greensboro, but I'll work hard while I'm here. How about it? You could use a good man."

Lavender picked up his paint scraper. *Click.* "Thanks, but Miss Retzyl would pin my ears back if I kept you out of school," he said. "We have laws, even in this 'two-bit town.'"

I clicked the shutter again just as Harm shifted to one side. Crud. A photo of Harm.

"Didn't mean anything by it," Harm told Lavender. "Some people like two-bit towns." He shoved his hands in his pockets. He might have looked cool if his fists hadn't strained against the fabric. "As for Miss Retzyl, I'm not worried about that backwoods nag."

Backwoods nag? Miss Retzyl?

"Take that back!" I shouted. "You ain't known her long enough to call her names."

"Sorry," Harm said, keeping his eyes on Lavender. "An after-school job? How about it? Minimum wage won't hurt my feelings."

"No thanks," Lavender said, his voice firm.

He shrugged. "Suit yourself," he said, heading for the door. "See you around, Ghost Girl."

Click. Just in case I ever need a photo for evidence, I thought.

"That kid's too much like his brother," Lavender said, watching him mount his bike. Harm zipped past the window and headed for the meadow.

I smiled at Lavender. "We'd love to stay and chat, but the Colonel has entrusted us with a critical task of an outdoor nature."

"We got to look around," Dale added, peeling off his sweatshirt.

Lavender picked up his sandpaper. "Watch out for snakes if you go down to the water."

Snakes. Great.

We crossed the front yard and headed for the trail leading to the creek.

"I don't understand ghosts any more than I understand girls," Dale said, kicking a pinecone ahead for Queen Elizabeth. "Why didn't she come? We even played her song."

"Maybe the Colonel makes her nervous," I answered.

The path twisted down the hill to a small brick building. Its sunken steps led to a door wearing a heavy chain and padlock.

"The springhouse," Dale said, circling the building. A ramble of kudzu draped the back wall; red bricks peeked between large, deep-green leaves. "Used to have a back door," he added. "Somebody filled it in with stacks of orange bricks. In a hurry too," he said, poking at a crooked brick. "Weird."

"Why would anybody do that?" I murmured. *Click.*

He looked toward the creek. "And there's the old pavilion where my granddaddy first danced with the girl he would marry." He gave me a shy smile. "My grandmother," he said, like I couldn't figure it out.

We picked our way down the steep, washed-out path to a large riverside platform riddled by water and time. A snake slithered into the still water and zigzagged away. Dale didn't even blink. "The band played at that end," he said, pointing to a pile of boards. "Mama says they hung lanterns between these poles so light skipped across the water, and they kept the floor polished so the ladies could glide."

I looked at the broad cypress-lined creek and wondered if my Upstream Grandmothers once danced—if they had more grace than me. *Click.*

A trace of rosemary drifted by. Queen Elizabeth sneezed and the hedge behind her moved against the breeze—just a glimmer of a form, a shimmer in the air, a rustle where a rustle shouldn't be.

Fear skated across my skin like heat lightning. "Dale," I whispered.

"I saw her," he said. And he took a step closer to me.

That night I settled into bed with the *Piggly Wiggly Chronicles*, Volume 6.

> Dear Upstream Mother,
>
> Today we saw the ghost.
>
> She followed Dale and me to the pavilion and stood behind a privet hedge, eavesdropping. Or watching. Seeing her froze me solid. I didn't even shoot her photo, which would have been proof positive. Also a certain A.
>
> It's hard when you got a ghost and nobody believes you. Not the Colonel, who searched. Not Miss Lana, who wants a Poster Ghost. Not even Lavender.
>
> Would you believe me? I think maybe you would.
>
> Mo

Chapter 11
The Alchemy of Light

On Monday, interview refusals flocked in from elders with second thoughts. Maybe the weekend had something to do with it, maybe the promise of autumn brought it on. Either way, Hannah Greene got shot down by travel.

"Grandmother went to Wrightsville Beach and decided to stay," she explained. "My great-aunt Tildy's subbing for me. She was at the Greensboro sit-ins." She smiled in Harm's direction. "You're from Greensboro. Maybe you've heard of them."

He didn't even look her way.

I opened my notebook to the empty section, the one marked math. *Harm = jerk.*

The Exums raised their hands. "Uncle Lewis remembered he can't stand us. He says we should get lost, maybe forever."

Miss Retzyl squeezed off a Pity Look. "I'm sure he didn't mean it."

Attila raised her hand. "I think he did."

"We're switching to Miss Delilah Exum," Jake replied. "She runs the best candy counter in the county."

"She has to like us," Jimmy added. "We're customers."

Thes raised his hand. "My uncle backed out too." He twisted in his desk, gazing hopefully at Attila. "Anybody want a partner?" Attila pretended to clean out her desk. "Fine," Thes sighed. "I'll take Mayor Little's mother."

The class gasped. Thes? And the meanest woman in town?

"I know," he said. "But she goes to our church and Daddy says I have to."

"She's a donut," Dale explained.

"Donor," Thes said. "She's a donor."

"I'm sure she'll be delighted," Miss Retzyl said. She looked at Harm, who sat with his eyes closed. "Harmond?" His snore zigzagged through the silence, soft and ragged as cotton. "Harmond Crenshaw!" she said, and he jumped like she'd Tasered him. "Whom will you interview? I need to know. Now."

"Interview?" Harm mumbled, his voice thick. "I'm working with Anna Celeste. She's got old what's-her-name."

Attila sat up. "Really?" she said. "I'm game if you are."

Thes gaped, his freckled face startled. "I thought you didn't want a partner."

"She doesn't want a partner with orange hair and

freckles," I explained. "Miss Retzyl, I object. I don't like Harm snooping around Grandmother Miss Lacy."

Miss Retzyl ignored me. "Harmond, you've already dropped a grade for taking so long to name an interview subject. The best you can make at this point is a B."

Anna's mouth fell open. "Does that apply to his partner too?"

"Oh no, not a B," Dale said, his voice quivering like a slap of lunchroom Jell-O.

"And how's *your* project coming?" Miss Retzyl asked, her stare ricocheting off me to hit Dale right between the eyes.

"Mo's got updates," he said, and stopped breathing.

"Thank you, Dale," I said. "Everything's going very smooth for Dale and me. We've introduced ourselves to our Entity, who prefers to remain anonymous for now, and presented our card. We've shot five rolls of film and we're working in the darkroom with Miss Lacy Thornton this afternoon."

"*I'm* interviewing Miss Thornton after school," Attila said. "She's not available for lesser endeavors until later."

Lesser endeavors? I hate Attila Celeste.

Miss Retzyl clapped her book shut. "Don't forget your science chapter tonight. Harmond, a word please," she said as the bell rang.

Yes. Detention for sleepy-headed Harm Crenshaw.

⋆⭒⋆⭒⋆

An hour later, I settled into Dale's beanbag chair. I pulled a clue pad from my bag and scrawled a title across the page: *Harm Crenshaw Investigation.*

"What do we know about the subject in question?" I asked.

Dale sat cross-legged on the floor, cradling his guitar. He twisted a key on the guitar's neck, sending the string's tone higher. He closed his eyes, listening. "If you're talking about science, I'm lost."

"I'm talking about Harm Crenshaw, our surveillance subject, who may be infiltrating Grandmother Miss Lacy's house as we speak."

He opened his music book and studied a diagram. "It's amazing how many songs you can play with just three chords. If you can sing, I mean. And I don't think Harm's infiltrating, Mo. I think he's just desperate not to fail history, same as us. Why else would he work with Attila?"

"What do we know about him, really?"

Dale looked up. "Okay, here's what I know: If Harm was any faster on that bicycle, we'd hear a sonic boom."

"First-class getaway vehicle. Check."

"He wears the same black pants and scuffed shoes every day, and has just three shirts. So he's poor. Which," he said, "poor happens."

Poor? I hadn't noticed, maybe because of the fancy bike.

He strummed his guitar. "That was a minor chord," he announced, strumming again. "Minor chords sound like Spanish moss." He was right. The sound felt lonely, like Spanish moss on a cloudy day. He played a cheerier chord. "Major chords sound like oak trees with their roots solid in the ground." He rested his arm against his guitar. "And Harm doesn't have a mother, same as you."

No mother? The words kicked me in the chest.

"What makes you say that?" I asked, my voice going tight as his guitar string.

"He eats a square meal every day," he said. "Orange four-cornered Nabs. Square, get it? He brings them from home the poor way instead of getting them out of a vending machine the flashy way. What mother gives you nothing but Nabs for lunch?" He strummed. Queen Elizabeth pawed at her ear. "That can't be right," he muttered.

He looked at me, his blue eyes serious. "Why do you care about Harm?"

"It's like Lavender says: Harm's trouble. I don't want him honing his evil skills on Grandmother Miss Lacy."

He shrugged. "Miss Thornton's smart. She can take care of herself."

I glanced at the clock. "Speaking of Grandmother Miss Lacy, she's expecting us at five o'clock to develop our photos. And I've shot enough photos of her and Miss Lana to paper the inn's lobby. With any luck I also got a portrait of our ghost. Academic jackpot. Feel free to applaud."

Instead of clapping, Dale squinted at Sir Isaac Newton. Newton stood on a piece of driftwood, staring at a fly. Even for an introvert, he looked moody. "I would go with you," Dale said, "but I promised Newton I'd write him a song." He lowered his voice. "He's going through an awkward stage and I'm the only friend he's got."

What? I'm being dumped for a newt?

"So far my entire life's an awkward stage, but you don't see me staring at flies," I said. "You're just afraid to see a possible ghost photo." I stood up, very dignified. "And since when can you write a song?"

"Since in about fifteen minutes from now."

Dale has an unusual grasp of time.

"Fine," I said. I closed the door behind me.

"Come in, dear," Grandmother Miss Lacy said, her carved oak door squeaking open. I peeped into the parlor. Attila perched on a velvet chair, a digital recorder at her side. "Anna Celeste is just finishing her interview," Grandmother Miss Lacy said loudly. She leaned close to my ear. "Thank heavens you're here. That child has interviewed me half to death."

I swept into the parlor. No Harm. "Hey Attila. Did you dump your partner?"

"*Dump* is an unattractive term, Moses."

Sometimes I could kill the Colonel for naming me Moses. I know I washed into town, but give me a break.

"Harmond and I agreed it's to our mutual advantage to work alone." A car horn tooted outside. "There's Mother. Thank you, Miss Thornton. I may have follow-up questions."

"Good glory," Grandmother Miss Lacy said, closing the door behind Attila. "I didn't know one girl could be so pushy." She smiled at me, her eyes twinkling. "Now you," she said. "I've been looking forward to this all day. I can't wait to introduce you to this form of . . . well, magic," she said, heading down the hall. "The alchemy of light."

She opened a door and I followed her into her tiny darkroom. She plucked two heavy rubber aprons from a hook. She put on hers, and handed me the other. Metal pans spanned the countertops, an old-fashioned machine crouched in the corner like a giant praying mantis. The air smelled mysterious and sharp.

"What *is* this stuff?" I asked, slipping the apron over my head. I wrapped the sash around, like the Colonel does with his cooking apron, and tied a half bow in front.

She closed the door, turned off the regular light, and flipped a red one on. "My darkroom," she said. I blinked in the eerie red glow. "Here's the film you've shot," she said, pointing to five strips of reddish brown negatives dangling from a line. "Some of your images mystify me, but I'd say you have a good eye, Mo. A very good eye.

"Now, let's see how things develop," she said, opening a pack of paper. She smiled like a schoolgirl. "Develop. Photography humor," she explained. "I haven't had this much fun in years. What expectations do you have, dear?"

"The Colonel says expectations are Fate's ambush," I said. "But I hope I've photographed a ghost."

I hadn't.

Two hours later my first batch of photos dangled from the wire, drying. "I don't get it," I said. "No ghost. And I've got all these nice crisp photos of Lavender, Dale, Miss Lana, the Colonel, the inn. But all my photos of you look like they're sprinkled with light. I don't have a single good photo of you in the inn, and you're half owner!"

"Perhaps I'm not photogenic," she said in the easy way of people who know they photograph good. I looked at my photos of Harm.

"Harm's came out just like yours," I said. "Like globs of light stuck to him."

"Maybe we splashed some chemicals," she murmured.

"Just on your photos and Harm's? If they were all on one roll that might make sense. And every time I photograph the piano, I get nothing but a blur."

"An exposure issue, I imagine. That piano's stood in that dark corner forever."

I grabbed a pair of tongs and swirled my last shot in its rinse. "Dale and me played 'Heart and Soul' on that piano the other day," I said, remembering her humming in the café. Her elbow clattered against the enlarger. "You know it?"

"Every child who's ever graced a piano bench knows that old song. I've played it many times, with many friends." She squinted at my library shots. "We'll reshoot the library too. It's as blurry as the piano. Don't worry, dear, I have beau-coodles of film."

"That reminds me, I got an old photo to show you," I said. "From the inn's library."

She hung her rubber apron on the door. I followed her to the kitchen, where she poured two glasses of milk. I hesitated, wanting to tell her about the glimmer at the pavilion, and the footsteps in the inn. I eased up to the subject, not sure she'd believe me.

"I'd hoped to photograph our ghost to prove things

to . . . people." She arranged our cookies on a plate. "You don't believe in ghosts," I said, sitting at her breakfast table. "I mean, I know you don't out loud, in the café. But just between you and me. When it's quiet. Do you?"

She shook her head. "There's all kinds of ghosts in this world, Mo, but the kind you mean? No, I don't believe. Oh, I'd like to," she added. "An unexplained breeze brushes my face or a sound turns my head, and I always hope to see someone I miss. So far, no one's come for me."

I scooted to the edge of my seat. "But you believe in other kinds?"

"In a way, I suppose," she said, putting the cookies on the table. "At my age, I sit down to breakfast with memories more often than with people I can touch," she said, and reached over to squeeze my hand.

"Memories aren't ghosts," I told her.

She smiled. "Perhaps not. I'm sure you'll sort it all out, dear. Eternity is no match for the Desperados. Here," she added, "try these cookies. They're my favorites."

I reached for a cookie. "They're homemade, I'm sure," I said, very polite.

"Mercy, no," she said. "When you're my age you don't waste time making cookies." We settled into a comfortable silence. "I wonder what a picture of a ghost would look like," she finally said. "Don't you?"

Actually, I'd given it zero thought. Or if negative numbers can hook up to that idea, less than zero thought. "Yes ma'am," I said, reaching for my milk. "Now that you mention it, I do. Speaking of photographs . . ."

I opened my messenger bag and lifted out the photo from the library: two girls looking into the camera, a skirt-tail, a blur of a boy. "We found this in the library," I said. "I hoped you might know who they are."

She grasped the photo in both hands and tilted it toward the lamp. "Will you look at that," she said. "Of course. That's me," she said, pointing to the thin, smiling girl. "The sourpuss is Myrt Little, the mayor's mother." She stared at the blurry figure. "The skirt's a mystery, but that's Red Baker," she said, tapping the boy's image. "Always moving, whirling, never could stand still. I probably photographed him twenty times, and didn't get more than two good photos for my trouble."

"Red Baker?" I said. "Why would you photograph *him?*"

She laughed. "We were children together—and friends." She propped her chin on her hand. "Don't look so surprised. Red was a very nice boy. Besides, I like to live a little on the edge. And Red Baker was certainly edgy—in an old-fashioned way."

Grandmother Miss Lacy and Red Baker, friends? Had the earth reversed its poles? "Red Baker used to be nice? What happened to him?"

"Anger, I suppose. Anger can corrode most anything if it sits still long enough."

Someone rapped at the door and she bustled down the hall. "Dale," she said, opening the door. "What a lovely surprise. And Queen Elizabeth. Do come in."

"We can't," Dale said. "Our paws are muddy. Excuse us, Miss Thornton, but is Mo here? Because I left my sweatshirt at the inn and Mama's gonna skin me alive if we don't get it back."

We? He wants me to go in a haunted inn at dusk for a *sweatshirt*?

"Mama's murderous careful about new clothes. And Mo *is* my best friend," he added. True. Being a best friend has its price.

I grabbed my messenger bag and headed for the door. The sun slanted low across Grandmother Miss Lacy's lawn, outlining her old garage in soft, golden light. "Thank you for the darkroom lesson," I said. "I loved it."

"So did I. You two be careful," she called as we crossed the porch. "It'll be dark before you know it."

I shivered. "She's right, Desperado," I said. "Let's fly."

Chapter 12
A Secret Uncovered

We pedaled frantic as bats on a rising moon. "Hurry," Dale panted as we swerved onto the inn's drive and bounced down the path, Queen Elizabeth galloping behind us. We jumped off our bikes and landed on our feet running across the lawn as the bikes spiraled to the earth behind us.

The inn's windows stared at us blank and empty. "At least nobody's looking at us this time," Dale said, glancing at the upstairs windows.

"Stop looking. She'll feel it and know we're here," I said.

"Right," he said, squinting up at the window.

"I said don't look!" I told him. "Where'd you leave your sweatshirt?"

"On the piano."

The one slammed shut by ghost hands?

"You know Dale, I've never actually taken something from a ghost. I'm not sure how they feel about that—as a people, I mean." He frowned. "Maybe you should let her have it," I said. "It *does* get cold when she's around. It could be a good deed."

He shook his head. "I promised Mama I'd bring it back."

Dale's a Mama's Boy through and through. Of course, with the daddy he's got, what choice does he have?

He pushed the front door open. "Hello? Anybody home?" He peeked inside. "There it is," he whispered. "I hope she hasn't been wearing it." He looked around the room. "Not that there's anything wrong with you having nice things," he said, louder. He turned to me. "I'll sneak in and grab it. You wait out here with Queen Elizabeth. But if I scream, come get me."

Wait out here? Joy surged through me.

"If anything happens, I'll save you," I said, hoping I wouldn't run the other way instead. He flexed his knees like he stood on the free-throw line. Then he tiptoed in, every muscle set to run. "Don't look at the stairs," I whispered. "Or touch the piano keys. And don't . . ."

He snagged the sweatshirt, wheeled, and sprinted toward me. "Did you see her?" I demanded, slamming the door behind him.

"No," he said. "But I feel her staring at us. Let's go."

I grabbed my bike. If we went the long way, it would

be pitch dark before we made the café. "The shortcut," I said, looking at Red Baker's path.

He gulped. "Stay close," he told Queen Elizabeth. "No trash-talking to Red's dogs. You ain't as big as you think."

We barreled across the meadow and onto the path, our tires crunching across a carpet of leaves. Near Red Baker's place, Dale hopped off his bike and waved toward the ground in the universally recognized signal for Dismount and Slink.

He swore softly as he peered across the yard. "Mr. Red's outside," he whispered. "Somebody's with him."

A man's harsh voice shoved through the silence. "They'll never make it," he said. A man stepped into the light. Flick Crenshaw! Flick spit in the grass. "That inn will bleed them dry. That wing nut and the old biddy . . ."

Mr. Red scowled. "Watch your mouth. I've known Lacy Thornton all my life."

Flick shrugged. "Have it your way." He got in his red sports car. It roared to life and sped toward us. "The bikes!" We yanked them into the bushes as Flick tore past, headed for the inn's driveway. The engine's sound faded away.

"Let's get out of here," Dale whispered. He stepped back, and a twig snapped.

Red Baker wheeled to face us. "Who's over there?" he

demanded, picking up a swing blade. We froze. "Detective Joe Starr? Come out where I can see you."

He took a step toward us. "I know you're there. Show yourself."

His front door scricked open. "Stew's ready, Gramps," a familiar voice said. "Is Flick staying? I made enough for all of us."

"Hush." Mr. Red's gaze patrolled the edge of his yard.

Behind us, a fox squirrel scampered along a tree limb and sprang to the ground. Dale grabbed Liz and clamped his hand over her muzzle.

Red stared at the squirrel, his face relaxing, and then turned toward the house. "Keep your shirt on, boy, I'm coming. You nag me worse than your mama ever did," he said, and headed for the house.

I bent the sassafras branch down. A dark-haired boy slouched tall and lanky in the doorway. Mr. Red clomped up the crooked cinderblock steps and across the porch. The boy at the door turned into the light.

"Crenshaw, Harm Crenshaw," I whispered. "He's Red Baker's grandson."

Chapter 13
Preemptive Strike

The next morning, we dropped our bikes and headed for the schoolhouse door. "Desperados," a voice called. "Wait up."

We turned to see Harm Crenshaw pedaling hard across the grounds. He hopped off his bike, chained it to the bicycle rack, and swaggered over to us. "Hey," he said.

"Hey," Dale replied, giving him a gunslinger look.

"I checked out your scarecrow," Harm said.

"Who cares?" I demanded.

"Good work," he told Dale. "The lederhosen are a nice touch."

"Of course it's nice work," I said. "Miss Lana says Dale's an artist. Like van Gogh, only with both ears."

He frowned and glanced at Dale's ears. "Right," he said. "Look, I'm sorry things didn't work out with Lavender. He seems like a nice guy. I'd like to help him and . . ." He hesitated and changed course. "Okay, I'll level with you. I could use the money. If either of you could put in a word for me. With Lavender or the Colonel . . ."

He stared at me, making his eyes soft and pleading.

"Puppy eyes," Dale warned, his voice scornful.

Harm Crenshaw was trying to play me! I swung my messenger bag over my shoulder. "If you need money, maybe your granddaddy can help you out," I said, heading toward the school.

Harm's puppy eyes disappeared. "Don't know what you're talking about."

"Red Baker dresses poor but people say he carries a roll of moonshine cash that would choke a mule." I looked at Dale.

"I know. Figure of speech," he said, beating me to it.

Harm hooked his thumb in his pocket and tried to smirk, but he moved jerky and off rhythm. "What's that got to do with me?"

"Red Baker," I said, heading up the steps. "He's your grandpa. Right?"

The door flew open. Attila stood with her hands on her hips, studying Harm with the gleam she usually reserves for research frogs. "You're Red Baker's grandson?"

"What if I am?" he asked, blushing. For a half second I felt sorry for him. I hate a blush. It's like a traitor riding beneath your skin.

"You eavesdropping, Attila?" I said. "Because where I come from, that's rude."

"Yes," she said. "And where *do* you come from?" She eyed Harm up and down. "That explains why you didn't want us to know where you live. I'd be ashamed too."

"Who says I'm ashamed?" Harm shot back.

"Actions speak louder than words," Attila retorted. "Excuse me, I'd hate to miss morning announcements. Wouldn't you, Harmond?" The door hissed closed behind her.

"What did you do to *her*?" Dale asked.

Harm shrugged. "She dumped me as her history partner, so I called her queen of the backwater brown-nosers."

Dale whistled. "She'll be gunning for you," he said as the three of us headed down the hall and settled into our desks.

Miss Retzyl claimed her place at the front of the room looking pretty in a regular pink dress and her own hair. She doesn't own a wig—I've asked. Dressing normal's a way of life for her—something I appreciate after a lifetime with Miss Lana. "Good morning," she sang.

Attila raised her hand. "I have an announcement. Normally I wouldn't say this, but I feel full disclosure's best in a small town. I'm sure we'd all agree."

Full disclosure? Has she lost her mind?

"She's ratting him out," Dale whispered, and I nodded.

I looked at Harm, who clenched his fist and took a deep breath. He wasn't going down without a fight. The Colonel says my enemy's enemy is my friend. I raised my hand, buying Harm some time. "I hear the Exums got in trouble last night," I said. "I thought I'd mention it in the interest of full disclosure."

"We did not!" Jake cried. "We don't even own any paint!"

Paint? What was that about?

Miss Retzyl clapped her hands. "Anna Celeste, you have the floor," she said.

Harm's voice boomed out. "Miss Retzyl, I've decided on my history paper. I'm interviewing my grandfather Mr. Red Baker, well-known moonshine consultant." The class gasped. Attila looked like a first grader who'd swallowed her ice cream money.

"Preemptive strike," Dale murmured. "Good."

"Your *grandfather*?" Sal said, studying him. "So that's who you are."

"You're interviewing Red Baker?" Hannah said, her voice tinted with admiration. "He's even meaner than Mayor Little's mother."

Harm's eyes never left Miss Retzyl's face. "I know I can only make a B at this point, but it's taken me this long to confirm my interview. Red's temperamental. I appreciate your patience and hope my paper's worth your wait."

The class swiveled to Miss Retzyl. "Thank you, Harmond," she said, her voice bland as vanilla pudding. "I look forward to your report."

He gave Attila a smile. "Sorry I interrupted you, Anna," he said. "What were you saying?"

Attila slammed her book report onto her desk. "Never mind."

I grinned. Anna Celeste Simpson had met her match.

Chapter 14
Somebody Screamed.
Maybe Me.

Labor Day—with Miss Lana's famous Farewell to Summer Parking Lot Cookout—came and went, clearing the way for the first quick breath of autumn. The next day—Tuesday—Dale and me dropped by the inn after school. We found Lavender fuming on the front porch.

"I've never seen anything like it," he said, grabbing an armload of tools and taking them to his truck. "Everybody we hire runs away. Even Sam and Tinks quit. I'm never going to get this place ready in time for the party." He raked his fingers through his hair. "What are you two doing out here, anyway?" he asked, slapping his cap against his knee. "I'm in such a bad mood, I forgot to ask."

Lavender's bad moods fall rare as snow and melt just as quick.

"We got to reshoot some photos," I said.

"Come in, then. Tell me what you think," he said, slamming the tailgate shut and heading up the steps.

He pushed the door open and we stepped inside. Without their skins of cobwebs and dust, the rooms stood sleek and elegant. The heart pine floorboards stretched on like rivers of honey, the windows flooded the rooms with afternoon light. We walked across the lobby, our steps echoing. "It's big as Kansas in here," Dale said as Queen Elizabeth sniffed the baseboards.

"Five rooms cleaned, seven to go. But without Sam and Tinks . . ." He slapped his cap against his leg again. "I might as well tell you. I don't believe in ghosts, but it looks like everybody else in the county does."

Including us, I thought.

"Ghosts?" Dale said, looking worried. "Plural?"

"They swear ghosts move their tools. They hear footsteps and voices. A girl's voice, men's voices . . ." I heard myself swallow. "Window glass that shouldn't break does break. It's ridiculous," he said. "I'm in and out of this place all the time and I haven't heard a thing. But I still have to hire again. *Because of ghosts.*"

"Are you sure they hear *voices*?" Dale asked, darting an anxious peek at the stairs. "Because there's only one ghost in Miss Lana's contract." He looked at me, his face grave. "We could have squatters from the other side."

Lavender snorted. "There's no ghost, little brother," he said. "Those guys are scaring themselves out of here.

Which means telling the ladies we got to post another ad. Are they at the café?"

"Miss Lana is," I said. "Grandmother Miss Lacy's gone to see her accountant."

"Again?"

"It's a full-time job being rich," I said. "That's what Miss Lana says."

He stuffed his shirttail in his jeans. "I wouldn't know about that, but I'd like to find out."

"You will, soon as you win Daytona," I told him.

"I do admire your confidence, Mo," he said. "You all want a ride to the café? I can put your bikes in the back of the truck."

Riding in the GMC with Lavender. Tempting. But I didn't want to see Miss Lana's face when he told her their workers had flaked like crescent rolls. "Thanks," I said, "but Attila's burning a DVD of Grandmother Miss Lacy and we got to get top-grade photos or risk Comparative Flunking. Skeeter can give us PowerPoint for a fee—if we get the photos in time."

"PowerPoint? Good name for a bird dog." He grinned. "Dale?"

"I'll stay," Dale said, his voice dull. "If I don't come out, tell Mama I love her."

"I think she's noticed," Lavender said. "Let me get this

over with." He hates giving Miss Lana bad news. Even his hair lost its luster.

I made my voice easy, the way Miss Lana does when I head for school shy a book report. "Lavender, even if you fail and ruin the biggest party in history and even if the entire town turns against you, Dale and me won't feel let down."

"I might," Dale said, putting his hands in his pockets. "A little."

Outside, the wind set the porch chairs rocking. Lavender stared at me a moment, possibly overwhelmed by my compassion.

"Thanks, Mo," he said. "I appreciate your support. Close the door on your way out," he added, and strolled out whistling.

"I'll be quick, Dale," I promised. I shot three fast ones of the piano, and headed for the dining room. The chandelier looked great against the high, pressed-tin ceiling. I focused on a tear-shaped prism. *Click.* "Let's get the library," I called, backtracking.

"No," Dale said. "I'm not going up there. Neither is Queen Elizabeth."

As I started toward him, a low voice rumbled through the room. My sneakers squeaked to a halt. The dining room stood empty and still. "Lavender?"

Dale called, turning to the door. "Did you forget something?"

Thank goodness. Lavender. A voice shivered through the silence: *"Get . . . out."*

My heart stuttered. That wasn't Lavender.

"Mo?" Dale called, his voice off pitch.

"Get . . . out . . . of . . . my . . . inn." Every nerve in my body jumped. My fingers went numb. The voice floated out of nowhere, louder, whispery rough. *"Get . . . out . . . now . . ."*

Somebody screamed. Maybe me.

"Run!" Dale shouted, pounding toward the door. He jerked it open as a second voice shot down the stairs. *"Help,"* a high-pitched voice called. *"Help!"* I twirled on the dining room threshold as the chandelier started swinging. *Click.*

"Wait for me, Dale!" I shouted. I bolted across the porch and jumped the steps. Dale wobbled down the drive, steering his bike with one arm. Liz dangled wildly beneath the other, all four paws trying to run.

Chapter 15
Not for Sale

The next afternoon, Dale sat in the café nursing a milkshake and poring over my photos. "What do you mean, what would a photo of a ghost look like?"

"Interesting question," Lavender said from the counter. He'd dropped by to pick up a couple checks for supplies. He'd lured Sam and Tinks back with the promise of a spin around the racetrack, once he's racing again.

"I see why you want to reshoot," Dale said. "We got blurry piano and library pictures, and Miss Lacy Thornton and Harm look like they got light blobs stuck to them." He smiled at Lavender. "At least she got some good shots of you," he said, thumbing through the stack. "This one's nice," he added, studying a photo of the Colonel and Lavender, side by side.

"It's yours," I said, and he slipped it into his pocket.

Miss Lana smiled. "Cousin Gideon might have some ideas about your photos, sugar," she said. "He dabbles in unusual things. Why don't you write to him? He loves letters, which he claims are a lost art."

The Colonel backed in from the kitchen carrying a tray of coffee cups. "With Gideon, working's a lost art," he said. "He should get a job."

Miss Lana ignored him. "And if Gideon can't answer your questions," she continued, signing the last check with a flourish, "he may know someone who can. He attracts interesting people."

"He attracts flakes," the Colonel said.

I nodded. I'd get Skeeter to email my note. It only cost a quarter, and it would save time.

Lavender slipped the checks in his pocket. "Thanks, Miss Lana," he said. "Ready, Colonel? We got a meeting with the building inspector in half an hour."

The Colonel sighed. "Roger." He headed for the Underbird.

Poor Colonel. Before his memory found him, he spent days plotting courses through wild forests and nights sleeping beneath the stars. Now he has mayors and building inspectors to deal with.

When you're not used to normal, it pinches like new shoes.

No sooner had Lavender and the Colonel rounded the curve than Red Baker's rattletrap truck wheeled into the parking lot. Mr. Red stepped out in his auction clothes: white shirt, red tie, pressed chinos, black shoes polished to a high sheen.

Now what?

"Good afternoon," Miss Lana said as he scuffed across the tiles to the counter. She patted her Marilyn Monroe wig into place. "How can we help you today?"

"You can't. I came to do you a favor." Miss Lana smiled so quick, I almost missed the suspicion in her eyes. I walked over beside her and stepped up on my Pepsi crate. Red Baker's eyes flickered over me. "Nobody wants to work for you," he told Miss Lana. "That inn's haunted, whether you got the eyes to see it or not."

"There's nothing wrong with Miss Lana's eyes," I told him.

"Didn't say there is." He ran a hand across his whiskers. "You got ghosts. People talk. You'll run out of money soon enough, and then what?"

He popped his knuckles. "I hate seeing Lacy Thornton struggle," he said. "If Lacy goes down, others go down. Lacy's a silent partner with his mama," he said, nodding at Dale. "And others besides."

Miss Lana's face went calm as porcelain. "How can I help you?" she asked. Miss Lana says when dealing with a person of Unknown Intentions, you should be double polite—once for them, once for you. The Colonel says you should look for a weapon. "Pear pie, perhaps?" she offered, removing the pie cover and picking up a knife.

"I'll take a piece if it will help," Dale offered, vaulting onto a stool.

"I didn't come for pie," Red Baker said. "I came to buy the inn."

She hesitated, the knife hovering over the crust. She cut a careful wedge and slipped it onto a saucer. Red Baker grinned like a snake smiling at a mouse. A shiver crept up the back of my neck. "Even if you fix that inn up, nobody will stay there," he said. "It's too haunted. I've seen them myself. I'll take the place off your hands, and pay you to boot."

"How much?" I asked.

"Uppity kid," he said without looking at me.

Miss Lana summoned a paper-thin smile. "Mo enjoys a certain *joi de vivre*. She also asks good questions."

"Twenty thousand dollars, cash on the barrelhead," he said. "Say the word."

"Twenty thousand dollars?" I said. "We paid ten times that."

"Good math," Dale whispered.

Miss Lana slid the pie to Dale. "Mr. Baker, if that inn's a bad investment, why would you buy it, even for that piddling amount?"

Another good question. *Pop-pop-pop.* "My pig operation bumps up against your property. I want to expand it."

Pig operation? What pig operation?

I looked at Dale as he shoved a forkful of pie into his mouth. "Ah nebba sthmel ana piiihs," he said, reaching for his milk.

"I never smelled any pigs either," I said.

"You won't." Mr. Red tugged a roll of dirt-streaked cash out of his pocket. "Here's my down payment. Take it or leave it."

This time, Miss Lana's smile was an out-and-out lie. "The inn's not for sale."

He shrugged. "Lacy Thornton can't keep you afloat forever," he said, stuffing his cash in his pocket. "She ain't as rich as people think."

"Grandmother Miss Lacy's plenty rich," I said.

"Really? Lacy Thornton's father drove a rich man's car," he said. "Lacy drives a Buick old as you are. You call yourself a detective. You figure it out."

He clomped to the door, leaving a trail of black shoe-prints.

Chapter 16
Footnotes from Charleston

Friday evening, as I sat in my room contemplating the evils of fractions in general and common denominators in particular, my vintage bedside phone jangled. "Mo's flat, Mo speaking," I said. I possess killer telephone skills.

"Is this Mo LoBeau of Desperado Detective Agency?" a man asked.

"That's right. Your life disaster is our pleasure. How can we help?"

"This is Cousin Gideon, Esquire."

I laughed. "Cousin Gideon! How are you?"

"Fine, sugar. I hope you are. I just got your Skee-mail. Sounds like big goings-on in little Tupelo Landing."

"Huge," I agreed. "Dale and me hope to bring you on board as a footnote for our ghost case."

He laughed liquid and slow. "I am scared to death of ghosts, sugar," he drawled, "but I have an absolutely intrepid friend who investigates haunted places for a living. I showed her your questions and I have her answers here. Got a pencil handy?"

"Shoot," I said, turning a page in my notebook.

"First, my friend prefers film cameras to digital ones. Ghosts generally show up like orbs of light."

My heart skipped.

"She also suggests setting up a voice-activated recorder in the inn at night. I know Lana has one because I gave her one for Christmas years ago. It's so old, it uses tapes, but it should work just fine."

I shivered. "Ghosts talk to each other at night?"

"Well, I'm no expert, but I don't see any reason to stop chatting just because you're dead. Do you?" Cousin Gideon's a notorious chatter.

"I saw that tape recorder in Miss Lana's doodad drawer the other day," I told him. "Did your friend mention seeing ghosts? Because Mr. Red says he's seen them and Lavender's workers claim ghosts move their tools. And Dale and me have heard things and seen a possible glimmer."

"Hmmm." Tap tap tap. Cousin Gideon taps his pen against his teeth when he's thinking. A bad habit. "Well, she says some people see ghosts and others can't. Others hear them, or smell them. She didn't mention moving things specifically, but I suppose they can. I mean, they have a reputation for that kind of mischief, don't they?"

"Right. Thanks, Cousin Gideon," I said, jotting a few notes. "This makes dynamite background." I made an executive decision. "In fact, I'm awarding you full foot-note status. Congratulations."

Miss Lana says people can hear you smile into the phone. She's right. I could hear Cousin Gideon beaming. "Appreciate it, darling," he said, and then hesitated. "You be careful with this stuff, Mo. You know what they say: Fools rush in where angels fear to tread. And you're no fool, Mo LoBeau."

"I ain't much of an angel either," I said, and he laughed.

"Come see me, sugar. Now, if Lana's nearby I'd love to hear her voice."

An hour later I pushed open the inn's door and tugged Miss Lana's tape recorder from my pocket. I crept across the lobby, Dale following so close, his toes snigged at my heels. "If Mama learns I snuck out, she'll kill me. Don't look at the chandelier. Or at the stairs," he whispered, putting his hand on my shoulder. *"Or the piano."*

I stopped and he slammed into me. "Open your eyes, Dale," I snapped. "I ain't a seeing eye friend." I tiptoed behind the reservation desk, clicked the recorder on, and put it under Lavender's dust mask. "We'll come back in the morning to see who we caught chatting."

I took Dale's cold, clammy hand and led him to the door.

* ⋆ * ⋆ *

The next morning, I called Dale the instant I opened my eyes. "Wake up," I said.

"Saturday morning. Ghost tape," he replied, and hung up.

The tape recorder sat right where we'd left it. Only one thing had changed: "It's nearly full," Dale said.

Ghost voices. On tape. Proof. Automatic A. The skin on the back of my neck crawled. "Let's hear it," I said.

He backed up, shoving his hands behind his back. "I don't touch ghost things. It's a rule."

"Fine." I hit rewind. Then play. We leaned toward the recorder, straining to hear. First, scrabbling. "Ghost fingers," Dale whispered. "Or mice." Then footsteps. My mouth went dry. "Ghost shoes," he whispered.

A man's voice jumped out at us: *"Will you look at this."*

"Ghost!" Dale cried, grabbing my arm. I yanked free. The voice sputtered, and I heard something heavy slide across the floor. Then: *"Where's that hammer?"*

"Ghost with hammer," Dale breathed. "Bad."

"Looks like they replaced that window glass again. Idiots."

"Hold on, Dale," I said, frowning. "I know that voice."

Pop-pop-pop.

"That's Red Baker popping his knuckles like always, and that's his hateful old voice."

"No," Dale whispered.

I leaned closer to the recorder. "He's dragging something," I said. I looked around the inn, at a faint double track across the heart pine floor. "A stepladder," I said, glancing at the ladder propped against the wall. On the tape, faint footsteps scuffed up the ladder's steps. Then a sharp whack.

I looked at the parlor window. A crack zigzagged across its face.

A wave of anger nearly swept me off my feet. I jabbed the recorder, turning it off, and stared at Dale. "You know what this means, don't you?"

"Yes," Dale whispered. He collapsed onto the stairs and rested his forehead against his palms. He drew a jagged breath.

Poor Dale. He'd known Red Baker all his life. Now this.

I sat beside him. "Are you okay?" I asked, trying to sound sensitive.

He looked up at me, his blue eyes glistening. "I think so. It's just shocking is all. I mean, Red Baker." He shook his head. "He looks so . . . lifelike."

Lifelike?

Sometimes I wonder what it would be like to live in Dale's world. Other times I think I wouldn't last five minutes in there. "He *is* lifelike, Desperado. He's alive."

"Right," he said, sagging with relief. "I think so too."

I hopped up and paced, my hands behind my back. "We ain't got ghosts, Dale. We got Red Baker tricking us. And you know what that means, don't you?"

"We're failing history. Again."

"It means we're on the verge of solving a major crime," I said. "We need backup."

Detective Joe Starr blasted through the café door a half hour later. He's dark and handsome in a plainclothes cop way, but I still think Miss Retzyl could do better. "What's wrong?" he demanded, looking around the empty café.

Miss Lana looked up from her recipe book. "Well, I'm thinking of going vegetarian on Tuesdays, which I suppose some people could see as wrong. What do you think? You're more of a meat-and-potatoes man, I believe."

True. Joe Starr's a carnivore, tooth and nail. "Pris said you have an emergency," he said. He zeroed in on me, and his hands went to his hips. "You," he said.

"Good afternoon Detective," I replied, very professional. "Allow me to compliment you on your response time." He waited, his sleet-gray eyes unsmiling. "The Desperados have solved another major crime and we'd like you to make an arrest. Lavender's waiting for us at the inn. There's just one more person we need to notify."

"And without him we're pretty much dead," Dale added.

True. I dialed. Fortunately, Mr. Red picked up. "This is Mo LoBeau of Desperado Detective Agency. Miss Lana's selling the inn," I said. "Meet us there in a half hour." I hung up before he could get a word out.

Twenty minutes later Red Baker ambled through the inn door and froze. Detective Starr simmered by the window, his arms crossed. Miss Lana perched on a sawhorse, filing her nails. Lavender leaned against the desk, looking good in corduroy.

"Thanks for dropping by," I said.

He edged back toward the door, bumping into Harm. "I didn't drop by. I came because you said Lana's selling the inn. Why's Starr here?"

I pulled the tape recorder from my pocket. "First Dale and me got something we'd like you to hear." I pressed play. His gravelly voice flooded the room. *"Left their tape measures out again. Idiots."* Pop-pop-pop.

Miss Lana stood up. "Sabotage," she said, her voice drizzling scorn over the word.

I turned off the tape. "There's more," I said. "Moving tools, breaking that window." I gave Starr a detective-to-detective smile. "We'll turn our evidence over to you and prepare a press release including the correct spelling of our names."

Starr slipped the recorder into his pocket. "If you have an explanation, Mr. Baker, this would be a good time," he said.

Mr. Red shrugged. "Don't know what you're talking about."

"That's your voice and your popping knuckles," Lavender said. "We know it, and a jury will know it." He glared at Harm. "And what's your role in this?" he demanded. "No wonder you wanted a job. Talk about easy access to your crime scene." Harm's mouth fell open. I'd seen him fake surprise in class, but this looked real.

Mr. Red stepped in front of Harm. "I'll pay for your darned window," he said. "Leave Harm out of this."

"Who are you talking to on that tape?" Starr demanded.

"Myself," Mr. Red growled. "I'm an old man."

Interesting. Maybe Red Baker does care about Harm, I thought. He shoved Harm toward the door. On the other hand, I thought, maybe he doesn't.

"What about the rest of it?" I asked. "What about the footsteps upstairs?"

"Don't know what you're talking about," Mr. Red said, heading for the door.

Starr reached for his handcuffs. "I take it you'll press charges, Lana? Take your pick: malicious mischief, breaking and entering, harassment, trespassing. Mr. Baker, this way to the patrol car."

Harm swallowed so hard, I could hear him from across the room. Miss Lana's eyes went softer. "I'd like to talk to Lacy Thornton first, if you don't mind. She's home today, a little under the weather."

"Let's go see her then," Starr said, glancing at Harm. "Stay where I can find you," he said. "If Mr. Baker goes to jail, we'll make arrangements for you."

"Arrangements," Dale mumbled under his breath. "Bad."

Starr walked Mr. Red to the Impala, Lavender and Miss Lana trailing behind. That left me, Dale, and Queen Elizabeth. Plus Harm, and an accusing silence.

The Impala pulled away. "You getting left on your own is an Unforeseen Consequence of our good detective work," I said. "It wasn't part of our plan."

"Same as Daddy staying in jail so long," Dale said.

Harm shrugged, walked to the piano, and opened the keyboard. "It's not the first time I been left. I always land on my feet."

"Just between us, how did Mr. Red do the rest of the haunting?" I asked.

Harm stretched his hands across the piano keys and a soft chord rippled through the silence. Cold flooded the room. He spun to face us. "What the . . ."

"Like, how did he rig *that*?" Dale asked, snuggling into his sweatshirt.

Harm looked around the room. "How did he deep-freeze this dump?" he said, crossing his arms and shivering. "He didn't. How *could* he?"

"And what about her?" Dale asked, pointing to the staircase. "How does Mr. Red make *her* happen?"

"Who?" Harm and I asked together, turning.

My heart jumped like a racer out of the blocks as a swirl of pale pink light wandered down the stairs, to the piano. It hovered, and then sailed straight for Harm.

Harm's thin face went gray as a raw plaster wall. He backed, backed, backed away as the pink moved closer, closer, and churned to a halt inches from his face.

Red Baker didn't concoct *that*. I grabbed my camera and pointed it with shaking hands.

"She's . . . gone," Dale said, looking around the room as the mist faded and the temperature rose.

"What was *that*?" Harm demanded.

"Our history interview," Dale said. "She acted like she knew you."

"Knew me? That's crazy."

Dale looked Harm up and down. "Ghost bait," he said, his voice thoughtful. He looked at me. "I told you we'd need some."

And Harm sat down on the floor. Hard.

Chapter 17
Spitting Image

Harm stood waiting for us Monday morning at the bicycle rack—a definite surprise. "Hey Ghoul Girl," he said. Not a surprise. I nudged my bike into the rack.

"Hey yourself, Ghost Bait. What's up?"

"Shhh," he said, his gaze lingering on Attila and Hannah, who leaned against an oak tree, chatting. "Don't call me that," he said. "And nothing's up. I mean, nobody pressed charges, which was . . . nice. I appreciate it."

Thes blasted past. "Going to storm tonight," he said. "Eighty percent chance. And a cold front drifting down, but no snow. It's way too early for snow."

"Thanks, Thes," I said, and he trotted away. I looked at Harm. "Thes is weather-obsessed. There's no way to stop him, so Miss Lana says to thank him."

Dale jammed his bike in the rack. "Hey Harm, you want to talk ghosts? Because ours likes you, and as Ghost Bait for our interview, you got a right to ask."

Harm crossed his arms. "You want me to help with

your paper?" he asked, and we nodded. "Sure, I'll do it. Cost you a hundred dollars," he said.

"A hundred dollars?" I said. "We don't have that kind of money."

"Your call. You can get back to me," he said, slipping back into his smirk, just like that. "You got your interview questions?" he asked. "After what I saw Saturday, I'm thinking they'd better be darned good ones."

"We got them," I said. "You first."

To my surprise, he opened his notebook. "Questions for Red Baker. One: What's your earliest memory of your father, Mr. Truman Baker? Two: What did Truman's distillery smell like and how did it work? Three: How did Truman's business affect local culture and commerce?"

"Fancy words and good questions," Dale said. "Miss Retzyl will like those."

Harm closed his notebook and stuffed it in his pack. "They're only good questions if Red answers them. And since he hasn't actually agreed to an interview, I see an F in my future."

Dale shook his head. "He won't want a grandson to flunk." He tilted his head like a curious owl. "Funny, I never knew Mr. Red had a grandson. And I been knowing him all my life."

"Well, you got me beat," Harm said. "I only met him at the auction."

My stomach fluttered like I'd stepped in an elevator going down too fast. *He just met him?* What if I met Upstream Mother and she turned out to be like Red Baker?

"So *that's* why Mr. Red dressed up for the auction," Dale said, his voice going soft. "To meet you. That was nice of him."

"Charming," Harm said. "What about you, Ghost Girl? You got questions?"

I knew them by heart. "One: What's your name? Two: What happened to you? Three: How much allowance do you get in the next world?"

"Allowance," Dale said, pulling a crumpled paper out of his pocket. "Good." He smoothed his paper against his leg and read out his questions.

"One: Why are you still here? Two: Do you get lonely? Three: Do you dream about people you used to know?"

Sometimes it surprises me, the things Dale thinks about.

"Pathetic," Attila said, brushing by. "Maybe you should try these. One: Who do I think I'm kidding? Two: Am I lying through my teeth? Three: How many times will I repeat sixth grade?"

She shot us a withering glare. "*My* paper's done. I only need to print it."

"Like we care, Metal Mouth," Harm said. He looked sheepish as she stomped away. "I guess I'd have braces too if I could afford them," he said. "Flick says a good smile's worth thousands of dollars later in life. Listen," he said, "what are you two doing this afternoon? Because I actually would like to talk about . . . things."

"We're going to Grandmother Miss Lacy's with our latest batch of film."

"*I'm* not," Dale said, backing away. "Not if you're carrying ghost film."

"You're just scared to look a ghost in the eye," I said. "But you are too going. If Miss Retzyl asks you about developing film, you got to answer. Besides, Grandmother Miss Lacy's not feeling good. It would be a good social skill to pay her a call."

For a split second I thought Harm would ask to come along. Then: "Thank her for me," he said. "For not pressing charges against Red. Thank Miss Lana too."

"Thank them yourself," I said, and headed up the steps.

That afternoon, Dale and I stood on Grandmother Miss Lacy's porch, shivering in a chill wind. Thes had nailed it: cold front. I knocked on the carved front door.

Dale stared at Queen Elizabeth hard enough to bend spoons. "Sit," he said. To my shock, she plopped down by the door. "Good girl. I can't believe you came to school," he told her, ruffling her ears. "She's never done that before, Mo."

"She's brilliant," I lied, and knocked again.

"Miss Thornton's yellow pansies look good," he said, peering at the wide-faced little flowers. "Mama says they're tougher than they look."

The door creaked open. "I thought I heard voices," Miss Lana said. "Miss Thornton's in the parlor. The doctor told her to rest and avoid stress. She's bored out of her mind. She'll be glad to see you." She kissed my face. "Don't get her too excited though, sugar," she said, and hurried toward the café.

"Too excited?" Dale echoed. "What does that mean, exactly?"

"No darkroom," I said, and he smiled like I'd yanked him out of detention.

"You go on in," he said. "I'll be there after Liz settles in."

I found Grandmother Miss Lacy thumbing through a photo album. She sat with a green shawl draped over her thin shoulders, her blue hair glinting in the glow of the fireplace. I knocked on the door casing. "Mo! Thank heavens. I'm bored within an inch of my life. Sit down and talk to me."

I filled her in on school faster than Lavender at the racetrack: word problems, analogies, book reports. "Plus I shot more film for history," I told her. "But it can wait."

Finally we turned to Red Baker and his fake ghost.

"I've known Red Baker all my life, and he has *never*

made me so furious," she fumed as Dale tiptoed by cradling something in his arms. "What did he hope to accomplish by scaring our workers away? He doesn't need land for his pigs."

"You're right," I said. "He's up to something."

"Red's been up to something since birth," she said, and then laughed like water breaking through a dam. She reached for her album and thumbed through the pages. "I have a photo I'd like you to see." I peeped at the pages. "Here I am with Father's Duesenberg," she said, showing me a black-and-white of a short, birdlike girl and a long, pale car. She turned the page. "And this blur in knickers is Red Baker."

She flipped the page. "Here's a rare image of him standing still." I peered at the photo as Dale walked into the room holding a clear bowl of suspiciously familiar yellow pansies.

"I hope you feel better soon," he said, trying not to slosh water on the floor.

Grandmother Miss Lacy blinked at her own pansies. "Thank you, dear," she said. "They'd look best on the marble-topped table, perhaps."

I turned back to the old photo of Mr. Red as a boy. Black hair, thin face. He wore a long-sleeve shirt and tie, knickers and argyles. He held a cap in his hand and stood lanky as a coyote, his thin shoulders sloping a modicum to the left. "*That's* Red Baker?" I asked. "He's a dead ringer for Harm Crenshaw."

"Or the other way around," Dale said, peering at the photo.

She laughed. "It took me a while to place Harm the day we drove to the auction. But you're right. Harm's the spitting image of his grandfather."

People say that like it's nothing—being the spitting image of somebody else.

"Can I borrow this?" I asked.

"I suppose," she said, sliding it out and handing it to me. "I'll want it back, though," she added as the phone jangled. "Could you get that, dear? It's probably another Azalea Woman calling to see if I'm dying and if so, who's in the will. Take a message," she called as I trotted down the hall. "I'll return calls tomorrow."

I swept into the kitchen. The supper plate Miss Lana brought over rested on the counter, covered with a neat white napkin. I grabbed the phone, the antique kind that clings to the wall. "Grandmother Miss Lacy's residence, honorary granddaughter Mo LoBeau speaking," I said.

"Who?" a woman said.

"Mo LoBeau, cofounder of Desperado Detective Agency. Who's this?"

"Miss Filch, manager at State Bank, calling for Lacy Thornton."

I frowned. The old "I got a title and you don't" trick. I'd used it before, mostly on third graders.

"Greetings, Filch," I replied. "Miss Thornton is resting. I am Miss LoBeau, her ambassador. May I help you?"

"I need *her,* sweetie. Call her to the phone."

I smiled so wide my lips hurt, in case Miss Lana was right and smiling might put Filch in a better mood. "I can take a message. She'll call you."

She huffed like she could blow my house down. "Tell her Miss Filch called. *Again.* Tell her we have *still* not received payment. Tell her she needs to call me by ten o'clock tomorrow morning or I'll start the paperwork. Understand?"

I gasped. "Paperwork? What's going on?"

The phone went dead in my hand.

Chapter 18
A Paying Customer, Sort Of

"Paperwork?" Dale said that evening as thunder galloped across the sky. We sat in my flat—me on the bed and Dale at my desk—schoolbooks scattered around us. "Paperwork's bad," he said. "Paperwork happens just before they take your car. Not that anybody would want Miss Thornton's old Buick. And what payment? And how come it's late? Miss Thornton's got more gold than Fort Knox."

"I don't know," I said, trying to dis-remember Red Baker's warnings.

"Did you ask her?"

"Not exactly. I told her State Bank called and I'd left the message in the kitchen. She said 'that terrible Filch woman again.' Then she said not to worry, she'd handle it."

"Well then," he said, swiveling back and forth on my desk chair. "We might as well not worry."

Dale kills me. He's got a worry switch he flips just

like that. It's something he got from his daddy, not from Miss Rose. "I hate English," he said. "Why do we have to study a foreign language anyway?"

"English ain't a foreign language," I told him.

"Are *you* English?" he demanded. "Because I'm not." I could see his point, which made me uncomfortable. "What's an analogy again?" he asked.

"A double-barreled comparison. Miss Retzyl's crazy about them. Here, try another one: Chicken is to feather as mink is to blank."

"Coat?" he guessed.

"Fur," I said, drawing a picture of a fluffy chicken and a slender mink. I turned my notebook toward him. "See?"

He frowned. "What's that supposed to be? Dwarves? Because you can't make fun of people, Mo. It isn't right."

I took a moment. Only the intrepid study with Dale.

"Forget the pictures," I said. "Chickens have feathers and minks have fur. Chicken is to feather as mink is to fur. You got to give it both barrels. Our test is tomorrow, Dale. Try again: Dark is to night as light is to . . ." Dale sucked his lip in and squeezed his eyebrows together. If I waited any longer, he might swallow his face. *"Day,"* I said, exasperated. "Dark is to night as light is to day."

I sighed. I needed a hot chocolate. Maybe a double.

Dale jumped. "What was that?"

"The storm," I said as a gust of wind hit the house and rain pounded the roof. "You want some hot chocolate?"

Footsteps clomped across the porch. "Mo, somebody's out there."

"Probably the Colonel. Who's there?" I called. "Colonel?"

The footsteps stopped at my door. "It's Harm. Let me in."

Crenshaw, Harm Crenshaw? Here?

I opened the door on a night wild with bluster and rain. "What are you doing out on a night like this?"

Harm shrugged out of his soggy jacket, stepped inside, and shook his head like a dog, splattering storm across my wall. "I need a detective, and I've got cash."

Cash?

I went into my bathroom and grabbed a towel. "Here," I said, tossing it to him. "Park your shoes by the door."

He kicked his shoes off, revealing bare feet. "Have a seat," I told him, nodding to my rocking chair. "Dale and me were just wrapping up some paperwork. We'll listen to your story. I can't promise the Desperados will take your case, but anything you say to us is confidential."

Dale nodded, and settled back.

Harm sank into the rocker, leaned forward, and tossed the towel over his head. He emerged tousled and a little drier, his dark hair curling around his pale face.

He should wear his hair curly more often, I thought.

Not that I care.

"What's this about?" Dale asked.

"It's about Red. And Joe Starr."

Dale leaned forward. "You call your granddaddy by his first name," he said. "Lavender calls Daddy by *his* first name too: Macon. Daddy can be hard to live with."

"I know the feeling," Harm muttered as I picked up my pen and clue pad. "Anyway, Detective Starr's watching Red. Watching him close."

I tapped my pen against my pad. "Starr's a law man. Mr. Red's a moonshiner."

"Mr. Red is to Joe Starr as a bone is to Queen Elizabeth," Dale announced. "Analogy," he added in the silence that followed. I gave him a thumbs-up.

"Plus Starr's probably professionally ticked by that stunt Mr. Red pulled at the inn. You can't tell by looking at him, but Starr likes us."

Harm settled back and crossed his legs. "I've been watching Red. I think he's got a still somewhere—but he swears he doesn't. He doesn't have a job, but every couple weeks he disappears at night. He leaves broke and comes home flush. I can't find his still, but I'm worried Joe Starr will."

"Probably," Dale said. "But moonshining's a federal

charge, and a federal pen's like a Hotel 6 with a good weight room. Mr. Red can do that time standing on his head."

Harm's voice cracked out like a shot: "No. I don't want him to do any time."

Could Harm actually care about Red Baker? Interesting.

"You can't undo time once you're down for it," Dale said. "If you could, Daddy would be out by now." Like I've said, if things were up to me, Mr. Macon would stay put. Nobody hits Dale and Miss Rose and walks free if I can help it.

"We've worked with Starr before," I told Harm. "He's smart. And stubborn. And Dale's right: If he's decided to take Mr. Red down, he's going down."

"Not if you find the still first," Harm said. "We could destroy it before Starr throws Red in jail."

"Even if we do destroy it, he'll go right back at it," Dale said. "Dogs don't change their spots."

"Leopards," Harm said, frowning. "*Leopards* don't change their spots."

"The animal of the saying can be changed," Dale said, very cool. "The spots cannot."

I studied Harm as silence settled around us. The night had washed the smirk off of him. Without it, he looked tender and thin, like bamboo growing too fast for its roots. "Why don't you want him doing time?" I asked.

"He can't," he said. "He's too old."

My stare pinned him to the chair the way Miss Lana's pins me when she waits for the truth. He did what I do: looked at my rug, my Elvis calendar, my NC wall map marking the many places I know my Upstream Mother ain't. Finally he looked at me.

"If Red goes to jail, I got nothing. And nowhere."

His words landed true as rain.

He reached into his pocket and pulled out a roll of dirt-streaked cash. "I've tried following him, but he's always watching me. Now you guys . . ." He drummed up a smile. "Don't ask me why, but he thinks you're idiots. You could watch him twenty-four/seven without him even caring."

"Automatic cover," I said.

"Excellent," Dale replied. "We'd need to come to your house," he added as Harm began counting the bills: $20, $30, $40. "A hundred dollars," Harm offered.

A hundred dollars? Dale's mouth fell open.

I narrowed my eyes. "That's what you wanted to charge *us* for being ghost bait."

"Really?" Harm said, grinning. "What a coincidence. If you still need my help with your interview, I'll put my money away and call it even."

Dale looked at me and I nodded. "Deal," Dale said.

"Done," Harm said, stuffing the cash in his pocket. "What's your ghost plan?"

"Stakeout," Dale replied faster than I could blink.

Dale's ideas often surprise me. Fortunately, this one made sense. "Dale's right," I said. "We'll treat the ghostly suspect like any other. We're going for proof of identification admissible in a court of law. Plus motive if we can find it."

"Motive?" Harm asked, looking puzzled.

"Motive for post-mortem loitering," I said. "I'll let you know when and where. Meanwhile, call us next time Mr. Red acts suspicious."

Harm slipped his feet into his shoes. "Come over Saturday if you want," he said. "You can check our place for clues. I'll be around all day."

As he headed into a blustery night, Dale looked at me. "Did he just do us a favor or did we do a favor for him?" he asked.

"Good question," I said. "Sometimes you got to wait and see."

Chapter 19
Mr. Red's Secret

After Saturday morning's breakfast rush, Dale and I climbed the crooked cinderblock steps to Red Baker's front door. "Stay sharp," I whispered as the door squeaked open.

"Hey," Harm said. "Come on in."

I stepped inside and blinked, waiting for my eyes to adjust to the dim light. The small, stuffy room smelled faintly of broccoli. Or worse. A gas heater sat in one corner. A fake leather couch the color of tired baloney hunkered against one wall, and a broke-down La-Z-Boy slumped beside it.

"Nice place," Dale lied.

"Not really, but have a seat anyway," Harm said, nodding to the sofa. I pushed a jacket out of the way and sat, ignoring the duct tape on the arm. Dale settled beside me. Harm slung himself into the La-Z-Boy, turned sideways, and draped his long legs over the arm. "I forgot to ask you if you wanted something to drink," he said, looking startled.

Dale grinned.

"What's so funny?"

"You're working on social skills." He raised one eyebrow. "Girls?" he guessed.

Harm shrugged. "Flick says they like manners. I got iced tea. I'd offer you something to eat, but . . ."

"Four-cornered Nabs would look nice on a plate," Dale suggested.

A few minutes later I brushed orange Nab crumbs off my shirt front. "We brought something," I said, opening my messenger bag. I handed him the photo from the library. "We found this in the inn."

"Who is it?"

"Sparrow-girl is Grandmother Miss Lacy," I said.

"She's pretty, in a birdy way," he said.

"And the scowling one's Myrt Little, the mayor's mom."

Harm barked out a laugh. "Thes's interview? She looks even meaner than Red."

Dale nodded happily. "Thes is doomed."

Harm squinted at the photo. "Who's the guy?"

"That's what we wanted to show you," I said. I waited for him to look at me—a trick Miss Lana taught me. "That's Red Baker."

"Get out of here." He turned a tiny knob on the lamp and clicked a switch. The lamp flared on as he shoved a pile of clutter off the table—old newspapers, a compass, a set of keys. He held the photo to the light.

"If you like that photo, try this," I said. I handed him Grandmother Miss Lacy's photo of Mr. Red standing still. Harm's mouth fell open.

"Spittin' image," Dale said, leaning back and lacing his fingers behind his head.

Harm snorted. "If I ever had any doubt . . ."

"Doubt about what?" Red Baker demanded, clomping in from the hall. He stopped dead as his eyes settled on me. "What the Sam Hill are you doing in my house?"

"I invited them," Harm said, jumping up. "Look." He held out the photo. "We could be twins out of time."

Mr. Red rubbed his whiskery face. "If that's so, you haven't got much to look forward to in your old age."

A joke? From Mr. Red?

"Here's another one," Harm said, handing him the library photo. Mr. Red tilted it toward the light.

"Where'd you get this?"

"The inn," I said. "Grandmother Miss Lacy says it's her and Myrt Little and you. And somebody running out of the photo—she didn't know who."

"That's the old Duesenberg in the background," Dale said.

Red Baker swiped the side of his face. "Lacy's daddy must have taken this photo. He stuck that car in every photo he took. Loved it like a baby." He handed the photo back. "How much longer you going to be?" he asked, staring at me. "Harm's got things to do."

"They just got here," Harm said. "We're doing homework. Which reminds me, I was hoping I could interview you about our family history. For school. It's half my history grade. It would mean a lot to me."

Mr. Red plucked his keys from the table. "My history's none of your business."

"Well . . . it's my history too," Harm said. "There's the evidence right there," he said, pointing to the photo and smiling. Mr. Red glared, and Harm's smile slipped.

"Don't fritter away the day," Mr. Red said, and stomped out the door.

"That went well," Harm muttered as the door slapped shut.

I slipped the photos into my pack and squinted at the lamp. "That lamp hasn't got an electric cord," I said, and looked around the room. "Nothing does. Is it all battery?"

"The house runs on methane," he said. "Red ran a gas line from the pig house."

Dale sat forward. "Pig house? That's a famous moonshiner's trick—putting your still in a pig house so nobody smells it. Have you looked in there?"

Harm nodded, and pushed his hair from his eyes. "It's

state-of-the-art, I'll say that for him. He treats the waste so it doesn't stink. But no still. I can show you."

An invitation to a pig parlor? My life has come to this?

"Another time maybe," I replied as Mr. Red slammed his truck door. I looked out the window. "How long before he comes back?"

Harm shrugged. "Your guess is as good as mine."

I looked at Dale. "We should come back when Mr. Red's not in and out."

"But we haven't seen Harm's room yet," Dale said. He lowered his voice. "You're supposed to show first-time visitors around," he told Harm. "It's a social skill."

Harm shot me a shifty look. "It's not exactly girl-ready."

"That's not a girl," Dale said. "That's Mo."

It grated, but a good detective can use anything for cover, even an annoyance of this magnitude. I drew myself to full height. "I have no interest in Harm's armpit of a room," I said. "But you go ahead, Dale. I'll wait."

Harm unfolded himself from the crippled La-Z-Boy. "Come on, then. Make yourself at home, Mo. Look around if you want to."

As Harm's door closed behind them, Mr. Red cranked his truck and rattled away. I'll never get a better chance, I thought. I wandered down the hall and pushed open a half-closed door. Mr. Red's room.

An uneven curtain hung across the window, the bed gaped half-made. A ladder-back chair faced a desk cluttered with pliers, wire, dirty socks. Gross. As I turned to leave, something in the corner caught my eye: blueprints. I carried them to the desk and unrolled them. The 1938 drawing of the Tupelo Inn.

But what were those?

Penciled-in numbers spidered across the blueprint: 14/238, 5/119, 12/142/, 4/84 . . . Some had been crossed out. "Fractions?" I murmured.

Laughter burst from Harm's room. I tucked the blueprints under my arm and headed down the hall, stopping to peek in a bathroom half the size of mine with a floor twice as slanty. The bare-pipe sink wore a faded yellow gingham skirt and the tub a rust-colored ring.

I wandered past Harm's room to the kitchen, past a sink piled with dishes, onto a screened-in back porch. An ancient washing machine stood at the far end of the porch, a shelf of dirty quart jars stretching above it. "Right," I heard Dale say, tromping down the hall. "What happened to Mo?"

I whirled to face them. "What's going on?" Harm asked.

"Just making myself at home, like you said." I spread the old blueprints over the top of the washer. "Any idea what these mean?"

Harm and Dale crowded close. I pointed out the numbers.

"Fractions, maybe?" Harm guessed. "But what do fractions have to do with the Tupelo Inn?"

"And why are some crossed out?" Dale asked, standing on his tiptoes to scan the farthest numbers.

"I found these by Mr. Red's bureau," I said, looking at Harm. "Keep an eye on them if you can. If he marks out more numbers, let us know which ones and when."

He nodded. "I'll put them back for you," he said.

I gazed across the backyard, past the sagging wash line, past the shovels and swing blade leaning against the shed. "Nice chickens," I told him, nodding toward the reds scratching up the yard. "How many you got?"

"About ten too many," he said. But he smiled when he said it. And his smile wasn't half bad.

Chapter 20
Ghost Stakeout

We set our stakeout for the next afternoon—Sunday. Dale and I pedaled down the inn's drive after church to find Harm rocking on the porch. "Nice truck," he said, nodding at Lavender's 1955 GMC pickup.

The GMC's a work of art, a mix of swooping lines, smooth blue paint, and salvaged parts. I toed my kickstand down. "Lavender's down at the pavilion putting in some overtime," I said. "That means we have complete access to the scene of the . . ."

Of the what?

"The encounter," Dale finished.

"Right. The scene of the encounter." I took my camera from my basket as Queen Elizabeth galloped up the steps and flopped down in the shade, her sides rising and falling like bellows. "We'll set up on the reservation desk," I said, and opened the door. "Hello? Anybody home?"

Nothing. I double-checked my camera.

Harm stepped gingerly through the door. "What's

the plan?" he asked, looking skittish. "Because I've been thinking. The other day was probably a fluke. The way the ghost acted, I mean."

"Denial," Dale whispered. "Show him the photos."

I spread my photos across the desk. "These are of you. These are Grandmother Miss Lacy."

Queen Elizabeth sneezed.

Dale leaned down to scritch her ears. "Liz is sneezing an awful lot lately," he said. "I hope she's not getting a cold."

I ignored him. So did Harm.

"These are ghost photos," I said, pointing to the speckles of light.

"*Ghost* photos?"

"According to Cousin Gideon, a footnoted source, ghosts show up like orbs of light. The ghost is all over you, every time."

Harm gulped.

"You and Miss Thornton," Dale said, fanning my photos out. He gave Harm a thoughtful look. "I'm thinking you two are our common denominators. Like in fractions," he said. "You're the bridge between us and the ghost."

Only Dale could turn ghosts into math.

Harm studied the black-and-whites, raked them into a stack, and tapped them against the desk. He's neat, I thought. How can he stand living with Mr. Red? "I still don't know why a ghost would be interested in me," he said, handing them back.

"Maybe we'll find out," I said. "Today I'm hoping to get a sharp ghost photo, and learn her name. Then we can start figuring out what happened."

Harm jammed his hands in his pockets. "What if she, you know—touches me?"

"A ghost touch?" Dale said, his eyebrows rising. "Speaking as a professional? I'd scream like a first grader and run for my life."

"Sounds good," he muttered.

"All right," I said, looking around the room. "Last time she dropped by . . ."

"I'd just played a chord on the piano," Harm said.

Now that he mentioned it, almost every time she visited, someone had just played the piano. "Exactly," I said. "We'll re-create the scene. If you're not scared."

Harm squared his shoulders. "Me? Nah."

"I am," Dale said. "But I'm more afraid of telling Mama I'm flunking history." He looked at me. "We could play 'Heart and Soul' again."

Harm stepped up to the piano. "You want the treble or the bass?"

"Bass," Dale said, looking surprised as Harm

scooted the bench out of the way. They stood side by side, their backs to me, Harm a head taller than Dale. Dale's bass chords rolled through the air smooth as sunset and Harm moved easily into the lilting melody. "Heart and soul," Harm sang in a strong, clear voice.

Dale chimed in, their voices swirling together like molasses and butter on a hot biscuit. "Mo," Dale whispered, looking over his shoulder. "The stairs."

Queen Elizabeth sneezed.

I stepped back as an eddy of mist drifted down the steps. The temperature dropped. I picked up my camera. The mist floated toward Harm. Closer, closer, backing Harm across the room until his back touched the wall.

The mist hovered inches from his face. "Who . . ." he rasped. He closed his eyes. If the ghost got any closer to Harm, he'd inhale her. That couldn't be good even if it *did* get us an A. *Click.*

"Mo, do something," Dale whispered.

What?

I stepped forward. "How do you do," I said. "I am Miss Moses LoBeau of Desperado Detective Agency. These are my associates, Dale Earnhardt Johnson III by the piano and Harm Crenshaw, who you got pinned against the wall."

Dale bowed. Queen Elizabeth sneezed.

"We're pleased to meet you," I said, and hesitated. Ghost etiquette is an intuitive art. "I don't believe we caught your name," I added.

The mist backed away from Harm. It floated across the room, through a closed window, and across the porch onto the lawn. As we ran to the window, the mist bobbed across the lawn, down the path leading to the springhouse.

"Follow her," I said.

We rushed the door, jumped off the porch, and sprinted across the yard, stopping to catch our breath at the head of the path, Queen Elizabeth at our heels.

"Where's she going?" Harm murmured.

"To the river, maybe, where Lavender is," Dale said, sounding hopeful. I heard the distant sound of a hammer against wood as I lined up a shot. *Click.*

"Maybe," I said. But I doubted it.

We trailed her until, near the springhouse, she veered into the forest. "I don't know," Dale said, rocking to a stop. "It looks dark in there."

Harm peered into the woods. "Aren't you curious?"

"Only about twenty percent," Dale said. "The other half of me is scared stiff."

Harm looked at me. "Ghost Girl?"

I peered into the dense woods, catching a quick glimmer of pink against the forest green. My heart pounded. I stepped off the path and into the woods.

"Watch that briar, Harm," Dale said, plowing in behind me.

We crept into the woods, the tree canopy swallowing the day. I followed the faint glow. Twice, I thought we lost her. Both times she came back, hovering just ahead. Finally she headed up a slight rise. Dead ahead a shaft of light sliced the forest. "What's that?" Dale whispered.

A wrought iron fence marked off a small clearing. "I think I know," I said, remembering the blueprint's prickle of crosses. We slipped closer and the hair on the back of my neck stood up. Sunlight glinted off a crooked gray army of stones. "The old cemetery," I whispered.

We crept across damp leaves, their perfume rising round and sweet. "Looks like somebody keeps this place up," Dale said, stepping gingerly through the gate. He knelt to look at the stubble. "Somebody with a swing blade," he added, his voice shaking.

To our right the tree limbs rustled, sending a shower of twigs and leaves to the ground. Queen Elizabeth took off like a rocket, ears back, yelping as she shot across the grave-yard and zipped into the woods. "Squirrel," Dale explained, his voice too high. "Liz!" he called. "Liz. Come here."

Her yelps faded into the forest.

I looked around the graveyard. "Over there," I said, pointing to a pale white stone towering above the rest. I ran my fingers across its chiseled letters: BLAKE.

"Here she comes," Dale whispered. The mist flowed through the gate and wound among the grave markers, settling at last over a small, sad stone. We crept closer.

"Nellie Blake," I read. "Beloved daughter and friend. 1927–1938."

Click.

"Hey Nellie," I said. "Nice to finally meet you."

> Dear Upstream Mother,
>   Tonight we got our first big break on our Ghost Case and met Nellie Blake, 1927-1938. Meeting her felt like electricity racing up and down my skin.
>   After we said hello, Nellie faded away. We stood around trying to look calm and then stampeded like wild horses. Formally meeting your first ghost can get on your nerves. So can swing blade stubble in a graveyard. If Tupelo Landing ever needs an Olympic sprint team, we already qualified.

When I got home I called Grandmother Miss Lacy to see if she remembered Nellie Blake. "Yes, I believe so," she said. "But old memories blur, Mo. I'm afraid I can't help." Then she asked to speak to Miss Lana and I lost control of the phone.

Despite this small strikeout, all we need is background on Nellie, and a break on Harm's case. That's our deal: Harm would be Ghost Bait for us and we'd hunt Red's still for him.

Miss Lana says life is full of checks and balances. I think our deal with Harm balances out pretty good.

Mo

Chapter 21
AhhoooOOOoooo-Gah

We got the break we needed on Harm's case at quarter past dark the next Friday night.

My phone jangled. "Mo LoBeau, Detective on Call," I said. "Felonies and misdemeanors are our pleasure. How may we assist you?"

"Red's getting ready to make his move," Harm whispered.

"How long have we got?"

"An hour, max. He waits until I start my homework, and slips out. Hurry."

Harm does homework on Friday night? Weird.

I hung up and dialed Dale's number. Busy. I tied my sneakers, found my jacket, and dialed again. Busy. I crammed a flashlight and clue pad in my bag. Still busy.

I rushed to the café, stuffed a take-out bag with scraps, and headed for Dale's.

"Come in, Mo," Miss Rose called, placing her phone in its cradle. That explained the busy signal. Miss Rose can talk a post deaf when she's lonely, which Miss Lana says is most of the time now that the idea of Mr. Macon is gone.

"Hey Miss Rose, you talking to your sister again? I hope her tomatoes are still producing and that you're not too lonely. Miss Lana says letting go of even a trace of somebody is hard."

She laughed. "I wasn't talking with my sister, the tomatoes are rolling in even this late in the season, I'm not *too* lonely, and Lana's right," she said. "It's hard. If you're looking for Dale, he's in his room."

The sound of Dale's guitar wandered through the house like smoke across still water. I tiptoed to his open door and found him sitting by Sir Isaac Newton's terrarium, his back to the door. He strummed the "lullaby and good night" Miss Lana sings to me when I dream wrong. But when he started singing, the words came out pure Dale—a terrifying mix of science and love.

> *Lullaby little newt,*
> *You are warty and look cute*
> *You're amphib-i-an, I'm not,*
> *You're cold-blood-ed, I'm hot.*
>
> *Born with gills you now breathe air*
> *I got thumbs and good hair*
> *Darwin says that we're still kin*
> *Glad I ain't got your chin.*

Dale laid his guitar down. "Sweet dreams, Newton," he whispered, and turned out the terrarium light.

It's hard to know what to say when your best friend serenades an amphibian. On one hand, Miss Lana likes me to be sensitive. On the other hand, the Colonel says most situations don't require my input. "Grab your flashlight, Dale," I said. "Mr. Red's on the prowl."

We blasted past Miss Rose with a promise not to miss Dale's curfew. A little later we ditched our bikes and crept across Mr. Red's barnyard. An owl hoo-hooed above us and flapped heavy and awkward as a flying encyclopedia to a nearby tree. "I don't see why we have to come over here *now*," Dale whispered. "Why don't we wait until Mr. Red checks his still in the daytime?"

"He's a *moon*shiner, not a sunshiner," I said. "He works nights. Besides, we're in school in the daytime."

"School," he muttered. "Why don't they have it when it's too dark for anything else?"

We froze as something—or someone—rustled behind us. I held my breath as it rustled closer, nearer . . . Queen Elizabeth jammed her nose between us and wedged her way in headfirst. "I told you to stay with Mama," Dale scolded.

"Shhhhh," I said, peering at the house. "You'll wake Mr. Red's dogs." Too late. Three rib-skinny dogs stared through the tall fence. A fourth slunk from a dense thicket in the center of their pen. The pen's sharp odor rose into the night.

"Nice dogs," Dale whispered. "Good dogs. Sit." They growled.

I looked at the house. Two figures moved around the kitchen, silhouetted in the lamplight. "They're finishing supper," I whispered.

"Wish I was," Dale said. He sniffed the air. "What's in that take-out bag? I'm starving."

Dale's like a newborn. He likes to eat every three hours.

"Table scraps," I said.

Harm left the kitchen and the light came on in his room. The back door swung open. Mr. Red walked to the shed, grabbed a shovel, and reached in his pocket. Keys! "The truck," I told Dale. "Hurry," I whispered, flinging the take-out bag over the fence.

The dogs hurled themselves on the food and we darted to the driveway. "Brilliant," Dale murmured, grabbing Queen Elizabeth and scrambling into the back of the truck. I rolled across the open tailgate and snagged the corner of a tarp. "Liz!" Dale hissed, grabbing for her as she squirted out of his arms. She shot into the shadows as Red Baker ambled toward us, a shovel over his shoulder.

"Let her go!" I whispered, shoving Dale under the old tarp and diving in beside him. Mr. Red swung the shovel into the truck bed beside us. He slammed the cab door, and the old truck shuddered to life.

"Good," I whispered. "Surveillance is going according to plan."

"Stop it," he said, his voice accusing. "We're under a smelly old tarp in the back of a truck going who-knows-where with a mean old man and Queen Elizabeth is AWOL. You ain't got a plan and I know it."

Undercover work can make Dale irritable.

We bounced down a rutted path in silence. The truck swerved, and brambles scraped their sharp green fingers down the sides of the truck. "We should be on the blacktop by now," Dale whispered as the truck swerved, slamming us against the cabin.

"We must be going the other way. Toward the inn."

"Nellie's house," Dale said, covering his head with his arm. "Great."

The truck hit a hole, throwing us into the air and jolting us down hard. Again, brambles squeaked along the truck's panels. Finally the brakes squealed, and we lurched to a halt. "Shhh," I whispered. The truck door slammed, and Mr. Red crunched to the side of the truck. I held my breath as he fumbled with the tarp.

The shovel!

I nudged it toward him with my foot. He brushed my shoe as he grabbed it. His footsteps faded away. "Come on," I whispered.

We eased out from under the tarp, and slipped off the tailgate smooth as water over a dam. "He's over there," I said, pointing.

Mr. Red held the shovel by his side. He looked right and left, the way the Colonel does when he's lining up on something. I looked behind me. Through the trees, I could just make out the glint of moonlight tiptoeing the inn's roofline. Mr. Red peered over his shoulder, tugged something out of his pocket, and studied it a moment. He started through the forest, stepping long and careful and mumbling under his breath.

"What's he doing?" Dale whispered.

"Counting," I guessed. Mr. Red stopped, made a neat turn, and took off again. We crept through the moonlight-silvered trees and settled behind a black-berry thicket.

"Where are we?" Dale asked, looking around.

Good question.

"Somewhere between the springhouse and town. Maybe. The inn's behind us. The cemetery would be over there," I said, pointing.

Dale yanked my hand down. "Don't point," he said. "It bothers . . . people."

Mr. Red tipped the shovel into the ground and jumped on it, driving it into the earth.

"What's he doing?" I whispered.

"Digging. With a shovel."

Why do I even ask?

Mr. Red grunted softly as he worked, lifting shovel after shovel of soil and heaving it to one side. Finally, the rough shriek of metal against metal. He knelt and reached into the earth. "Flashlights. Now," I whispered, and we clicked on our lights.

Mr. Red looked up like an animal snared. "Who's there?" he asked, scrambling to his feet, a dirty Mason jar in his hands.

"Desperado Detective Agency. Mo and Dale at your service."

He shielded his eyes. "Turn those blasted things off. You're blinding me."

Dale clicked his light off and I tilted mine to the ground. "Hey Mr. Red," Dale said. "Nice night for digging. What did you find?"

"None of your business," he said.

"Moonshine, maybe?" I guessed.

"I wish you'd tell us," Dale said. "Because this doesn't look good, you digging up things on somebody else's land."

"I take care of my own. That's all you need to know," he said, settling the jar in the crook of his arm. "Get lost."

"We already are," Dale said, very even. A tree frog chirped.

"This land ain't yours," I added. "What's in that jar?"

Dale grabbed my arm. "Mo," he whispered.

"Not now," I told him. "I'm questioning a suspect."

"Mo," Dale said, pointing through the forest. "Look."

"What?" I peered through the trees. In the distance, a set of headlights charged toward us. "Is there a path through here?" I asked, looking at Mr. Red. "Maybe I'm turned around."

"Path? There's no path, not anymore," Red Baker said, staring at the lights. "That's . . . No . . . It can't be."

"Those are headlights," Dale said.

The hair on my arms stood up and my fingers tingled. "That car's driving right *through* those trees," I said. The headlights zoomed toward us like the trees didn't exist. The car roared closer, lights and engine blaring brighter and brighter, louder and louder.

"Move!" Dale cried.

Red Baker dropped his shovel and ran. My feet felt rooted as pines.

"AhhoooOOOoooo-Gah."

"MOVE!" Dale shouted, shoving me hard.

I slammed onto the forest floor and rolled, briars

ripping at my skin. Dale somersaulted past. The car thundered so near, I smelled its exhaust.

Dale jumped up. "That's a Model T!" he said, staring at the taillights.

Another horn blared as a second car zoomed by. "And an old Duesenberg." He looked at me. "Ghost cars."

"Ghost cars?"

"I just hope they don't turn around."

My heart pounded. We stood close, watching the lights disappear. The engine's roar faded away, swallowed by the uneven song of tree frogs. I peered into the dark. "Mr. Red? Are you okay?"

No answer.

"Mr. Baker?"

"I hope he ain't run over by ghosts," Dale whispered, slapping at a mosquito. "That would be hard to explain at the emergency room."

"Mr. Red?"

A truck door slammed somewhere distant. "Son of a gun," Dale said as Mr. Red's headlights flared and his truck choked to life. "He's leaving us."

His truck roared away, and we stood alone in the forest.

Chapter 22
The Judas Trail

I trained my light along the ghost cars' mysterious path—a path thick with trees and brambles—and then tilted my beam to the treetops. "These trees stand shorter than the others."

"The old Judas Trail from the inn to the store at the edge of town," Dale said. "The path they let grow up when the inn closed. It has to be."

A raw scream jolted the night, bouncing off trees, zinging my nerves. I hit the ground and looked over at Dale's feet.

"Screech owl," Dale whispered. "Get up."

Crud.

I jumped up and dusted myself off. "I knew that," I said, zipping my light along the forest floor. Something glinted: Mr. Red's jar. "It doesn't slosh," Dale said, picking it up. He tried the lid. "Rusted shut."

"We'll open it later. Turn your flashlight off," I whispered. "Somebody might come hunting us."

Mr. Red lay in wait behind us, probably at the inn, blocking two ways out—the inn's drive and his own path. The ghost cars had barreled toward the inn too. I made an executive decision. "We'll take the Judas Trail. I just hope we can find it in the dark."

As my words died, a mist gathered in the distance. "It's Nellie," I whispered.

Dale gulped. "That would be sweeter if she had a pulse." Nellie crept closer. "Don't crowd me," he called. "I'm ghost-shy." She faded back. "She has social skills," he whispered. "That's good." We began the slow trek following Nellie back to town.

"Cash," the Colonel said an hour later, wiping earth from the jar.

"Of course," Miss Lana said, pouring two glasses of milk and sliding them to Dale and me. "Moonshine is a cash-only business." She laughed. "No wonder Red wants the inn. It's his bank account."

I looked around the deserted café. The 7UP clock on the wall said five to nine. We hadn't mentioned Nellie or the ghost cars. Not yet. Talking solids seemed easier: We had the jar as proof.

The Colonel shook two dirt-streaked rolls of cash onto the table, each held tight by a rubber band. He counted slowly, peeling each bill from the roll. "Three thousand dollars." He drummed his long fingers against the counter. "It was on your property," he said, glancing at Miss Lana. "It's yours."

Miss Lana adjusted her *Gone with the Wind* bed jacket on her shoulders. The Colonel and me gave it to her for Christmas last year. It looks good. "Technically it's ours, but Red put it there. I'll talk to Miss Thornton in the morning, and we'll decide what to do."

"There's something else," I said.

How to describe ghost cars to people who don't believe in ghosts?

"That's right," Dale said, looking dapper in a milk mustache. "I can't believe we didn't already say it."

Good. I'd let Dale take the lead.

He took a deep breath. "Queen Elizabeth got lost and she's not outdoorsy. We got to find her."

Queen Elizabeth, who can find Dale no matter where he is? Can't she find her own way home?

"Actually," I said, "I meant . . ."

The phone jangled and the Colonel scooped it up. "This is the Colonel. We're closed. Don't beg." He squinted. "I see." He lowered the phone. "It's Red Baker. He's taken Queen Elizabeth into custody."

Dale went six shades of pale.

The Colonel turned back to the phone. "Where was she when the alleged offense . . . I see. The charges?" He winced. "No, Mo and Dale are here. In fact, they have something you dropped. We can talk about it tomorrow morning when we pick up Queen Elizabeth. And Red," he said, making his voice level as moonlight, "we expect to find her in good health and good spirits when we get there."

He hung up. "Red says Queen Elizabeth killed a chicken. He's penned her for the night."

"He's a liar!" Dale shouted. "She's never killed a chicken in her life."

Miss Lana, who says never say never, raised her eyebrows.

I tried to think ahead. "Dale's right—unless maybe Queen Elizabeth yawned and a hen impaled herself," I added. Just in case.

"Red claims he has proof," the Colonel replied.

He put his hand on Dale's shoulder. "There's no point going over there when Red's angry. Let him cool off until morning. He'll keep her safe—he has to."

"Don't worry," Miss Lana said. "We'll get her back. Call Rose and tell her you're staying here tonight."

Dale dragged himself to the phone. I slipped my arm around the Colonel's waist. He's sinewy as an old oak, the Colonel, with a heart just as true. He'd have Queen Elizabeth sprung by lunchtime.

Next to Lavender, he's the best father Dale's got.

That night, I couldn't sleep. Could have been the ghost cars, could have been Queen Elizabeth's capture, could have been the Colonel's snores rattling the house.

I clicked on my light. Miss Lana says insomnia is life's invitation to overachieve.

I grabbed Volume 6 and my homework list. In a diabolical display of teacher cunning, Miss Retzyl had combined our language arts and history assignments: *Write a polite business letter setting up a time for your history interview. Use good style.* I picked up my pencil.

DESPERADO DETECTIVE AGENCY
Paranormal Division
Mo and Dale, Chief Investigators

Miss Nellie Blake, Ghost
The Tupelo Inn
Tupelo Landing, NC

Dear Nellie,
Dale and me (or I, whichever is correct)

cordially invite you to meet with us on the evening of the next full moon. At that time we hope to immortalize you with a history interview and a few photos.

We look forward to hearing from you in a non-terrifying way.

Sincerely,

Mo LoBeau, Esquire

PS: We'll invite Harm too. I think he likes you.

I turned the page and licked the tip of my pencil.

DESPERADO DETECTIVE AGENCY
Paranormal Division
Mo and Dale, Chief Investigators

Mr. Red Baker, Moonshiner
Tupelo Landing, NC

Dear Mr. Red Baker,

Dale and me found your stupid jar and counted what you'd hid inside. Miss Lana or Grandmother Miss Lacy will be in touch soon.

I figured out what those little numbers are on your map, but I haven't mentioned it to anyone, not even Detective Joe Starr.

Not yet.

Harm needs a history interview and Dale and me do too. I hope you feel like helping us right away.

Mo

I turned the page one more time.

Dear Upstream Mother,

Today I wrote my first blackmail note. Tomorrow I will leave it in Mr. Red's truck. They say blackmail's wrong, but to me it felt good. Is persuasion in our blood? Please let me know.

Yours truly,

Mo

Chapter 23
Freedom!

"It's Liz!" Dale shouted the next morning, slamming a bowl of grits au red-eye on the café counter and bolting for the door. "She's free!"

I looked up from the toaster and my half loaf of Wonder Bread. Harm strolled across the parking lot, Queen Elizabeth trotting by his side. I slapped two slices of cold bread on a saucer and slid it to Tinks. "Today's special: Toast Tartare. Enjoy."

I ran across the parking lot as Dale dropped to his knees to hug Queen Elizabeth. He looked up at Harm. "Thanks. I owe you. And the . . . late chicken?" he asked, his voice tiptoeing up to the words.

Harm shrugged. "A weasel got that hen. Red knows that. For some reason, he came home in a bad mood last night."

A bad mood? Good, I thought. "I'd like to take a look at Mr. Red's blueprints again. Can you set it up?" He shook his head.

"He locked them in his dresser drawer last night.

Maybe he got antsy, with you all coming over." He scanned the packed parking lot. "Speaking of Red, any updates?"

Across the lot a car door opened, and an Azalea Woman popped out. "Yes, but we're not yet prepared to discuss the details," I whispered as she sashayed toward us.

"A jar full of money," Dale added. "And two ghost cars."

"Money and ghost cars?" Harm said, looking like Liz when she smells a squirrel.

Dale stood and dusted his knees. "We'll fill you in later. Breakfast is on me, to thank you for taking care of Liz. The special today's Miss Lana's Georgia toast and bacon."

"We've reserved a table overlooking the jukebox," I added. "We recommend reservations Saturday mornings. The place fills up fast."

He shoved his hands in his pockets and grinned. "Best offer I've had all day."

Harm had just settled in when Thes bellied up to the counter, his smile crinkling his freckled nose. "Better take your plants in, Miss Lana, I'm predicting frost."

"Frost?" an Azalea Woman chirped. "Already?"

"A light one," Thes said. "Don't worry, we'll be back in the seventies day after tomorrow. You know what they say: If you don't like the weather in North Carolina, just wait a few minutes." He studied the Specials Board. "Georgia toast, please. And okra."

I tried not to retch. "Coming up," I said, scribbling on my order pad.

"I'll have the same," his father called from the other side of the room. Nobody works a room like Reverend Thompson. He'd already shaken a half-dozen hands and cornered the Exums by the jukebox.

"What did the Exums do this time?" Dale asked, pouring Thes a water.

Thes lowered his voice. "Spray painted a bad word on the church pump house." He glanced at me. "One I can't repeat in front of girls."

I studied the Exums. Jimmy's shoulders quivered. Jake hung his head. "What makes your daddy think they did it?"

"They signed it," Thes said.

Dale snickered and headed for Harm's table as I turned toward the kitchen. "Wait, Mo," Thes said. "I got to interview Mrs. Little and I'm hoping you Desperados might go with me. Like bodyguards."

"Mayor Little's mother?" I looked down the counter.

Mayor Little had spun backward on his stool. He leaned against the counter, his elbows back. "Mother simply dotes on the thorny plant family," he was telling the Azalea Women. "She calls them nature's barbed wire." He laughed. "Mother's such a hoot."

"Sorry Thes, but I ain't inspired for it. An excellent interview requires virtuoso-level questioning, plus Dale and me got a couple other cases under way. Don't worry. Your daddy can pray you out of there."

He cast a worried look at his father, who shook a finger in Jake Exum's face. "You're supposed to have a buddy in a dangerous situation," Thes said.

"That's when swimming over your head."

"I *am* in over my head," he said, his green eyes pleading. "Daddy set my interview up for this afternoon. All I got's three questions and a throw-up feeling."

I grabbed a Biscuit Carnivore for table six. "Sorry," I said, "but we already got all the *pro bono* work we can handle."

Skeeter looked up from her law book, one stool over. "That means for free."

Thes frowned. "Who said anything about free? I got seventeen dollars saved up. Cash. Bodyguard me this afternoon and it's yours."

Seventeen dollars? Why didn't he say so?

"You're on. I'll even throw in a photo."

Chapter 24
Murdered Sure as Sin

That afternoon, Dale and I headed for the neat cottage Mayor Little shares with his mother, Myrt. Queen Elizabeth pranced at our side.

A chilly wind whipped along the street. I buttoned my sweater and put my hands in my pockets. "I wrote to Nellie Blake requesting a full-moon interview, but I don't know how to mail it," I told Dale.

He took a hank of yellow yarn from his pocket and tied Liz to the fence post. "Maybe you could leave it on the piano." He nibbled his lower lip. "But a full-moon interview," he said, his voice doubtful. "I don't know."

"Don't worry, I got a plan."

"Am I in it?"

"Of course you're in it."

"Then I'm worried," he said as Thes wandered up.

"Thanks for coming," Thes said, handing me a wad of crumpled dollar bills. "We might as well get this over with." We trailed him up the walk. The door opened as he raised his fist to knock.

"Good afternoon, Thes and Desperados," Mayor Little said, smoothing his tie. "Welcome. Mother will receive you in the drawing room."

"Thanks," I said, unbuttoning my sweater. I smiled. "We're hoping you'll sit in on the interview since we assume she likes you."

"Well, for a few minutes," he said, ushering us to a hot, crowded room that smelled faintly of mothballs and cat. "Mother, your guests have arrived."

She looked up from her rocking chair.

As a member of Tupelo Landing's First Family, Mrs. Little naturally dresses good. Shiny dress with a ruffle at the collar, neat stockings, polished shoes. But above the collar floated a lemony face and yellow-gray hair pulled into a bitter bun.

We perched on her flowery sofa, me in the middle. "Good afternoon," I said. She stared at me with hooded eyes. "I think you know us, but in case Old Age ironed the wrinkles out of your brain, allow me. I'm Mo LoBeau of Desperado Detective Agency. To my left you got my partner Dale, and to my right, Thes. You know us from church."

I looked at Thes. Silence.

"On behalf of Thes, I'd like to say you look lovely," I added.

She rapped on her chair arm. "Get on with it."

The mayor chuckled. "I'm sure Mother meant to offer refreshments. Let me see what I can rummage up," he said, scurrying away. "Mother's been looking forward to this for days."

Thes smiled. "Thank you for talking to me today," he said, sounding like a robot. He placed a recorder on the coffee table. "It's for history."

Silence. His smile slid off his face.

"I got a few questions. First, how old are you? Extra credit's at stake."

"None of your business."

"Okay. Thanks for that," he said, marking an X on his paper. "What's your first memory of Tupelo Landing?"

"Pigs. We fenced in the town to keep them out."

Thes looked at his paper. "What's the most important thing you learned in life?"

"Drink water."

Mayor Little tipped in with a tray of soft drinks. We settled into a silence prickly as the cactus on the windowsill. The glasses sweated. So did Thes. "That's all the questions I got," he told me, looking worried. I opened my camera. Mrs. Little stared at Thes like a vulture eying carrion. *Click.*

"I got something," I said. I reached into my pocket and pulled out the old photo from the library. "Do you recognize these kids?"

Her face came to life. "Heavens yes," she said, her gnarled hand going to her throat. "That's Goody Two-Shoes Lacy Thornton grinning into the camera like a little gargoyle. I'm the pretty one standing next to her. The blurry boy's Red Baker, and the skirt-tail and shoe at the edge of the photo . . . Why, that's Nellie Blake."

I sloshed my Coke onto my pants. "Nellie Blake? Are you sure?"

"Of course I'm sure. See how that skirt's torn? Looks like a kite tail flapping behind her. Nellie had the prettiest clothes in town. Never did take care of them. She probably tore that climbing a tree or chasing her dog. Besides, where Lacy went, Nellie followed. They were practically joined at the hip."

Really? Grandmother Miss Lacy made it seem like she hardly knew Nellie.

"Nellie's folks owned the inn," she continued. "Nouveau riche. Not old money like Lacy Thornton's family. But nice enough."

"Nouveau riche?" Thes repeated.

"New money. Flashy money. Nellie was smart as a whip, but troublesome. Quick tempered. A pain in the sit bone." She jabbed a crooked finger at me. "Reminds me of you."

I counted to ten. "Thank you," I said. "Was she a good

reader? I mean, could she read invitations left on a piano for instance?"

"Of course she was a good reader," she said. "We all were." She laughed sudden as a swift flying up a chimney. "Nellie made Lacy drink that spring water like it was going out of style. Lacy's strung tighter than a warped fiddle, you know. Spring water calmed her down, I always thought."

She looked at Mayor Little. "Where's that musty old paper I found the other day?"

Mayor Little jumped up and rushed to the desk. "Here we go," he said, handing a time-yellowed pamphlet to me. "An old ad for the inn." I gave it a quick scan.

TUPELO SPRINGS
CURE YOUR ILLS

SPRING 1. Cools fevers.

SPRING 2. Cures depression and illusions.

SPRING 3. Quickens faint hearts.

SPRING 4. Eases breathing.

SPRING 5. Invigorates the liver.

SPRING 6. Calms indigestion.

SPRING 7. Steadies the nerves.

"A footnote," Dale said. He smiled at her. "Thank you."

She leaned forward. "Nellie was murdered, you know."

Murdered? Is that why Nellie's still here? To solve her own murder?

"Mother! How unpleasant!" Mayor Little cried, jumping to his feet. "Well, this has been nice," he told us. "But I'm sure you need to run."

"No," Dale said, "we're good."

She ignored them. "Most people called it an automobile accident. Not me. I say someone sabotaged her car. Nellie was murdered sure as sin."

I gulped. "Why would somebody murder Nellie Blake?"

She looked at me, her eyes sharp. "Maybe they didn't want to. Maybe Nellie died in someone else's place. Maybe there's a Judas in our town," she said, and my heart pumped ice.

"Ask Red Baker. He was the first one there." She looked at her son. "I'm tired," she said. "Show these children to the door."

Chapter 25
Blackmail

Whoever says blackmail doesn't pay hasn't tried it. To everyone's surprise but my own, Red Baker agreed to see us the very next afternoon—Sunday.

"We'll pump Mr. Red for information on Nellie's murder and the ghost cars, plus his still," I told Dale as we walked across Mr. Red's front yard. "I just hope he's in a halfway decent mood."

He wasn't.

"I don't know what's got into him," Harm said as Dale and I tossed our jackets on an old footstool and settled on the duct-tape couch. "All I know is Red slammed his truck door this morning and stomped in here crumpling a piece of notebook paper. He said, 'Call those blasted friends of yours and tell them I'll do their dad-blamed interviews at four o'clock this afternoon. Yours too. You got twenty minutes. But that's the last I want to hear about it. Ever.'"

"That was real thoughtful," I said, slipping my tape

recorder out of my bag. Dale pulled a tape out of his pocket, blew off the lint, and popped it in.

"Gives me a chance to pass history," Harm said. "It's a long shot, but . . ."

"Life's a long shot," Red Baker growled from the hallway door. He stomped into the room, sank into the crippled La-Z-Boy and glared at me. "Twenty minutes. Go."

I turned Miss Lana's old tape recorder on and hit the record key. "Mo and Dale interview with Mr. Red Baker, Harm Crenshaw assisting. Take one.

"Thanks for inviting us," I said. "I'm glad Miss Lana and Grandmother Miss Lacy decided to let you have the money we found even if the Colonel says it's theirs."

"I see it different," Mr. Red snapped.

"There's a lot of 'seeing different' going around lately," I said, giving him a faux smile. "For instance, seeing ghost cars is different for Dale and me."

"Way different," Dale said, leaning forward. "You seen them before, Mr. Red?"

The same question had been pacing my mind, followed by others: Who'd drive dead cars down a forgotten path? Where were they going? Were they running away from or flying to?

Red Baker looked at us, his eyes like steel. "What cars?" he said.

Harm frowned. "You know what they're talking about."

"The ghost cars that ran us down," Dale said. "The ones you ran away from."

Red Baker crossed his arms. "Don't know what you're talking about."

"Really?" I said. "Because I figure you been in those woods plenty of times digging for treasure."

"You're crazy," he said, and pointed to the recorder. "You got fifteen minutes."

"Fine," I said, thrusting the word like a bayonet.

Harm wiped his palms on the legs of his pants. "Here's the deal. We need interviews," he said, looking at his grandfather. "All of us do. I'm writing about you, and our family's distillery. And they're writing about a girl you used to know."

Mr. Red slouched sideways. The sunshine cut a dusty beam through the window and across his grizzled face. "Dale and me are writing about Nellie Blake. Mayor Little's mom thought you could help us with some details."

Dale took out his clue pad. "We need thoughts from Nellie's friends because Nellie's . . . well, I hate to say dead exactly, but . . ."

"I know what she is," he said, his voice sharp. "You leave her alone."

I pictured the cemetery, every blade of grass just so.

Then I pictured the swing blade leaning against the shed. The room wobbled.

It's one thing knowing a ghost. It's another thing when an adult knows her too—even if that adult's Red Baker.

"Mrs. Little says you were first on the scene the night Nellie died," I said. "That makes you an eyewitness to history."

"Yes," he said, his voice going dull. "I was that."

"She also says somebody tampered with Nellie's car," I added. "That Nellie died in someone else's place."

He shrugged. "People say all kinds of things."

Dead end. I went another way.

"Your daddy and Nellie's daddy worked together. Yours owned the distillery," I prompted.

He nodded. "That's right. Blake supplied the spring water and the tavern inside the inn; Papa supplied the recipe and the know-how. We were as legit as they come—until Congress outlawed distilleries back in the 1920s and '30s.

"Old Man Blake threw us out like trash and tore the distillery down. It was on his land. We couldn't do a thing to stop him."

Dale whistled. "So Nellie's daddy ended up nouveau riche and yours . . ."

". . . Didn't. So what? You saying we tampered with

Nellie's car?" he said, his voice rising. "That we killed her? Over money? You wouldn't be the first to say it."

"Gramps," Harm said, reaching for his arm. "Calm down."

He snatched his arm away. "It's a bald-faced lie," he said, glaring at Dale.

Dale scooted to the edge of the settee. A ready-to-run move. "We're not saying anything mean, Mr. Red," Dale said. "We're just trying to pass history. Right Mo?"

"Right."

Mr. Red simmered like the Colonel's sauce pot. I changed tack. "What kind of car did Nellie's father drive?"

"Don't know. A Chevy, maybe. Why?"

He didn't know? *That* was a bald-faced lie. If people accuse you of tampering with a car and killing somebody, you remember.

"How about your daddy?" I asked, very easy. "What did he drive?"

"We drive Fords. Family tradition. He drove a Model A."

"Like in the woods," Dale said, his voice soft.

Mr. Red flushed. "Stop bringing up those woods, confound you."

Dale stood up. "We better go. Thanks Mr. Red, but I can see we're barking in the wrong direction on this."

"Barking up the wrong tree," Harm and me said at the same time.

Red Baker sprang to his feet. "Why did you follow me into those woods?" he shouted. I snatched up the recorder. "You couldn't have known I'd be there unless . . ."

He wheezed like somebody'd punched him in the gut and looked at Harm. His old face sagged. "You," he said, his voice going gray. "A traitor under my own roof."

"A traitor? No! I'm not," Harm said, rising uncertainly to his feet.

"Get out," Mr. Red said. "Get *out*!" he snarled, grabbing Harm's shirt and twisting it in his fist. He shoved him. Harm staggered toward us like an out-of-kilter scarecrow, his long legs scrambling. Red lunged forward and snatched the tape recorder from my hand.

"Go," he yelled.

He shoved all three of us out and slammed the door behind us.

We stood on the porch, stunned by sudden light. Harm stared out across the yard, blinking fast. The chickens clucked and scratched by the shed.

I straightened my messenger bag on my shoulder. "That didn't go quite as good as I hoped it would," I said.

"No," Dale sighed. "Probably not."

I looked at the closed door. Bully. "Hey!" I shouted, pounding the door with both fists. "Give us our jackets and Miss Lana's tape recorder. Don't, I'm calling the law." Silence. "You want Joe Starr over here? I'll have him here before sundown."

Mr. Red yanked the door open and hurled a pile of jackets to the porch. Miss Lana's tape recorder sailed by, landing on top. "Leave that fancy bike I paid for right where it is or *I'm* calling the law, you ungrateful whelp." He slammed the door and clicked the dead bolt into place.

I picked up the recorder. He'd kept the tape.

"Old people," Dale said, handing out the jackets.

Mr. Red jerked the window shade down.

"Let's go to the café," I said. "The special tonight's Goulash-a-Go-Go. Miss Lana's wearing her white go-go boots and a tie-dye outfit. Probably can't hold a candle to whatever you're planning," I told Harm, "but you might enjoy it. You too, Dale."

Dale shook his head. "I promised Mama I'd be home before dark." He gave Harm a shy smile. "I've been hoping you'd come see my room. You could meet Mama and Newton. It would be nice if you could spend the night."

Harm shrugged into his slate-gray jacket, not meeting our eyes.

"You'd be doing Dale a favor," I added. "His social

skills need work. And you could do your homework together."

I didn't mention it, but Harm's books were inside and when it comes to homework, the only excuse Miss Retzyl takes is Precise Death—death that happens to the Precise Student and not to a relative. If they have known relatives.

Harm zipped his thin jacket to his chin. He stood for a minute, scanning the bramble-and-trash dog pen, the old shed, the chicken house.

"I hate this place," he said, and tromped down the steps.

Chapter 26
Bad News or Worse?

Next morning, Miss Rose dropped Harm and Dale off at school, her ancient Pinto belching smoke as she turned toward the Piggly Wiggly. "Talk about ghost cars. I didn't know Pintos still roamed the earth," Harm said as they joined me by my bike.

Dale grinned. "Lavender's brought that old car back from the dead so many times, he named it Lazarus."

Harm went blank as sand.

"Sunday school joke," I explained, slinging my messenger bag over my shoulder.

"Right." He gave me a sleepy smile and headed for the door. He veered around Attila, who sat in the sun preening like a pigeon.

"Where's he going?" I asked.

"To ask Miss Retzyl for new books. Mr. Red might never take him back."

It could be true, I thought. The Colonel says Red Baker holds a grudge better than anybody in Tupelo Landing, including me. "How'd it go last night?"

"Good," he said, combing his fingers through his hair. "I like company." Nights wear thin at Dale's house, where Miss Rose keeps the TV dark to fend off brain rot.

Dale yawned. "Of course, Mr. Red kicking Harm out might be a sheep in wolf's clothing," he said. My brain did an unexpected backbend as I tried to follow. "You know, when something good is dressed up bad," he explained, heading inside and down the hall. "Maybe Harm's lucky to escape. Just too bad Mr. Red kept his stuff."

I looked across the classroom at Harm, who wore yesterday's rumpled clothes. "Good stuff's hard to come by," Dale said as we slid into our desks. "Especially if you're poor. And honest."

Miss Retzyl, dressed in a normal brown skirt and a blouse the colors of autumn, walked to the center of the room. She smiled like an angel. "Pop test—word problems," she said. An Exum retched. "Take out a clean sheet of paper."

When the lunch bell finally jangled, I cut Dale from the stampede and edged him toward the hall. I didn't ask about the test. Dale is to word problems as ship is to the Bermuda Triangle.

"Come on, Desperado," I said. "Skeeter's on office duty today and I got to make a call. Walk like you're innocent."

"I *am* innocent," he said.

"Pass, please," Skeeter said, looking up from her desk. I flashed a hall pass with Miss Retzyl's name on the bottom. Her signature's the only cursive the Exums know, but they know it perfect.

"Nice," she said, holding the forgery to the light. "You got a story for the log?"

I clutched my belly. "I may have caught something during math. I got to call Miss Lana for medical advice."

"She's been burping," Dale added, stepping away from me.

"Potential barf event. Check," Skeeter said, making a note. She tapped her pen against the log book. "Real reason? Anything you say to me is confidential."

"Property dispute," I said. "We got to make a call on our client's behalf."

"Bike-napping case," Dale added.

Skeeter studied her fingernails. "Have we discussed my fee? I can't recall."

I'd prepared a proposal during science. "Miss Lana's contemplating an online order: Her outfit for The Bash *and* the Colonel's." And mine, I thought, if I'm not careful. "She's planning on visiting a library, where the Internet's free," I said.

Skeeter frowned.

"But I can try to turn her business your way. Miss Lana's word-of-mouth is unstoppable."

She raised an eyebrow. "Deal. You have two minutes. I'll stand watch," she added, and we shot to the phone. Red Baker picked up on the fourth ring. I heard him slurp something. Maybe soup.

"Thanks for the half-interview," I said. The slurping stopped. "Give Harm his stuff, and we're even."

Red Baker slammed the phone down.

That afternoon when we left school, Harm's silver bike sat in the rack, a note duct taped to the handlebar. "It's from Red," Harm said, peeling it off. He read it and shoved it into his pocket. "Bad news and worse. Which you want first?"

"The bad news," Dale said.

He looked at Dale. "Looks like you're stuck with me," he said. "Until Gramps calms down, anyway, which could be never."

"That's not bad news," Dale told him. "You can take Lavender's room."

Lavender's room? That's like taking in boarders at Graceland.

"What's the worse news?" Dale asked.

"Gramps dropped off my stuff," he said, nodding to a

backpack propped at the end of the rack. "Including my books. No excuse not to do our homework."

I grabbed my bike. "Let's hit the café," I said. "I'm suffering from an ice cream deficiency."

Dale shook his head. "We told Mama we'd help in the garden." Miss Rose grows the vegetables for the café. That and her Tobacco Culture Tours keep her and Dale afloat. "You want to come?" Dale asked. "We could make notes for our Nellie Blake interview."

I nodded as Harm swung a long leg over his bike's narrow seat. "Hop on," he told Dale. Dale sprang like a cricket onto Harm's handlebars, and we took off.

That evening, Miss Lana cornered me behind the café counter. "Mo, we need to discuss costumes for The Bash," she said.

My universe screamed into slow motion, like a bad bicycle crash at the top of a steep hill. Outfits From The Past flashed before my eyes. My Heidi outfit from Oktoberfest two years back: blue dress, flowered apron, white anklets. Dale in his yodel-boy outfit: clunky shirt, knee socks, lederhosen.

The inside of my arms broke out in hives.

"Miss Lana, I thought I might go as a regular sixth grader. Maybe Miss Retzyl can point me in the right direction."

"Order up!" the Colonel barked.

"We'll talk, sugar," she said, and winked. She stacked three steaming plates along her arm and swayed to Skeeter's family, at a window table. Skeeter's little sister, Gray, a proven biter, slouched in a high chair like a sabertooth troll.

"How's the inn coming?" Skeeter asked as Miss Lana dealt the plates around.

"Don't worry," Miss Lana said. "We'll be ready."

"Excellent," Skeeter replied. "Let me know when you're ready to talk outfits. Skeeter-Bay is at your service."

Crud.

I draped a napkin over my arm and tried to smile at Tinks Williams. "Welcome," I said, my heart flat as a failed soufflé. "Tonight we're offering two specials. The Vegan Crunch—a delicate veggie pileup with a side of apple jerky—for seven dollars. Our Omnivore Odyssey features an epic chicken and broccoli stir-fry on a sea of rice for nine. What can I start you with?"

"Omnivore with sweet tea," he said, tossing his John Deere cap on the counter. "Anna Celeste tells me you're ghost hunting on the next full moon," he said. "You be careful, Mo, things aren't right in that inn. I'm used to you. I don't want to break in somebody new."

"Thanks," I said, giving him a smile. "I'm used to you too."

"Order up," the Colonel sang, and I whirled away.

⁺₊⁺₊⁺

That night, I grabbed the interview notes we'd made in Miss Rose's cabbage row and scanned our assignment. *"Outline your history interview. Answer these questions: Who? What? When? Where? Why? Tell me when your interview will take place."*

I picked up my pencil.

> Outline. Interview with A Ghost. By Mo and Dale
>
> Who's the Ghost of Tupelo Landing? (Photo of Nellie Blake's tombstone PLUS proof admissible in a court of law. Maybe.)
>
> What happened? (Interviews with Nellie's mortal friends: Grandmother Miss Lacy Thornton, Mrs. Myrt Little, and Red Baker.)
>
> When and where did Nellie go ghostly? (Sad story. I'll tell you later.)
>
> Why is she still here? (To Be Discovered.)
>
> Desperado Detective Agency plans to interview Nellie Blake on the next full moon, with Harm Crenshaw as Ghost Bait. Extra credit welcome.

I walked over to my Elvis calendar and circled the next full moon—a little over two weeks away.

Chapter 27
Wrong. Dead Wrong.

I thought organizing our interview would be easy with Harm and Dale living in the same house. I was wrong. Dead wrong.

"Dale and Harm hide out after school like outlaws," I fumed a week later as Sal and I crossed the playground.

"Boy stuff," she said, very worldly. Her soft curls glistened in the autumn light. "Mama says they outgrow it in fifty years, give or take a decade."

"*Fifty years?* But our interview's on . . ."

"The full moon," she said. "Next week, Mo. It's all over school. The Exums are offering ten to one odds that you flake. Poor Dale."

Poor Dale? What about me?

She slipped her red Piggly Wiggly sunglasses to the top of her head. "Maybe you can spend time with Miss Lana while Dale's doing boy stuff," she suggested. "Mama says Miss Lana's worried about you."

"She's worried about outfits." I shot her a look. "For The Bash."

Dale trotted up, his backpack slung over his shoulder like a bandolier. "Hey, Salamander," he said. "Nice glasses." He leaned close, examining the tiny white pig faces along the rims. "I never saw them up close. Good art." Sal dropped her books. Dale scooped them up and handed them back.

"Dale, have you asked anyone to The Bash?" she asked. "Because I'd hate for you to be lonely."

"Lonely?" he said, frowning. "How could I be lonely? The whole town's going."

Sal pulled her sunglasses back over her eyes. "I'll get back to you," she said, and hurried away.

Dale tilted his head, watching her go. "I like Sal," he said, "but she thinks funny." He turned toward the school and cupped his hands around his mouth. "Harm, come on," he shouted. "I got to show Mama my math paper."

"Math paper?" I said, my heart diving. "Does Miss Rose have to sign it again? We should have studied. Fractions are tricky, and when you start trying to multiply . . ."

He grinned rakish as Lavender after a good race. "I got a B. Same as we got on our history outline. I'm doing good."

My world tilted. Dale got a B in math? "That's . . ." Actually, it practically ranked as a miracle, but it didn't seem right to say it. "Congratulations."

"Harm helped me," he said, rocking back on his heels. "He's a natural teacher."

A natural teacher? And what am I?

I counted to ten.

"Dale, the full moon's next week. We got to get ready."

He scuffed his sneakers. "Right." He looked across the playground, at Harm. "You want to come over after supper? You can see Mama's new dishwasher and we can talk to Ghost Bait about the interview."

What? Miss Rose had a dishwasher installation and didn't invite me?

I held my head high as I stalked away.

"Mo!" Miss Rose cried, looking up from her desk. "Come in!"

"Hey Miss Rose," I said. I crossed her neat living room to give her a hug. "I hear you had a dishwasher installation. I'm sorry I didn't immortalize you with an Appliance Portrait, but I'll stage one at no charge on my way out. A major appliance is a milestone."

She blinked her eyes, which are emerald. "An appliance portrait?"

"You may want to comb your hair," I replied. "Is Dale home?"

"He's in his room." She slid her glasses down her nose and studied me. Miss Rose reads me like yesterday's news. "I'm sorry I didn't call about the dishwasher, Mo.

I know you like to help Lavender. I've been so busy getting next year's tours lined up, it slipped my mind. We're starting the tours with planting next spring and heading straight through to harvest. I may even fire up that old barn and go into autumn, if we have enough interest. With any luck, I'll be able to keep Lana's inn full half the year."

Like me, Miss Rose has a head for business. The Colonel says her tours will make her rich once she picks up steam.

"I'm glad it's just business distracting you," I said, businesswoman to businesswoman. "I'd hate to see you fall into a crippling emotional spiral on account of divorcing Mr. Macon, which I feel like I speak for the entire town when I say you're better off without him."

Her smile went flat as a nailed tire.

I took a framed photo from her piano—an old one taken on a good day. In it, Mr. Macon looks near handsome as Lavender. Miss Rose leans against him, beaming. Dale, who's pre-first-grade, looks big-headed and scrawny as a kitten.

"Nice photo," I said. "I can burn Mr. Macon out of there if you want me to. I got darkroom skills."

Silence fell over us like a cloak of nettles.

"Or," I said, putting it back on the piano, "I could leave it alone."

"Thank you, Mo. Lavender's dropping by in a little while to take a look at my dishwasher," she said, turning back to her desk. "Something's squeaking . . . Perhaps you could take a mother-son-appliance portrait?"

Lavender? Here?

"You're on," I said. I trotted to Dale's room, pausing with my hand on the doorknob.

I could hear him through the door: "Take it from the top." The music leaped from his guitar strong and clear. His voice followed easy as swinging on the porch:

"Nothing could be finer than to be in Carolina in the morn-ing."

A second voice piped up:

"Nothing could be sweeter than my sweetie when I meet her in the morn-ing."

They both chimed in:

"If I had Aladdin's lamp for only a day
I'd make a wish and here's what I'd say
Nothing could be finer than to be in Carolina in the morn-ing."

I opened the door. Dale and Harm looked around like I'd caught them steeling hubcaps. "Hey. I need that blue T-shirt you borrowed last week," I said, for cover.

Queen Elizabeth wagged over and I scratched her head. "Was that you singing?" It was a stupid question, but Miss Lana says even stupid questions start conversations.

"Guilty," Harm said.

"We don't say that in this house," Dale told him.

"You sound good," I said. "*Real* good."

"See?" Dale said, beaming at Harm. "Told you so." He grabbed my T-shirt off his chair and tossed it to me. It smelled like Queen Elizabeth's shampoo. "I'm sorry we've been scarce, but we been practicing. We wanted to surprise you."

A surprise? For me?

"Actually, we want to surprise everybody at The Bash," he said. "If we can get good enough. We've been working up to letting you hear us face-to-face. Harm never sang in front of anybody before."

"You sang in the inn the other day," I told Harm. "You sounded good."

"Yeah," he said. "But I had my back to you. That's different."

Interesting. Harm has a shy spot. I sprinkled a bug buffet in Newton's terrarium.

"And Mo," Dale added, "we need a manager."

"Somebody used to dealing with the public," Harm said.

Dale nodded. "Somebody that can spell and make posters."

Manager Mo LoBeau? I smiled at Newton, who blinked. "I don't know," I lied. "I'd need to hear your material before I could commit."

"Right," Harm mumbled, and shoved his shaking hands deep in his pockets.

"Take it from the top," I said. "And impress me."

They did.

> Dear Upstream Mother,
> Tonight after Lavender fixed Miss Rose's dishwasher (guitar pick in the spin-around), I shot my first Mother-Son-Appliance Portrait. Lavender stood with one arm across Miss Rose's shoulders. I never noticed before, but he has Miss Rose's smile.
> Lavender invited me to meet him at the inn tomorrow afternoon—but don't get your hopes up. He also invited Dale and Harm. Harm said no but Dale and me said yes. Then Harm changed his mind, and shook Lavender's hand.
> We'll ride over with Grandmother Miss Lacy and Miss Lana. I hope to ask Grandmother Miss Lacy about Nellie while we're there, but Miss Lana says we can't wear her out. Rebuilding an old inn is more stressful than you'd think, and Dale says my questions can get on your nerves.
> I wonder if you and me share the same smile.
> Mo

Chapter 28
Return of the Rat

"Hey," Lavender said the next afternoon, opening the inn's door. "Come on in."

Grandmother Miss Lacy and Miss Lana breezed in. Harm, Dale, Queen Elizabeth, and me followed. The late-afternoon sun slanted through the tall windows, casting the floors in red and gold. "The Colonel should be here in a minute," he said.

"You've worked miracles in here," Grandmother Miss Lacy said, admiring the dining room's chandelier.

"The electricity's not hooked up yet," Lavender said, "but she'll sparkle like diamonds when it is." He nudged Harm. "I found out how Red made that old light fixture swing," he added. "Remote control."

"Cool," Dale murmured. Miss Lana frowned. "But bad," he added. "Very bad."

Harm shoved his hands in his pockets. "Yeah. I'm sorry Red—"

Miss Lana popped his arm with her fan. "Red's like the weather. There's no point in apologizing for it."

Lavender led us across the room. "Glad you like the dining room," he said, opening a small door. "Because the kitchen's a different story."

"Oh my," Miss Lana said, stepping through the door. "I'd forgotten."

If the dining room sang, the kitchen cried. The dining room stood high-ceilinged and open; the kitchen fought for breath beneath a ceiling so low, Harm could almost touch it. A rickety counter ran along the front wall, and a sloping, tin-lined sink drained toward the corner of the building.

"I didn't remember it being quite this bad," Grandmother Miss Lacy said.

I lifted my camera and focused on the grimy windows over the sink. *Click.* Dingy cupboards lined one wall. An ancient wood stove crouched at the far end of the room, its oven door hanging open, a rack spewing out like a crooked tongue. *Click.*

Dale gingerly opened a cabinet door. "Brown paint used to be cheap."

"Ugly is always on sale," Miss Lana said.

Lavender dusted off a chair for Grandmother Miss Lacy. "My goodness," she said, sitting. "Can you fix this?"

Lavender crossed his arms and leaned against the counter. "The building inspector says we have to tear it out and start over."

Miss Lana's face went the color of mashed potatoes. "Start over? How much?"

"Fifty thousand dollars," the Colonel said from the door. Even Grandmother Miss Lacy gasped. "We need special ovens, freezers, sinks, plumbing . . ."

Dale wheeled to me. "Fifty thousand dollars? How many pizzas is that?"

When it comes to math, Dale thinks in pictures. He needs numbers he can see. "This room full, give or take," I said.

"Where will we get fifty thousand dollars?" Miss Lana wailed. "Even with Rose booking her tours here, we can't . . ." Her eyes filled with tears. "Why did I buy this place?"

"We," Grandmother Miss Lacy said, sounding far away. "We bought this place. And . . . I might as well tell you. It seems I've made some . . . unfortunate investments."

Miss Lana gasped. "How unfortunate?"

"Very unfortunate, I'm afraid."

Dale slipped close to her. "Are you . . . nouveau broke?"

She bit her lip. "Not quite, dear," she said. "But I don't have another fifty thousand to put into this project. In fact, I've had to borrow to do what I've done. And that's becoming . . . problematic."

Problematic? My Detective's Instinct told me her

problematic drove a silver BMW. "Filch at State Bank," I guessed.

Her eyes swelled with tears. "The Colonel's doing what he can. But I can't imagine where the money for this kitchen's coming from. Or how we'll pay off the inn."

Not pay off the inn?

"You'll rebound," the Colonel said. He used the same tone he used to use on me when I'd receive time off from school, for fighting. "You need time to get your bearings in the new economy," he told her.

"Time? She's out of time," an ugly voice said behind us.

"Anita Filch," I said, wheeling to find Rat Face standing in the door.

She looked over her shoulder at someone behind her, and barked, "For heaven's sakes, hurry!"

Flick Crenshaw stepped through the door, and my stomach flopped. "Nice work, Lavender," he said. "We'll enjoy owning the place."

He smirked at his little brother. "Red told me you were running with a new crowd, Harm," he said, looking us up and down. "Can't say much for your taste."

Harm flushed dark as a summer storm.

"This would be a good time to say something nice about us," Dale whispered.

Harm nodded and took a breath. "Flick, these are my friends, and—"

"Meet your future sister-in-law," Flick interrupted. "Anita Filch." Harm gulped.

Miss Lana says love is blind. She never mentioned it being stupid.

Rat Face simpered and held out a limp hand. "Pleasure," she said. A shivery silence settled over the room.

Flick punched Harm's shoulder. "Say hello to my fiancée."

Harm shoved his hair back. "But I thought you were with that blond woman—old what's-her-name," he said, his voice low. "What happened?"

"Say hello, kid. You're embarrassing me."

Harm stuck out his hand. She grazed it like he had poison ivy and stalked across the kitchen, her stiletto heels clicking against the floor. "Lacy, you haven't returned my calls, so I thought I'd drop by," she said, running a finger along the old counter. "We've been discussing your situation at the bank. Yours too, Lana."

Miss Lana watched her the way she watches a garden snake.

The Colonel cleared his throat. "Miss Filch, I believe Miss Thornton's accountant and I have put something together that will satisfy your bank and—"

"Too late," she snarled. "We're calling the note. Pay off the inn in full by November first, or my bank takes it. If my bank takes it, the deed will be in my pocket before sundown. Bet on it." Upstairs, a door slammed.

Nellie! Dale and Harm looked at me, their eyes wide.

Rat Face tapped her foot. "Are we clear, neighbors?" She said *neighbors* like a curse. Which the Colonel says maybe it is.

"November first?" Miss Lana cried as Nellie padded along the upstairs hall. "That's just weeks away. We can't possibly . . ."

"Pay up or get out," Rat Face snapped. Stealthy footsteps headed down the stairs. The Colonel looked toward the sound, curiosity playing like flame across his face.

"Hold it," Harm said, grabbing his brother's arm. "You're talking about my friends, Flick. You'll ruin them," he said. "And Red too. Red has—"

"I know what he has. Keep your mouth shut."

Harm looked like Flick had slapped him.

So that's it, I thought, remembering Flick and Rat Face chatting at the auction. They want Red Baker's money. And they'll take the inn to get it.

Nellie crept down the stairs and paused at the foot of the staircase. Dale gulped as Queen Elizabeth sneezed.

"Miss Filch," the Colonel said, basting his voice with calm the way he bastes a turkey, "Lacy Thornton's been a customer at your bank all her life. Surely . . ."

Rat Face put her hands on her hips. "We're calling the note," she said. A smile twitched at her lips. "There's nothing you can do. But I do think it's nice for an attorney of your caliber to have the skills of a fry cook to fall back on."

"A *fry* cook," Miss Lana said, putting *her* hands on *her* hips.

"Uh-oh," Dale said, stepping back.

"The Colonel is a chef, Rat Face," I shouted. "With the skills of an *attorney* to fall back on."

"Thank you, Soldier," the Colonel said.

Rat Face's beady eyes flickered over him. "*Rat Face?* You let your foundling call people names?"

Foundling?

The Colonel sprang toward her, his hands balled into fists, the planes of his face white with rage. "*What* did you say?"

Rat Face backed up. The Colonel stepped forward and lowered his face to her level. "You get your skinny little streak of mean out of here. Now. And don't come back unless you have the deed in your hand. *Rat Face.*"

She scurried to the door—which creaked open for her. "November first," she shouted.

She stomped out. A wind tumbled leaves across the porch and across the dining room floor as Flick backed away from the Colonel. He stopped to glare at Lavender. "If you know what's good for you . . ."

"I do know. Get out," Lavender said, his voice like a razor blade.

Flick marched across the dining room and out the door. It slammed hard enough to rattle the windows.

Lavender frowned at Miss Lana. "The wind?" he guessed as Rat Face's silver BMW flashed by the window, her headlights playing against the cedars.

Grandmother Miss Lacy teetered to the window, panting like she'd run a relay. "What a terrible woman . . ." Her voice trailed away and her knees buckled.

"Catch her!" I shouted. Lavender got there just in time.

"Miss Thornton?" he said as a tide of frigid air swept across the room.

"The hospital," the Colonel ordered. "Now."

Grandmother Miss Lacy's shoe clattered to the floor as Lavender rushed across the dining room. Overhead, the chandelier hissed and sputtered like an angry cat. "Stop it, Nellie," Dale yelled, running behind the Colonel. "You'll set the place on fire!"

Miss Lana and Dale bolted for the car. Harm and I skidded to a halt at the door, our breath clouding in the inn's freezing air.

"It's okay, Nellie," I shouted. "We'll help her."

"We promise," Harm said.

The chandelier crackled and one by one, every door in the inn slammed shut.

It took forever for the ER doctor to come out. "She'll be fine," she said, and a million tight-wound springs inside me gave way.

"Thank you and amen," Dale whispered.

The doctor looked at Miss Lana. "Are you Lacy Thornton's daughter?"

Miss Lana didn't bat an eye. "I am."

"We'll keep her overnight for a few tests," the doctor said, leading her down the hall. "I need you to sign . . ."

Lavender stretched like a big cat. "Told you she'd be okay," he said, but he'd looked as scared as the rest of us on that putrid green plastic couch. "Excuse me, Desperados. I owe the Colonel and Harm a call. Mama too." He headed for the phone.

"Come on, Dale," I whispered. "We got to work fast."

We found Grandmother Miss Lacy dozing in a crank-up hospital bed. She looked fragile as a baby wren fallen from the nest. "Grandmother Miss Lacy?"

Her eyes fluttered open. "Mo," she said. "Oh. And Dale." She squeezed my hand. "Don't worry, I'll be good as new. What did the doctor say?"

"You're spending the night for more tests."

She yawned. "Don't worry, dear, doctors always overreact so they can overcharge. Thank you for coming. Perhaps we could talk in the morning."

I kissed her face. "I love you," I said, nestling her navy pump by her side.

"Me too," Dale said. He leaned over her, his lips hovering over her face.

She laughed. "The kiss is optional," she told him, giving him a little push.

Dale gave her a shy smile. "Miss Thornton, emergency room sofas make you think. If I was you, I'd send out for pizzas every day before I'd spend fifty thousand dollars on a kitchen."

She sat bolt upright. "What did you say?"

Dale turned to me. "Has she gone deaf?" he whispered.

Take-out! Dale's brilliant, no matter how much evidence teachers stack up against him. "Dale's right," I said. "The café can cater the inn."

She beamed at Dale. "You're a genius."

"Thank you," he said, very modest.

She settled against her pillow as Miss Lana walked in. "Good news," Miss Lana said. "You'll go home tomorrow if the tests go well and you promise not to get stressed."

Grandmother Miss Lacy nodded. "And Lana, Dale's come up with a brilliant plan: The café can cater meals until the inn's on its feet. You don't need a kitchen."

Miss Lana tousled Dale's hair. "My little business-man," she said, and he blushed.

"As for *my* bad news . . ." Grandmother Miss Lacy took a deep breath. "I'm afraid you'll have to do the best you can until I get back."

"What bad news?" I asked. "You'll be fine."

She lay back on her pillow. "I'm broke, Mo. By now, the news is all over town."

Chapter 29
Harder Than if the Sky
Lost Its Blue

Grandmother Miss Lacy nailed it: The next morning her financial disaster was the topic du jour. Nobody could remember Grandmother Miss Lacy not having money. People took it harder than if the sky lost its blue.

Even Miss Rose came to town seeking comfort. She sat at the counter, her back straight. "Hey Miss Rose," I said, sliding biscuits her way. Worry had lined her eyes. Grandmother Miss Lacy is her partner too. "Nice posture. I'm more of a slumpist myself. What can I get you?"

"The special, please," she said. "Has Miss Thornton called this morning?" She twisted her wedding band—a nervous habit. Old habits die hard, Miss Lana says, and Mr. Macon's a very old habit.

Miss Lana stopped beside me. "Not yet, but we're fine, Rose," she said in her "this-better-be-true" voice. She splashed coffee into Miss Rose's cup. "Pass the biscuits around, sugar," she told me. "Nothing comforts people like hot biscuits."

I darted through the crowd, delivering biscuits and taking in news. Grandmother Miss Lacy's woes had spread across town like ripples across a pond. She'd helped so many people, she owned a quiet slice of near every business in town.

Mayor Little, at the counter, poked a hole in his biscuit and filled it with molasses. "If Lacy Thornton goes under, Tupelo Landing goes under," he said, sending a tidal wave of worry cascading across the café. He stared longingly at the biscuits. "Are you offering seconds?"

I looked at his round belly. "I'd hate to see you lose your figure, but I'll see what I can do," I said as Miss Lana stepped to the counter and clapped her hands. Her Ava Gardner wig shimmered as the café clattered to silence.

"As most of you know, Miss Lacy's coming home today. As you may not know, she's worried about us," she said. Miss Rose and Sal's mother looked up. So did Skeeter's mom. And Hannah's father, who owns the service station at the edge of town. "She'll talk to each of us when she's ready. Until we have more details, I suggest we do what we've always done in difficult times: our best."

The café murmured like pigeons.

"If we lose the inn, we'll go out with style. I'm sure you all know what that means." She gave me a regal nod. "Mo?"

I stepped up on my Pepsi crate and waited for all eyes to find me. "Party," I said.

The café cheered.

"We'll throw the best bash ever," she said. "We'll set the scene. We'll laugh and dance and eat old-fashioned treats. Mo and I will don authentic 1938 costumes. . . ."

"What?" I cried, staggering.

Dale gasped. "Costumes?" He shoved Harm behind the jukebox and dove after him, out of the line of fire.

Attila stood up. "Costumes suit *Mo and Dale,*" she said, her eyes glinting. "But Mother and I draw the line at costuming. So will our friends."

I hate Attila Celeste Simpson.

Buddha Jackson put his fork down. "I'll MC the event," he offered.

Miss Lana blanched. I knew she was picturing him prancing across the stage like a tubby Mick Jagger. "Thank you," she said, glancing toward the kitchen. "But the Colonel has already volunteered."

A pan hit the kitchen floor. Poor Colonel.

I waited for the crowd to settle. "Plus I got a bonus announcement," I said. "We've signed the hottest musical group this side of Raleigh for The Bash."

"Excellent! Who?" the mayor asked, jumping to his feet.

Crud.

When Lavender showed up at Miss Rose's for his Mother-Son-Appliance Portrait, we'd been on the verge of choosing a name for Dale and Harm's group.

I grinned. That's it.

"On the Verge!" I cried. "Live at The Bash! A big round of applause!"

Sal's applause spattered lonely and uncertain in the silence. The mayor stared blankly, his jaw sagging.

Dale peeped over the jukebox. "Who?" Harm pulled him back down.

"On the Verge!" I shouted. "Don't miss it!"

I hopped down and wound my way through murmuring Tupelites. Dale beamed up at me from behind the jukebox. "On the Verge. It's us, isn't it?" he asked, his eyes glistening.

"It's you, Desperado," I said. "Break a leg."

"Figure of speech," Harm told him, and he nodded.

"We're going ahead with the party? Impossible," Lavender said later that morning as Miss Lana poured his coffee. "I can't get ready in time."

Miss Lana settled beside Lavender. Without the excitement of the café crowd to sustain her, she looked as tired and worried as Miss Rose had. "Everything takes as long as you've got, Lavender. We have two weeks. The show must go on, even if Rat Face rolls up the stage at the end of it."

I looked around the café. The crowd had bolted, chatting about party clothes and financial ruin. The Colonel had rumbled off in the Underbird to collect Grandmother Miss Lacy. Dale and Harm had caught a ride with Miss Rose. Only Thes sat at the counter, polishing off his special.

"I'm sorry," Lavender said, his voice firm. "I can't do it."

Miss Lana heaved her Report Card Sigh.

"What about the pavilion?" I asked. "We can have The Bash there."

"Outside?" Lavender said. He tilted his head, which means he's thinking, and opened his egg sandwich, which means he needs pepper. "In October?"

Good point. Autumn here's like the water in my flat: It runs hot and cold.

Thes spun on his stool. "My forecast *is* trending warmer," he said as I nudged the pepper to Lavender. "I'll check the specifics for you, Miss Lana." Like me, he'd taken a Personal Day from school.

"Thank you, Thes," she said. "With good weather, all we need's a dance floor and a stage. The river and the stars will do the rest."

Lavender peppered his sandwich. Three sharp shakes. "We've already got the pavilion shored up," he said. "That may be doable."

Lavender loves doable. He's like the Colonel that way.

He peeked at Thes and lowered his voice. "Miss Lana, I checked the electric lines after . . . what happened last night. The sparks, I mean. I can't find an explanation."

Miss Lana shrugged. "Apparently the contract's right. We're ghosty," she said, easy as if she'd said "we're toasty." Lavender choked. Miss Lana grew up in Charleston, where they take ghosts in stride. Lavender grew up at Miss Rose's place.

"C'est la vie," she added. "Live and let . . . whatever."

"Let whatever?" he said.

"So," she said. "Let's pick a theme for our dance."

My stomach lurched. "Dance? Do you mean with boys?"

She laughed a laugh full and sweet as a stolen pear. "A party then, sugar. People can dance or not."

"Great," I said. "Because Dale and me got a strict non-dance policy."

"Are you sure, Miss LoBeau?" Lavender asked, giving me a wicked grin. "Because all the Johnson men dance, including Dale. Mama sees to it. In fact, I'm hoping you'll do me the honor."

Me? Dance with Lavender?

I waited a beat for dramatic effect, like Miss Lana taught me. "You're on."

Chapter 30
The Horror Unfolds

As the week rolled on and Grandmother Miss Lacy slowly picked up strength, the horror of Miss Retzyl's academic scheme continued to unfold. "It's time to wrap up your interviews and get your rough drafts together," she said on Friday afternoon.

Attila raised her hand. "The full moon's Wednesday night," she said, turning to look at me. The Exums grinned and rubbed their hands together. Traitors.

"I'll expect to see everyone's rough draft a week from today, for Fishbowl Friday," Miss Retzyl continued.

"Fishbowl Friday?" Dale said, looking blank.

"On Fishbowl Friday, everyone's name goes in the bowl," she said with a normal smile. "I'll draw three lucky students to present oral reports."

Hannah raised her hand. "How can oral reports be lucky? In this universe, I mean." Hannah reads science fiction.

"Lucky because they receive extra credit," Miss Retzyl

replied, and the Exums whipped around to stare at each other.

"Excuse me, Miss Retzyl," I said, "but the entire town's trembling from financial stress. Oral reports could tip us over the edge, which could mean not only personal heartbreak, but a class action lawsuit. I'd hate to see you embroiled."

She smiled. I adore Miss Retzyl. "I'll risk it, Mo. Any questions about the assignment? Wonderful," she said as the bell rang. "Have a lovely evening."

"A lovely evening of homework," Harm droned as he headed for the door.

"Maybe not," I said. "I feel a plan coming on."

After two glasses of Miss Rose's iced tea and three Oreos, my plan pulled itself together. I looked up from my notebook. Dale, who'd slung his guitar over his shoulder, was practicing moonwalking across the room. Harm, who'd staked out the ladder-back chair, sat with his feet propped up on the bed.

The Colonel says being a leader means risking an occasional plunge in popularity. I strapped on my emotional parachute. "You know what Wednesday night is, don't you?"

"Full moon," Dale said, backing into his dresser and

setting a photo wobbling—the photo of him and his parents, from Miss Rose's piano. Interesting.

Harm looked up from his library book, *Moonshiners I Have Known*. He'd given up on interviewing Mr. Red and gone generic. "You guys don't really need me," he said.

"Yes we do," I said. "You're Ghost Bait."

"Isn't there a better way to say that?" he asked. "One where it sounds like I'm human and I survive?"

"The Exum boys are giving odds we don't show on the full moon," I announced, and waited for their outrage. Harm went back to his book. Dale moonwalked into his beanbag chair. "Sal told me," I added. "A reliable source."

Dale twirled. "We know," he said. "Harm bet against us. So did I."

"What?"

He shrugged. "If we cave on the full-moon interview, we'll use our winnings to go to a movie in Greenville. You like movies." He looked at me. "We might as well forget it, Mo. The Exums will try to scare us out to cover their bets. And if the Exums show, Nellie probably won't. She doesn't like strangers. So, no interview."

I tapped my pencil against my notebook. Newton rolled his warty head toward me and blinked. "Fine," I said. "We'll do the interview tonight."

"Tonight?"

"If we don't show on the full moon, you two collect on your bet, we go to the movies, and we *still* get our interview and pass history."

Harm looked up and grinned. "I'm glad you use your mind for good, Ghost Girl, because if you ever go bad, you'll be diabolical."

"Thank you," I said. "Dale, don't forget your questions. Harm, please wear a clean shirt. Nellie will like that. Queen Elizabeth, I hope you can make it. Your howls really help.

"You all bring flashlights and your notebooks. I got the tape recorder and the camera. And don't tell a soul. Especially not an Exum. I'll drop off a note for Nellie on the way home, advising her of our change in plans.

"Meet me at moonrise," I added, and headed for the door.

On my way home, I swung by the inn and dropped my note on the piano.

> Nellie Blake, Ghost
> The Tupelo Inn
> Tupelo Landing, NC
>
> Dear Nellie,
> Emergency change in plans. Due to Exums,
> Dale and me got to change our interview to
> tonight at moonrise. We'll meet you near the

piano. Harm looks forward to seeing you and
will dress nice.
 Sincerely,
 Mo

That evening, I squinted at my glow-in-the-dark Elvis watch. 7:45 p.m. "Nellie's late," I said. "It's at least half past moonrise."

"She's not coming," Harm said. "Let's go home."

"And get laughed out of sixth grade? *And* flunk history? You're just nervous," I told him. "Relax, Nellie likes you."

He sighed. "That's what worries me."

I popped a tape into Miss Lana's old tape recorder. "We'll give her an hour," I told them. "Eternity could be in a different time zone."

The wind's bony fingers rattled the shutters as I leaned over the recorder. "Testing, one two three. Paranormal History Interview, Extra Credit Edition. Mo and Dale presiding. Harm Crenshaw, Ghost Bait."

"I wish you'd stop saying that," Harm muttered.

Dale propped his light against his pack, casting a soft glow across the old parlor. I looked past the old desk, beyond the piano to a tall window overlooking the river. Moonlight skated across the black water quick and bold. "You got your interview questions ready?" I asked, placing the camera in easy grabbing distance.

Dale tugged a crumpled paper from his pocket and placed it on the floor. Then he pulled four neatly wrapped slices of cake from his pack. "Angel food," he explained, placing the cake by my camera. "I hated to bring devil's food."

I hesitated. "Good social skills," I said, and he gave me a modest nod. "Now we just got to act polite when she gets here."

We waited. Nothing. Finally I shifted my legs. "My feet went dead asleep," I said, bumping my heels against the floor.

"Don't say dead," Dale whispered.

I sighed. "Okay, let's try the piano. I hoped she'd drift in on her own, but I'm not proud." Nobody moved. "Just one song," I said. "If she doesn't show, we'll take off."

Dale tiptoed to the piano. A graceful river of sound rolled through the silence. I listened for footsteps. Nothing. Crud.

"Come on, Harm," Dale said. Harm trudged to the piano. Suddenly it felt lonely on my side of the room. Very lonely. I grabbed my camera and casually sprinted to the piano as they sang: "Heart and soul . . ."

Queen Elizabeth sneezed and the temperature dropped like stepping off a cliff. Footsteps clattered along the upstairs hall as a pink glow swept down the stairs, hovered over our recorder and notebooks, and moved toward us.

"Say something polite," Dale whispered, his breath steaming in the frigid air.

"Hey Nellie," I said. "Thanks for dropping by."

The cloud slowed into a vaguely human form, a slender girl in pigtails and an old-fashioned dress. Dale elbowed me. "Grandmother Miss Lacy Thornton says hey," I lied. "She'd probably say more, but she's under the weather."

"Nerves," Dale explained, his voice pale. "We get on them."

A laugh soft as wind chimes flowed across the still room.

"I told you we'd take care of her," Harm added, his voice shaking.

She floated toward him. He backed up. She covered his hand. He pulled it away. Again, a laugh like wind chimes floated across the dark room.

"Nellie," I said, "we want to ask you some questions. For history. We're hoping we can help you too," I said, and Dale gave me a puzzled look. "Maybe you're tired of this lonely old inn. Maybe you want a different place to call home. We'll try to help you, only we don't know why you're still here."

Dale nodded. "A paranormal win-win," he explained.

Nellie almost looked at me. Then the swirls came faster and thicker, like cotton candy pulling itself into being. She floated to the window and whispered against the glass.

The pane frosted over. I lifted my camera. *Click.*

"Why . . . why did she do that?" Dale stammered.

She started toward us. "Back up, Dale," Harm whispered.

Nellie's chill stung my face as she rolled by us, to the inn's old desk. One by one the desk drawers scraped open . . . all but the little one, at the top. The one Lavender couldn't open. *Click.*

She drifted back to Harm, lingered—and floated away.

"She's gone?" Dale said in the silence. "We risked our souls on a practically full moon for an icy window and a messy desk? What about our interview questions? What about my history grade?"

I crossed to the frosted windowpane—a patchwork of tiny snowflakes already melting in the warming room. "A clue," I said, staring at it.

"Clue?" Harm said, walking up beside me. "What's it mean?"

"I don't know yet. It's a clue," I said. "Not an answer."

"I'll tell you what it means," Dale said. "It means girls are a big fat mystery, dead or alive." He leaned closer to the frosty windowpane and tilted his head, squinting at the frost. His breath fogged the pane next to it. Harm and I saw it at the same time.

I grabbed Dale's jacket. "Dale," I said, yanking him back. "Watch out."

"What?" he asked, scrambling backward. "Is she here again?" He looked wild-eyed around the room. "Because I didn't mean anything bad by whatever I said. I think Nellie's sweet."

"Look," I said, pointing to the breath-fogged pane. On it, an unseen finger had traced a single number.

7.

"A definite clue," I said as water collected in the base of the 7 and picked a jagged path down the pane.

"But a clue about what?" Harm asked.

I turned to look at the oak desk, its drawers gaping open—all save one. I tugged the drawer. It didn't budge. "Locked," I said, tapping it.

Harm crouched in front of it, shining a flashlight on the tiny keyhole. "I can open it if I have the right tools." He straightened up. "We can come back tomorrow," he said.

Dale passed his cake around. "If Nellie has something to say, why doesn't she just *say* it?" he asked.

"Maybe she doesn't know how," Harm said, staring at the frosted window. "Or maybe she's saying it and we don't know how to hear her."

Dale wolfed his cake down and placed the last piece

on the piano. "Let's get out of here," he said. "I want to see people with skin on."

That night I woke up sharp as lightning. That ice on the window wasn't a snowflake. It was lace. *Lace*-y Thornton, Nellie's best friend. And the 7 . . .

I sprang out of bed and rummaged through the odd books on my bookshelf: *The Piggly Wiggly Chronicles, Karate for Beginners, Geometry.* "Here it is," I whispered, sliding out Mrs. Little's old pamphlet.

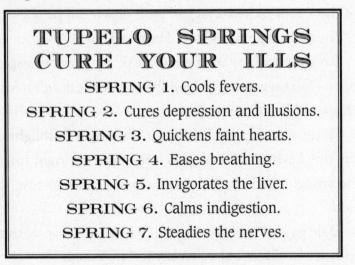

TUPELO SPRINGS
CURE YOUR ILLS

SPRING 1. Cools fevers.

SPRING 2. Cures depression and illusions.

SPRING 3. Quickens faint hearts.

SPRING 4. Eases breathing.

SPRING 5. Invigorates the liver.

SPRING 6. Calms indigestion.

SPRING 7. Steadies the nerves.

"That's it," I said. "Spring Number Seven. For Grandmother Miss Lacy's nerves." I squinted at the clock: 4:00 a.m. I grabbed my phone and dialed.

Dale picked up on the second ring, mumbled, and

dropped his receiver. "Hello?" I said as it bounced against the floor. "Dale?"

Queen Elizabeth II growled into the phone—an unexpected development. "Dale," I called. "I'm down here with Liz!" Nothing. Queen Elizabeth's toenails scrabbled against the receiver as I whipped up a quick Plan B. "Liz," I hissed. "Squirrel!"

She yelped like a dog possessed.

"Hush, Liz!" Dale said. "You'll wake up Mama." He grabbed the phone.

"Dale, wake up. It's me. This is maybe life and death. Meet me at the inn. We ain't got a moment to spare."

A half hour later the three of us—me, Dale, and Queen Elizabeth—crept down the path to the springhouse. I wore jeans and a windbreaker, and carried a quart jar. Dale wore cowboy pajamas and red snow boots, and carried a hammer. I didn't ask why.

"Where's Harm?"

Dale shrugged. "Snuck out an hour before you called. Said he had business."

I skidded to a halt. "In the middle of the night?"

Dale nodded. "He went out the same way Lavender used to. Through the bedroom window. He said he'd be back by sunrise."

Lavender had a secret exit? I made a mental note.

"I'd have gone with him if I'd known you were going to drag me over here again," Dale said. "This better be good, Mo. Like A-plus good."

A breeze wafted across the river. "There's the springhouse," I whispered as we rounded a bend. Its pale walls and slate roof looked serene in the moon's flat light. The breeze shifted and I caught the scent of rosemary. Queen Elizabeth sneezed.

"And there *she* is," Dale said. "Nellie Blake, standing by the door." The pink mist slowed. Nellie looked at us, turned, and walked through the closed door.

"Show-off," Dale muttered. Like I said, Dale doesn't wake up good.

I marched to the springhouse, grabbed the door's chain, and gave the padlock a yank. "Stand back," Dale said. He lifted his hammer. *Crack.* The lock fell to the ground and the plank door creaked open.

Dale pulled a small flashlight from his left boot and clicked it on. Its beam crawled across the floor, across seven basins that marked the inn's springs.

Queen Elizabeth's hackles rose.

"It's okay, Liz," I said. "If Nellie wanted to hurt us, she'd have hurt us long ago."

"Where did those come from?" Dale whispered, spotlighting a single set of footprints in the middle of the red-clay floor.

"The question is, where are they going?"

The footprints marched across the clay floor. Dale's light beam shook as he followed them to a spring. "That's Spring Number Seven. I saw it on the blueprints," I told him. "She wants that water for Grandmother Miss Lacy."

The pink flared.

I knelt by the spring. Out of the corner of my eye I watched Nellie's footprints pad to the back of the spring-house—and through a door bricked shut seventy years ago.

Chapter 31
A Business Offer

"Grandmother Miss Lacy," I shouted later that morning, pounding up her steps. "We got your cure!"

"Over here, dear," she called from behind a potted fern. I skidded to a halt.

"Water," I announced, holding out the jar.

"From Spring Number Seven," Dale added, and she jumped like he'd pinched her.

The front door squeaked open. Harm Crenshaw? Here?

"There you are, dear," Grandmother Miss Lacy said like having him there was normal as permanent teeth. "Do you mind bringing four glasses? They're in the cupboard by the sink."

"What are *you* doing here?" I asked, staring at Harm. He smiled at me bleary-eyed, still wearing last night's clothes.

"He's cheering up an old woman," Grandmother Miss Lacy replied.

Harm leaned against the doorframe. "Actually I came

over with a business offer from Gramps, but she turned me down," he said. He looked at her. "You sure you won't change your mind?"

"Positive," she said. "That money is Red's. But he'd best move it if he wants it. Filch won't be as generous as Lana and I are."

"Think it over," he said. "If you change your mind, I'll bring the blueprints."

Red Baker's treasure map. Since when would Mr. Red part with *that?* And why would he give it to Harm?

"Excuse me if I'm accidentally not sensitive," I said, and Dale went tense beside me. "But Mr. Red's a hateful old miser, which thank heavens you only got part of his DNA, giving you a scientific shot at being nice. So how did you get those blueprints? He won't even let you in the house."

"Red and I had a heart-to-heart last night," he said, not quite meeting my eyes.

Not likely. For that to be true, Red Baker would have to have a heart.

"A fifty-fifty split makes sense, Miss Thornton," he said. "Red owns the map. You own the land."

Harm might be lying about Mr. Red, but his plan made sense. I looked at Grandmother Miss Lacy. "You need the money," I told her.

She patted her blue hair into place. "It's a wonderful offer, Harm. I'll call Red and thank him."

"No!" Harm said. "I mean, that would embarrass him. I'll tell him for you."

"Fine. Now if you would fetch those glasses . . ."

Moments later the door swung open, and Harm backed onto the porch awkwardly balancing four juice glasses on a small tray.

"Thank you," she said as he set them on a table. "Spring Number Seven. Mo, would you pour?"

I filled the glasses, and passed them around. She lifted hers. "To your health, my friends." She closed her eyes and sipped like she could taste her childhood. "Delicious."

"Glad you like it," I said, giving the swing a nudge and setting it rocking. "We can bring you water every day if you want. To steady your nerves."

"It's way better than you dying," Dale added, giving her a smile.

"*Dying?* I'm not dying," she said, reaching over to knock on the porch rail. Grandmother Miss Lacy's superstitious. "Who on earth told you I'm dying?"

Dale turned to me, his blue eyes accusing. "You said life or death. Me and Liz got up at *four o'clock* this morning."

"I said *maybe*. Besides, it felt like life or death at four o'clock."

"Many things feel like life or death at four a.m.," she said. "They generally look better in their day clothes."

Harm poured himself another glass of water. "No," Dale whispered. "You're supposed to fill their glasses first." Harm topped off our glasses.

"Yes, I'm fit as a fiddle," she said. "Just ashamed of letting everyone down."

My heart sank a little. "We're really going to lose the inn, then?"

"Probably," she said. "I'm sorry, Mo."

She closed her eyes. For a minute I thought she was praying. "My yard's an absolute mess," she said, sitting up straight. I scanned the yard, which stood ankle deep in red maple leaves and sweet gum balls. "I can't do yard work at the moment . . . Doctor's orders. What would you three charge me to do it?"

Harm hopped to his feet. "Nothing. Where do you keep the rakes?"

"In the garage," she said. "And certainly I'll pay you. I'm not that broke, but I *am* tired. Why don't you come back this afternoon," she said. "We'll have refreshments, and straighten this place out."

"Besides," I told Harm. "We got some work to do."

"At the inn," Dale prompted.

"Right," he said, and yawned. "Let's go."

··*·*·*

We soon dumped our bikes on the inn's lawn and headed for the steps. "Hold it, Harm," I said. "How'd you get those blueprints? Mr. Red would never give them to you. He probably wouldn't even let you see them."

"That's right," Dale said. "He pretty much hates your guts."

"Thanks for reminding me," Harm muttered, heading up the steps. "Give me time to settle things, okay? I'll tell you when I can."

I looked at Dale, who shrugged.

"Thanks," Harm said, opening the inn's door. "Let's get this done." It took less than a minute to pull out the open drawers and search them. Nothing.

Harm squinted at the lock on the last drawer and reached into his pocket. He pulled out Miss Rose's tiny screwdriver, the one she uses on her eyeglasses. Funny he thought to bring that, I thought, since he'd planned to be back at Dale's before morning.

He leaned over the desk, at eye level with the lock. He slid the tiny screwdriver into the keyhole and jiggled it. "Come on, baby," he whispered, sounding too much like Flick. "Got it!" he cried, and slid the drawer open.

Dale and I crowded close. "What's in there?" I asked.

"Nothing," Harm said, looking bewildered.

"Check the outsides then," I said. "Nellie wanted us to see *something*."

Dale pulled the drawer out and flipped it over. Nothing on the bottom, the sides, the back. He slid the drawer into place and opened it again. It snagged. I thought of my Salvation Army desk. "Let me try," I said. I grabbed the small brass knob, slid the drawer out, and slipped my arm all the way into the space.

"Good idea," Harm said as my fingers closed around a paper in the very back of the desk. I tugged the old paper free and smoothed it against the desk.

"A letter," I said, staring at the faded brown ink. "To Nellie."

Dale gulped. "I hope she doesn't mind us reading it." He nibbled his lip. "Aren't there laws about opening other people's mail?"

The cursive slanted tall and even across the paper. "It's from her father," I said.

Upstairs, a door slammed. We looked up as footsteps hurried along the hall and down the steps. Nellie clattered to a halt halfway down. I didn't blame her. I'd be too nervous to come closer too. I turned toward her and read:

"Darling Nellie, Forgive my greed, forgive my temper, forgive my ridiculous disagreement with Truman. How I wish he'd killed me and not you. I'd give my world to hear you laugh again. Father."

Nellie plunked down on the stairs. "I'd sit down too," I said softly.

"Looks like Truman Baker *did* tamper with Nellie's car," Dale whispered. The room went ice cold. Dale crossed his arms. "Please Nellie," he said. "I didn't bring a jacket."

"Truman Baker," Harm said. "That's Red's father. And my great-grandfather."

He took a deep breath. "I'm sorry, Nellie," he said, his voice going soft.

"We all are," Dale added.

From the stairs, the soft rustling of cloth. The sound of footsteps turning and plodding up the steps and down the hall. A heartbeat later a door closed and a key clicked a lock tight.

"I didn't know those doors had keys," Dale whispered.

"They don't," I told him. "Not anymore."

I folded Mr. Blake's letter and slipped it in my bag. "Maybe Truman Baker did tamper with that car," I said. "But there's no way to prove it. Not now."

"No way to prove what?" a voice behind us asked. I wheeled to the open door. There stood Detective Joe Starr, Red Baker by his side.

"Arrest her," Red Baker said, and pointed at me.

Chapter 32
True or False?

"Arrest *me*?" I cried. "For what?"

"Whatever it is, Mo didn't do it. Plus she has an alibi," Dale said.

I brain-scanned the last few days, searching for crimes.

Dale glared at Detective Starr. "Besides, you can't go around arresting kids."

"If Mo didn't do it, he did," Red Baker said, pointing at Harm. "One of these little bandits took my blueprints and I know it."

Harm went pale around the gills. So Harm *did* take those blueprints.

To my relief, Detective Starr turned on Red Baker. "Now you're saying *one of them* has your blueprints? A half hour ago you said you saw Mo running across your yard with them. Which is it?"

"And *what* blueprints?" Dale demanded. Smart move. Would Mr. Red actually accuse me of stealing his moonshine map in front of a lawman?

"You know what I'm talking about," Mr. Red shouted, flushing beneath his stubble. "My blueprints."

"Blueprints of what?" I said, innocent as rain. "You mean a map? A map from where to where?"

He clamped his mouth shut and I smiled.

Starr took out his notepad. "According to Mr. Baker's statement, someone slipped through his bedroom window last night, jimmied the lock on his dresser, and stole his blueprints." I glimpsed the desk out of the corner of my eye. Crud. Miss Rose's tiny screwdriver lay there bold as day. *That's* why Harm had it in his pocket. He broke in and jimmied that lock. I looked away.

"So?" Dale said. "What's that got to do with Mo?"

"I dusted Mr. Baker's dresser for fingerprints. Found a couple kid-size prints."

Fingerprints? I tried to remember what I'd touched. The blueprints, for sure . . .

"I'd like to check these prints against yours, if you don't mind," Starr said. "To eliminate you as suspects. That way I won't have to take you in."

"That's all you got?" Dale demanded. "Red Baker's no-good word?" He sounded angry, but his eyes had gone glassy with fear. Dale getting fingerprinted would break Miss Rose's heart.

Harm shoved his hands in his pockets. "You'll find my prints all over that house," he said. "I used to live there.

You'll find Mo's and Dale's too. I showed them around the first time they came, to make them feel welcome."

"It's a social skill," Dale explained.

"Dale's prints might be in Red's room, but I'll bet money you find Mo's. She picked up everything in sight. You know how she is," he said.

What was *that* supposed to mean? But like Miss Lana says: Any port in a storm. "Harm's right," I said. "Picking up things and setting them down is a habit I got."

"A bad habit," Dale said, his voice stern. "Very bad."

Starr wavered.

I took a chance. A big one. "The Desperados always cooperate with fellow law enforcement. Go ahead," I said, holding out my hands. "I been hoping to see your fingerprint kit. We're thinking of ordering one, aren't we, Dale?"

"Yes," Dale said, looking totally baffled. "I feel that could be true."

Starr squinted at me, and then at Mr. Red. "Mr. Baker, did Harm have access to your room? Did these two visit your home?"

Mr. Red scowled.

"I wish you'd told me earlier," Starr said, closing his note-pad. "It would have saved me tracking these kids down."

"These scoundrels robbed me," Mr. Red snarled. "Do your job, confound you."

The pulse on Starr's forehead jumped. "Mr. Baker, these kids could worry the bark off a tree, but I don't appreciate you calling them names."

"Thank you," I said, very dignified.

"Do you kids have Mr. Baker's blueprints?" Starr demanded.

"No," we sang out like a choir of heavenly hosts.

"Search me," I offered, spreading my wings.

Starr ignored me. "Let's go back to your place, Mr. Baker," he said. "I'd like to take another look around."

I bet he would. Another look—for a still. Mr. Red seemed to have the same idea. "Forget it," he said, heading for the door. "I'll handle it myself."

"Fine. But stay away from these kids," Starr said.

Like I said, Starr secretly likes us.

Detective Starr stood by the window, watching Red Baker stomp across the yard. "Stay clear of him," he said, putting his notepad back in his shirt pocket. "You wouldn't know anything about his still, would you?" he asked.

"No," I said. Unfortunately it was true. I was beginning to wonder if we'd ever get another break on Harm's case.

"If you hear anything, let me know," he said. "I'm offering a reward."

"A . . . reward?" Harm said. "How much?"

Starr smiled the way Dale smiles when he hooks a fish. "Five hundred dollars for information leading to an arrest."

"Five hundred dollars? *American?*" I said, my heart pounding.

"Any thoughts you'd like to share?" Starr asked, clicking his pen.

"No sir," Harm said. Dale and me shook our heads.

Starr handed Harm his card. "Call if you think of anything." We trailed him to the porch and watched him climb into his dirt-colored Impala.

"That's a lot of money," Harm said as Starr pulled away. "Hope it's not enough to give you any ideas."

"I'm blank," Dale said.

"The Desperados never turn their back on a client," I told him. "Besides, he gave the card to you. Not us." Harm snorted and headed for his bike. "Hold it. Where's those blueprints?" I demanded.

He threw his leg across the seat, and studied us like he was balancing an equation. "I hid them in Miss Thornton's garage early this morning. Sorry I didn't make it back to your place by sunrise, Dale. Red surprised me and I had to hide."

"That's okay, I left Mama a note for both of us," Dale said.

"You better keep those blueprints hid or else get rid

of them, Harm Crenshaw," I said. "Starr won't give up as easy as he pretends he will."

"Neither will Red," he replied.

Early that afternoon we snuck around Grandmother Miss Lacy's house, past the Buick, to the old garage nestled in her juniper grove. Harm unfastened the door's clasp and it squawked open. "Shhhh," I whispered. "Grandmother Miss Lacy's napping."

My eyes adjusted to the dim light. We edged around a tarp-covered pile of machinery, slipped past some old luggage, and skirted a stack of empty buckets. Harm reached behind a stack of fertilizer bags and pulled out the blueprints.

"Over here," I said, motioning to the tarp. "Dale—your flashlight."

Harm and I spread the blueprints across the tarp. We leaned over the map, staring at the tiny fractions spattered across the page—some crossed out, some not. "Which cross-out looks newest?" I asked.

Harm squinted at the page. "This one, I think." *12/256 x 17/89.*

"The top numbers must be step-offs," I said. I nudged Dale. "We heard Mr. Red counting off steps in the forest. Remember?"

"Right," he said.

"But the numbers on the bottom," Harm said. "What the deuce . . ."

I tapped the page. "He got out of the truck here, and lined up with the roofline of the inn, here. And . . ." I hated to say it. "He looked over his shoulder, this way. I think he lined up with the cemetery," I said, and Dale gulped. "Then he started walking."

"The bottom numbers must be his which-way numbers," Dale said, and tilted the flashlight up into his own face. He looked like a freckle-faced ghoul. I tilted it back down. "They help him get his bearings, somehow."

Bearings. "That's it," I said so loud, they both jumped.

"The bottom numbers are compass bearings," I said, picturing the Colonel blazing a trail through the forest. "A compass is an old-timey GPS," I explained. "It's magnet-powered. You line the arrow up with north and then read the numbers around the compass rim. Those are your which-way numbers," I added, and Dale nodded.

"Right," Harm murmured. "Red keeps a compass lying around. These aren't fractions, they're locations. You step it off and dig."

Dale whistled. "Each number's a money jar? No wonder he called a lawman. Mr. Red's rich—if he can dig up his bank account."

He studied Harm. "Why'd you take it?" he asked. "For the money? I never figured you for a thief."

The word stretched between them flat and sad.

"*Thief?*" Harm said, his voice rising. The blueprints slipped, and I scooted them back in place, hoisting the edge of the tarp like the hem of a skirt.

Harm glared in the semi-dark. "True or false," he said. "If Flick and his rodent-faced girlfriend get their claws on his money, Red will never see another penny. Neither will Miss Lana or Miss Lacy."

"True," Dale said.

"True or false? Without his buried bank account, Red's broke."

"True," Dale said. "Most likely."

"True or false? If Red's broke, I'm never going home. If that's . . . really home, I mean," he added, his voice trailing away.

Dale didn't answer. "If you ain't taking the money, why take the blueprints?"

"I thought Miss Thornton could use some of the money and we'd keep the rest for Red. Besides, Red's the last person I'd figure to call the cops."

Dale frowned. I could practically see the wheels turning and smell the smoke. "You haven't been officially caught, which means you're still in a family-borrowing situation," he said. He looked at him, his blue eyes serious. "But you better give them back before you get caught, Harm. I mean it. Starr will take you in."

Harm gulped. "I'll put them in Red's truck," he said as the blueprints skidded.

"Dag this tarp," Dale griped, shoving the blueprints into place and dragging a handful of tarp with it. "What's under there, anyway? Lawnmowers?" Harm lifted the corner of the tarp and peeped underneath.

"Noooo way," Harm said. "Dale, give me a hand."

Dale grabbed a corner. Together they peeled the tarp back. A chrome bumper. A pale blue sculpted hood. An elegantly swooped fender. A whitewall tire yellowed by time. A running board, a cab, a handsome boot. "Ghost car," Dale announced, his eyes like saucers.

"*Ghost* car? That's a Duesenberg," Harm said.

Dale pressed his finger against the fender and looked at me. "It's 3-D," he said. "It's worth . . . I don't know. A lot."

Harm ran his hand along the sleek fender. "*Running,* it's worth a fortune. Broke down, I'm not so sure. Is the key in it?" Dale shone his light through the window, and whistled.

"Original leather, inlaid dash . . . She's a beauty."

"You're early," Grandmother Miss Lacy said, strolling through the door. I shoved the blueprints behind me. "I see you found Father's car."

"Does she run?" Dale asked.

"I doubt it," she said. "It's been here for years. It

reminded me so much of Father, I just couldn't part with it. The rakes are over here," she said, edging past me. I turned like a rotisserie chicken as she passed, keeping the blueprints hidden.

"Miss Thornton," Harm said. "This is a *Duesenberg*."

"I know, dear. A 1933 Model J. Father told me a thousand times."

"Do you know what it's worth?" he asked.

She turned to him, and I shoved the blueprints behind a cob-webby trunk. "Value's relative, dear. It's worth the world to me, because Father loved it. But in dollars? I'd have to pay somebody to haul it off, I imagine."

Harm's mouth fell open. So did Dale's. It wasn't a good look. "Miss Thornton, Duesenbergs sell for real money," Harm said.

"Tens of thousands of dollars, maybe," Dale added.

"Or more," Harm said. "Way more. Especially if they run."

"Do you think so?" she said, her hand fluttering to her throat.

"I know so," Dale said.

"Dale's people know cars," I added.

She sat down on the old trunk. "Thank you, Father," she whispered, and blinked back quick tears. "Perhaps we should have an expert look at it before we get too excited," she said.

"Lavender," I told her. "He'll know what to do."

Chapter 33
Jailhouse Interview

Lavender went to work on the Duesenberg that afternoon. "She hasn't budged since World War II," he warned. "The tires have dry-rotted and the seals need to be replaced, but if you can invest a little money in her, Sam and I will do the rest. No guarantees, but it *could* pay off big."

She gave him a crisp nod. "If it pays off, it pays off for all of us," she said. "Tell me what you need and I'll manage it somehow. Let's get started."

While Lavender and Sam set up in the garage, we raked leaves and watched for a chance to snag the blueprints from behind the trunk.

Our chance never came.

That evening, Dale and Harm practiced their performance pieces—again. "It's amazing what you can do with three chords and good harmony," Dale said, grinning at Harm. "I wish you could sing, Mo. If you could, you'd sound good."

Miss Lana says Dale's compliments are an acquired taste.

He plopped into his beanbag chair as Harm grabbed his science book.

"We need to talk about Nellie," I said.

Harm turned a page in his book.

"I know. Murdered, or not murdered?" Dale replied. "I hate to ask her straight out," he continued. "It seems so . . . personal. Mama wouldn't like it."

While I digested that, he moved on. "Who's the hands-down expert on local crime? Not rhetorical," he prompted.

"Detective Joe Starr?"

He shook his head. "Daddy. And murder's the kind of story that gets passed down at family reunions."

"It is?" Harm and I said together.

"Tomorrow's Sunday," Dale continued. "Visiting Day. We could pay a visit and ask him, if you want."

I felt like magnetic north wobbled. "I didn't think you wanted to see your daddy—not after the way he treated you and Miss Rose."

Dale leaned over to tie his shoe. "It's always going to be *after* the way he treated us, Mo. You only get one daddy and he's the one I got." He looked up at me. "I got to talk to Macon again sometime. This is as good a time as any."

Hearing Dale call his daddy by his first name made me feel older than stone. "I'm with you, Desperado," I said.

"Me too," Harm said. "Didn't he do business with Red?"

"I ain't confessing him to anything," Dale said. "But you can ask him. Only thing is, Lavender won't leave the Duesenberg unless we got a 911 situation, and I can't ask Mama to take us."

"We'll ask the Colonel," I said.

The next afternoon, we climbed into the Underbird. "Used to be a Thunderbird, but the *T* and *h* fell off," I told Harm as he slammed the door.

A half hour later, the three of us sat across a lunch-room table from Mr. Macon. The Colonel and Queen Elizabeth waited outside.

Mr. Macon looked lean and tough as wire cable and his blue eyes glinted like glass. I remembered what Miss Lana had said just before we left: "Be positive, my intrepids. Remember: A caged bird warbles sweetest in sunshine."

"Why does she talk like that?" Dale had whispered as we headed for the Underbird.

"The Colonel says it's in her blood," I'd told him.

He'd nodded. "Maybe they'll find a cure."

Now, as I studied the stark room and the guard at the door, I thought I knew what she meant. I slapped on my sunniest smile. "Hey Mr. Macon," I said, taking out my clue pad. "Miss Lana says jumpsuits are making a comeback this season, but even if they don't, orange is a real good color for you."

"Shut up Mo," he growled.

I smiled like he didn't mean it. I've never been his favorite, and getting him thrown in the slammer hadn't honeyed him up. Still, if my Detective's Instinct was right, he secretly longed for conversation. I nudged Dale. Silence. I moved on to Harm. "Mr. Macon, this is Harm Crenshaw," I said. "Red Baker's grandson."

"Pleased to meet you, sir," Harm said, very smooth. "I understand you and my grandfather go back a ways."

Mr. Macon sliced a look at the guard. "We speak, that's about it." His ice-blue eyes found Dale's. "Hey, Dale. How are you, son?"

Dale looked up. "Hey Daddy," he said. "I'm good."

"How's fifth grade treating you?"

"Dale's in sixth," I said. "It's nosebleed difficult."

Dale nodded. "Very hard. Harm and me started a singing group. We're good."

Mr. Macon crossed his arms. "School's wasted on some folks. You're one of them."

Shock shot across Harm's face like lightning across

an unguarded sky. "Nothing's wasted on Dale," he said. "He's making B's. And we *are* good."

Mr. Macon leaned on the table. "How'd you get here?" he asked, darting a look toward the door. "Is Rose outside?"

A stupid question. Why would Miss Rose divorce him, and then come calling? "The Colonel brought us," I said. "He's outside with Queen Elizabeth."

"How's your mother, Dale?"

"Good. She got a dishwasher."

He leaned back and watched Dale through narrowed eyes. "Tell her I miss her. You hear me, son? Tell her I miss her."

Dale froze like a fox smelling metal. "We came because we got a question," he said. "For our history paper."

Good. A side-step.

I pulled the recorder out. "It's about Nellie Blake. You ever heard of her?"

Mr. Macon took a cigarette out of his chest pocket and tapped the filter end on the table. "Sure. My old man liked to talk. Nellie getting killed ripped the town apart. But that was lifetimes ago."

"Ripped apart how?" I asked.

He twirled the cigarette in his fingers. "Lacy Thornton's people claimed her death was an accident. But most folks blamed Truman Baker."

"Red's father? Why blame him?" Harm asked.

"Truman rigged the brakes." He said it flat and simple. The earth is round, the sky is blue, Truman rigged the brakes.

Harm flushed. I guess it's hard hearing you carry murder in your genes.

Mr. Macon smiled. "Don't take it so hard, kid. There's degrees of murder. First-degree, second-degree, manslaughter."

"Right," Harm said. "But there's only one degree of dead."

"Why would Truman Baker want to hurt Nellie or her father?" I asked as the guard started toward us.

"Ask Red Baker," he said as the guard stopped beside us. "He saw what happened. That's the way I hear it, anyway."

Red Baker? An eyewitness to murder?

"You got another visitor, Macon," the guard said, nodding toward the door. A slight man in a shiny suit stood tapping his foot. "Says he's your attorney."

"Send him away. I'm busy."

That's Mr. Macon for you. He bosses people around even when he's the one wearing orange. He stood up and slipped the cigarette back in his pocket. "I got to get back inside," he told us.

He reached over to tousle Dale's hair. Dale ducked.

"See you, Daddy," Dale said, a blush creeping up his neck.

I hate Mr. Macon.

"Tell your mama . . ."

"Tell her yourself," I said standing up. "Dale and me are busy."

"Hey Mo," Mr. Macon called as we reached the door, "tell the Colonel I'm grateful." I turned. He looked smaller standing there in Prison Issue, like a pocketknife folded to hide the cutting edge.

"Grateful for what?"

"He'll know," Mr. Macon said, and nodded at the guard, who led him away.

Chapter 34
A Perfect Match

The next day, Monday, I thumb-tacked a flyer to the school bulletin board:

ON THE VERGE!
Tupelo Landing's hottest musical duo!
Command Performance!
Where? The Tupelo Bash
When? October 22, 8 PM
For interviews and autographs, contact
Manager Mo LoBeau

Dale and I stepped back to admire my work. He'd been quiet since our jailhouse interview, but he was starting to come back around.

Hannah Greene skidded around the corner, her arms spilling over with library books. Hannah never studies. She doesn't need to. "Hey, where you been?" I asked.

"Dentist," she said. She tugged a note from her Ray Bradbury. "Mama and I stopped at the café. The Colonel sent this." I unfolded the note as she sped off.

Soldier. You have a UPS package from that weirdo Cousin

Gideon. It's by the jukebox. I'm going to Winston-Salem for a few days to pick up records from my old office. I'll call tonight, and I'll see you when I get back. Keep a low profile: Lana's plotting costumes. Love, the Colonel.

"Cool," Dale said. "UPS."

After school, we ripped into the box. "Wow," Dale exclaimed, pushing the packing away. "It's . . . one of those."

"Right." I lifted the black box onto a table. Dale squinted at its white gauge. I placed the electronic wand beside it. "A Geiger counter?" he guessed.

A letter fluttered to the floor.

Dearest Mo,

I borrowed this vintage do-flop from my ghost-hunting friend. It measures electromagnetic charge in the air. She says ghosts are made of it. Just place the wand in ghostly spots and the energy registers on the dial. Happy hunting!

Cousin Gideon

PS: Hope this gets you a footnote.

"This could get us more than a footnote," I told Dale. "This could get us hard evidence versus what we got so far—circumstantial and hearsay."

"We *are* pretty much eyewitnesses," Dale said. "Won't that count?"

I shook my head. "Miss Retzyl's sweet, but she'll

believe we saw a ghost like she'd believe we rowed George Washington across the Delaware," I told him. "We need proof."

"What on earth?" Miss Lana asked, rushing in from the kitchen in her parrot-colored fiesta outfit and Cher wig.

"Ghostometer," Dale replied. "From Cousin Gideon."

She smiled like a ghostometer's normal as a slip-cover—one of the things I like about her. "Mo, could you set out the chili bowls, please? And Dale, if you'd move the cactus out of the kitchen and string the lights?"

"*Sí*, ma'am," Dale replied.

"*Gracias*, honey," she said. "Oh, and Mo. You'll be glad to know I've found a gorgeous 1938 party dress on Skeeter-Bay—just my color and size."

Costuming? My heart sped up like Lavender's foot had hit the accelerator. "That's great, Miss Lana. I wanted to talk to you about clothes. For The Bash."

"Oh no," Dale said, veering toward the cactus.

"Costuming's the chili powder of life, sugar," she said. "Wait 'til you see what else I found. I had to guess the Colonel's size, of course, but I think he'll be pleased. And you're going to *love* what I found for you." The skin on my back tingled. "Don't thank me," she said as Dale dragged a potted cactus across the floor.

"Miss Lana, I think I might go regular," I said. "You know. As a sixth grader."

She put her hands on her hips, her bracelets clanking. She studied me, her gray eyes puzzled. "*Regular?* But why?" She sighed. "Perhaps you're rebelling."

"Yes," Dale said, squinting at me. "I think that could be it."

She shrugged and gave me a smile. "Well, we all know what Bill says."

Crud.

Miss Lana's on a pet-name basis with William Shakespeare.

I didn't have to ask what she meant. She's said it so often, I hear it in my sleep: "All the world's a stage, sugar, so hop on up there."

I tried not to imagine what she'd ordered for me. "Yes ma'am. I'll take the ghostometer to my flat."

The next day—Tuesday, a so-called teachers' workday—dawned bright and cool. I met Dale in the inn's polished parlor, after breakfast. "Harm says he has an errand," he reported.

"I hope that means he's putting the blueprints back," I said.

Dale shook his head. "He can't spring them from the garage. Lavender and Sam are working in there around the clock."

"Hey Desperados, what's *that?*" Lavender asked, elbowing his way through the inn's front door with an armload of boxes.

"Ghostometer," I said. "What are you doing here? I thought you'd moved in with the Duesenberg."

His eyes sparkled like Dale's when Queen Elizabeth learns a trick. "You know me going and coming," he said. "That car's a thing of absolute beauty. But I promised Miss Lana I'd work on the pavilion today. With The Bash just around the corner, she's on edge. So Sam's working on the car and I'm over here, trying not to be jealous."

Dale eyed Lavender's boxes. "You need help?"

Lavender tied a nail apron around his waist. "Now that you mention it, I could use some muscle and a woman's eye down at the pavilion for a few minutes."

A WOMAN'S EYE? MINE?

I grabbed my camera. "Mo LoBeau, at your service."

"I'll help," Dale said, and peered into a box. "Nice . . . plain old lightbulbs."

Lavender grinned. "Like me, they dress up good. Miss Lana splurged on paper lanterns for them. You two grab the boxes, and I'll get the ladder. How long since you've seen the pavilion?"

"A couple weeks, maybe."

"You're in for a surprise."

Surprise didn't come close. The trail sloped to the springhouse, turned, and headed down to the pavilion as always. But the weeds and washouts were gone, replaced by neat timbers and crunchy white gravel. Lavender stopped at the bottom of the trail. "We'll add a fancy archway here for folks to walk through. Miss Lana's idea."

Miss Lana loves to make an entrance.

"But for now, feast your eyes on Tupelo Landing's newest night spot," he said, with the flourish of a circus acrobat. "The Tupelo Pavilion—an outdoor paradise."

"It looks more like a huge platform with rails around the edges so we don't fall off," Dale said, worry skating across his face.

"You're a natural poet," Lavender teased. "It'll look better with the finishing touches. Note the stage for the talent," he said, setting his ladder by a tall corner post. "That would be you and Harm."

"I'm their manager," I said, like he didn't know. I picked up my camera and framed the small stage at the far end of the pavilion. *Click.*

Lavender scampered up the ladder. "Who are you guys coming with?"

Dale looked up at him. "What do you mean?"

"It's a social occasion," he said as I unraveled a string of lights. "You can come with somebody if you want to." He looked at Dale. "Like, a girl?"

"He's coming with Sal," I said. "He just doesn't know it yet."

Dale popped open a box of bulbs. "I am?"

Lavender shot his brother a grin. "Sal's sweet. Hand me that hammer, would you? How about you, Mo?"

"I'm available, if you're asking."

"Me? Go out with you?" He grinned like he always does when I ask him, which I've been asking ever since I turned six. He said what he always says: "You're a baby. Besides, I've already got a date."

I passed him the hammer. "Not the big-haired twins again. They're an environmental hazard," I said. "They use enough hairspray to shellac a lizard in its tracks. You need somebody ecological. Somebody like me."

He moved his ladder down. "How do these lights look, Mo?" he asked, holding the string of lights against the next post. "Does that seem about right?"

Everything seems about right when I'm talking to Lavender, but I backed up and unfocused my eyes, trying to get the feel of the lights against the river's soft lines. "They need to be looser," I said, and he let the line dip. "Like that. Miss Lana says everything about a party's got to flow."

An hour or so later I dusted my hands. "I'd love to

stay and enchant you further," I said. "But Dale and me got to wind up our investigation. We got rough drafts due Friday, with the possibility of oral reports hanging over us like guillotines."

"Oral reports. Ouch."

Dale gave Lavender a careful look. "I went to see Daddy," he said, very casual. "I didn't ask you because I knew you wouldn't want to go."

There's no love between Lavender and Mr. Macon. Not for a long time.

Lavender laid his hammer on top of the ladder. "How's he doing?"

Dale shrugged. "Same dog, same spots." Lavender's face went soft as Miss Rose's when she thinks I'm not looking.

"He means leopard," I explained. "A leopard doesn't . . ."

"I know what he means," Lavender said. "I'm sorry, Dale." He looked at Dale the way he looks at an engine when he's trying to figure out why it's running ragged. "Macon's broke inside. It's not our fault. It's just the way it is."

Dale nodded.

Lavender picked up his hammer. "If I thought you were the one that landed him in jail, little brother, I'd thank you for it," he said.

Dale jumped like he'd stepped on a live wire. "Thank me?"

"Sure. Mama's safe, you're safe. Macon's looking at hard time—which means he might find time to take a hard look at himself. It's tough knowing what's good and what's bad the first time you see things."

The river lapped against the pavilion, and the wind sent a shower of scarlet maple leaves cartwheeling to the water. Dale squared his shoulders. "That's what I was thinking too," he said. "More or less. Come on, Mo. Nellie's waiting."

Moments later, as we scampered up the inn's steps, I caught the glint of sun-on-chrome behind the cedars. I squinted. Detective Joe Starr's Impala! "What's Starr doing here?" I asked. Queen Elizabeth II, who'd been napping in the sun, lifted her head.

"Stalking Mr. Red's still, most likely," Dale said. "Which I wonder if he even has a still. Because if he's not out digging up money, seems like he's hanging around the house. Maybe he's retired," he said, reaching down to smooth Queen Elizabeth's ears.

I pushed the front door open. "Nellie? You home?"

Silence.

"Let's ghostometer the desk and piano," I said, veering to our equipment. I found a note stuck to the dial:

Meet me at the garage at high noon.
Lavender's away and Sam's going to the
café for lunch.
Harm

"He's moving Mr. Red's blueprints," I said. "Finally." I peeked at my Elvis watch. 11:25. "But that doesn't give us much time."

I clicked on the ghostometer. The needle on the dial quivered, and lay still. Dale ran the wand along the desk. Nothing.

I held the wand while Dale played a few chords on the piano and hummed.

Still nothing.

"I hope she's not depressed about her daddy's letter," Dale said, looking worried. "Depression kills. Of course, Nellie's already . . . you know."

"Maybe she's in the library," I said, turning the ghostometer off.

We trudged up the stairs, Queen Elizabeth bobbing behind. Dale eased the door open. "Nellie?"

I set up on the library table. "Maybe she's scared of the ghostometer," I said as Dale ran the wand along a shelf of books. "It *is* ugly," I added as his wand snagged on a book, toppling it to the floor. "I got it, Dale. You keep scanning."

The book, with its faded green cover, fit my hands. "*A*

Girl's Book of Poems," I read, and opened it. "It's Nellie's!" I ran my finger across a signature written in faded brown ink. "Look, she smudged this one too," I said. "Just like her geometry book. I guess clumsy is forever."

The room went ice cold and the ghostometer's needle shot across the dial. "She's here!" I cried. Queen Elizabeth sneezed.

Dale spun in a circle. "But where . . . She's gone," he said. "What happened?" Queen Elizabeth snuffled and he scratched her ears. "I think Liz is allergic to her."

"Liz is allergic to rosemary," I said, tapping the ghostometer to see if that might help. Nothing. I tapped it harder. Still nothing.

"What rosemary?" he asked.

What rosemary?

"Don't you smell it? It always smells like rosemary when Nellie's around."

Dale narrowed his eyes. "I never smell rosemary. You two got ghost noses," he said. "Like ghost eyes, only with nostrils." While I took that in, he ran the wand along the other bookshelves.

"She's gone," I said, slap-tuning the ghostometer. The needle didn't flinch. "Why was she even here?" I asked, trying not to picture Attila's sneer if we had to give an oral report without hard evidence.

"Maybe she liked your joke: 'Clumsy is forever,'" Dale said.

The needle jumped.

"Why? It's not that funny," I said, staring at the dial. "Clumsy is forever."

Again, the needle jumped.

"What on earth?" Dale asked, padding to me.

"Or not on earth," I said. "Let's restage the scene. You knocked this book down, I picked it up . . ." I opened *A Girl's Book of Poems* with its ink smudge across the title page. I stared at the ink, every cell in my body tingling.

Of course. The ink.

"Dale, get Starr."

Dale let the wand swing to his side. "Why?"

"Because I know what Nellie wants. Are you ready to make an A in history and go Paranormal Famous? Because we got scientific ghost proof that will hold up in a court of law," I said, heading for the door.

"What scientific proof?" he demanded. "What court of law?"

"Give me time to go to the café and back. Find Starr and keep him here," I shouted, sprinting down the stairs. "You're practically Honor Roll!"

"I am? Why?" he shouted from the top of the stairs. "How did I do it?"

I jumped on my bike and sped away.

⁺₊⁺₊⁺

"Fingerprints?" Detective Joe Starr said fifteen minutes later, staring at me like I'd sprouted wings—which, if I'd biked any faster, I would have. "You can't fingerprint a ghost."

"We can," I said. "This is foolproof, isn't it Dale?"

"I hope so," he said.

"We'd do it ourselves if our fingerprint kit had come in," I said.

Dale nodded. "It's been delayed by we didn't order it," he explained.

Joe Starr looked at his watch—a gift from Miss Retzyl. "I know you got a kit in your car," I said. "Normally I wouldn't ask, but this is a 911 history situation. It's for Miss Retzyl."

Starr tapped his foot. He keeps his shoes polished to a high sheen.

"Girls like guys who help kids," Dale added. "Miss Retzyl is a girl. Sort of."

Starr sighed. "She already likes me," he said, "but let's see what you got."

As Starr crossed the porch, Dale lunged and pinched my arm like an anxious crab. "Fingerprinting a ghost?" he said. "Have you lost your mind?"

"Trust me," I replied.

"Those words again," he muttered, but he followed

me to the window overlooking the river as Starr bustled back in with his kit.

"All right," Starr said. "Where's your print?"

I breathed heavy on the windowpane. Starr squinted.

7.

I pointed to the period. "Right there," I said.

Starr flitted a fine powder across the pane. A fingerprint stared back at us. We held our breath as Starr placed a wide piece of tape over the print and carefully peeled it from the glass.

"Looks like a good print," he said, holding it to the light. "But anybody could have put it here."

"But anybody didn't," I said. "That's Nellie Blake's print."

Starr snorted. "Not likely. She hasn't lived here in decades. And even if it *was* hers, you couldn't prove it. She wouldn't have a print in my data bank."

"It's in *our* data bank," I said, reaching into my messenger bag and pulling out Nellie's geometry book—the one we found our first day in the library. I opened it and handed it to Starr. He read the inscription:

"I hate math. N.B.—August 28, 1937."

Beneath her initials were Nellie's inky prints.

Starr frowned. "What the . . ." He held his tape over one print, the next . . . and stopped over her index finger. "This can't be right," he said.

I opened *A Girl's Book of Poems*. "Here's her signature, if you want to match the handwriting samples."

Starr shifted the captured fingerprint away from Nellie's print and back. "I'll have an expert take a look. But if you ask me, these prints are a perfect match."

Chapter 35
We Forgot About Harm!

"Harm!" Dale cried, smacking himself on the forehead as Detective Starr drove away. "We forgot about Harm!" He swung my arm up like I wasn't attached and stared at my Elvis watch. "It's already quarter past lunch," he said. "Hurry!"

A few minutes later, we dropped our bikes and rushed the garage door. Inside, tools littered the floor and the old Duesenberg's hood gaped open. Harm crouched over a workbench, his notebook open on Mr. Red's blueprints.

"Took you long enough," he said, shoving his hair from his eyes. "I've got Red's numbers down. I need you two to distract him while I put the blueprints in his truck."

"Distract who?" Grandmother Miss Lacy asked, strolling in with a lunch tray. "Oh. Hello dears, where's Sam?"

I stepped in front of Harm as he swept the blueprints to the ground. "Is that lunch?" I asked. "Because I'm starved."

"Me too," Dale said, lining up shoulder to shoulder beside me.

"Mo LoBeau, are you hiding something from me?" she asked, her voice playful. She leaned around me, and zeroed in on the blueprints. Her smile collapsed like last year's rusty lawn chair. "What have you got there, Harm?"

"Nothing," he mumbled.

"Wonderful. Because for a moment I thought those were Red Baker's purloined blueprints. The ones Detective Starr called me about. The ones I swore the three of you had nothing to do with."

If her voice got any colder, I'd need earmuffs. I lowered my eyes to the Duesenberg's disemboweled carburetor at my feet.

She slammed the tray on the workbench, grabbed the blueprints, and rolled them up. "I have never been so disappointed," she said. "I stood up for you, Harm Crenshaw. And for you two. What have you got to say for yourselves?"

Harm took a deep breath. "I'm sorry, Miss Thornton," he said. She didn't answer—the Waiting For Confession trick. It worked, as usual. "I haven't been completely honest with you. I hope you'll give me a chance to make things right."

"I'm not sure you can make this right," she said as

Dale slipped a sandwich off Sam's lunch tray. "But please come up on the porch and try."

A half hour later, she had the whole ugly story minus the ghosts: Red Baker in the forest, marking off steps. The blueprints with their mysterious code. Harm swiping the blueprints in the middle of the night.

"He was trying to protect Mr. Red and you from Flick and Rat Face," I said. "It's almost good in a Robin Hood way if you hold your head right."

"I don't believe my neck bends that way," she replied.

"No, ma'am," Dale whispered. "I expect not."

We needed a mega change of subject. I went for the ghost.

"We got good news too," I said. "We're close to naming the entity. We got proof that will hold up in a court of law—well, once Joe Starr brings it back to us: Nellie Blake's fingerprint." I watched Grandmother Miss Lacy's face, which went pale.

"Nellie Blake's fingerprint?" she said, rocking forward in her chair. "But how . . ."

"We got them off a windowpane she touched the other night. Joe Starr helped us," I said, and Harm whistled.

"Plus Nellie smells like rosemary," Dale added. "We have a witness to that—one that's not me or Mo."

I hesitated. That would make Queen Elizabeth our witness. I moved on.

"Rosemary?" Grandmother Miss Lacy said. "Are you sure?"

"Yes ma'am," I told her. "Sure on both counts."

Her old eyes filled with tears, and Dale's shoulders slumped. "I didn't know rosemary would make you cry," he said. "Girls," he muttered. "Even wrinkled they're a mystery."

"It's all right, dear," she said, pulling a handkerchief from her sweater pocket. "It's just that Nellie and I were good friends. And she did rinse her hair in rosemary water. There's no way you could have known that—I'd forgotten it myself. That's how we lose people . . . detail by detail, day by day, until they're pale, pale memories."

She blew her nose. "You three haven't been honest with me about the blueprints. But I'm afraid I haven't been very honest with you, either—about your ghost. I never dreamed she could be real."

"Nellie's real, all right," I said.

She dabbed the corner of her eye. "Come inside," she said. "I have something to show you." And she led us to her parlor. She crossed to her bookshelves and plucked down a small photo album. "Meet my best friend," she said. "Nellie Blake."

She opened the album, and a pretty, dark-haired girl

smiled at us. Nellie licking an ice-cream cone. Posing for a portrait with a one-eyed dog. Reading by the springhouse's shady back door. "We must have read a hundred books there," Grandmother Miss Lacy said. "Her father had that door bricked shut after Nellie died. He said he couldn't stand to see anyone use it ever again."

That explained why Nellie walked through that bricked-up door, I thought. I studied the next photo: two girls sitting at the piano in the inn. Nellie and Grandmother Miss Lacy. "You're playing 'Heart and Soul,'" I said, and Dale gasped.

Grandmother Miss Lacy nodded. "Probably. We all played it. Me, Nellie, Red, Myrt...But it's Nellie I think of when I hear it now."

Harm looked from the photos to me. "You look like her," he said.

"A little, perhaps," Grandmother Miss Lacy agreed. "But my word, you act like her, Mo," she said, blinking away sudden tears. "Always thinking, always meddling." She reached over and patted Dale's hand. "Always getting friends in trouble. Such kindred spirits."

"And Nellie's dog?" Dale asked. Dale's a sucker for a dog story.

"Oh, that's Right-Turn Wilma," she said, laughing back tears. "Wilma had just one eye. She only turned right. That's the only way she could see to go, I suppose."

"You hid these photos from us," I said, trying not to sound hurt.

She brushed her fingertip across Nellie's photo like she could brush the messy hair from Nellie's face. "I did," she said. "Please forgive me, Mo."

"She does," Dale said, and I nodded.

She gave me a quick smile. "It never occurred to me the ghost rumors were true, and I certainly didn't want to breathe new life into Nellie's sad, sad story. You've discovered that story by now, I imagine."

"An automobile accident," I prompted, and the light slipped from her eyes.

"Yes, this time of year," she said, looking out the window. "Nellie was so excited. It was to be her first dance that night. Nellie and her father were speeding from the old store to the inn when their brakes gave way in a curve. We heard the crash at the store.

"Red Baker looked like a ghost, climbing into his daddy's Ford. I piled into the Duesenberg with Father and we flew along the Judas Trail, one behind the other."

"The ghost cars," Dale whispered.

"Red and his father arrived first," she said, looking at Harm. "Red found Mr. Blake hurt and dazed, but Nellie . . ." She sank to the settee. "Later, Red told me she said, 'Tell Lacy . . .'"

Harm sat beside her. "Tell you what?" he asked, his voice soft.

"That's all," she said, opening her hands and letting them fall. "She was gone." Her voice cracked. "She was my best friend," she said, her voice rising like a hurt child's. "I've wished a thousand times I had a chance to say good-bye."

Her eyes glittered with tears. "This goes back on my shelf," she said, closing the photo album. "Now that you've uncovered her story, I'll make you copies for your history paper—or for you to keep. You two are so much alike, Mo."

Usually I have a river of words flowing in me. Now my river ran dry.

"Maybe that's why Nellie likes us," Dale said.

Or because Grandmother Miss Lacy loves us, I thought.

"Thank you for the copies," I said. "We'll footnote you. We got something to show you too," I said, pulling Mr. Blake's letter from my bag.

She read the letter. "That poor man," she murmured, handing it back. "Was Nellie murdered? Mr. Blake certainly thought so, and other people did too. But Truman Baker swore he didn't touch their car. My parents believed him and tried to stop the gossip. Even with no proof, the rumors swirled on day after day, keeping our pain so fresh, it felt like Nellie died day after day too. One day her parents had had enough. They packed up and left, and all I had of Nellie was gone." She closed her eyes and leaned into the curve of the settee.

"I'm sorry," I whispered. The moment felt rare and tender, delicate as a moth cupped in my hands. We rose and tiptoed toward the door.

Her eyes flew open.

"Not so fast," she snapped. "We still have those blueprints to deal with."

Crud.

She stared at Harm, her eyes icy sharp. "I've given you time to think, young man. What are your plans?" she demanded.

"Young man," Dale whispered. "That's not good."

"I'm . . . trying to come . . . to come up with a plan," Harm stammered.

She stood, snatched her navy blue purse from the secretary, and hooked it over her arm. "Fortunately for you I already have one," she said. "Get in the Buick, all three of you. We're paying Red Baker a call."

Chapter 36
The Ghost of the Boy He Used to Be

We rode in silence—past the school, over Fool's Bridge, past the old store. Harm sat in the front seat clutching the blueprints. Dale and me sat in back, Queen Elizabeth lounging between us. "She's getting a little pudgy," I whispered, poking her tummy. "Is she okay?"

"Ignore her, Liz," Dale said, and they both turned to stare out the window.

"Maybe we should rethink this," Harm said, his voice thin and brittle as old paper. "I thought I'd slip the blueprints in his truck, and let him think he's gone senile. Red has a temper."

"Who has a temper?" Grandmother Miss Lacy demanded.

"Gramps," he said as we bounced down the lane. "Gramps has a temper."

She slowed for a deep rut. "So did Nellie. I'd be surprised if either of them ever learned to count past ten."

I smiled. Something else me and Nellie have in common.

Mr. Red was crossing his dirt yard with a galvanized pail when we pulled in. He pushed into his dog pen, emptied the bucket into a trough, and headed for us, wiping his hands on a blue bandana. "Afternoon, Lacy," he said, opening her door.

"Hello, Red." She stepped out of the car, ignoring the pen's stench. "I'm sorry to disturb you, but these children have something to say."

Harm gulped.

"Act innocent," I whispered, climbing out of the Buick. "Hey, Mr. Red."

"I made a sweet potato pie, Lacy," he said like I hadn't spoken. "Come in and I'll cut you a piece."

Harm's mouth fell open. "I didn't know you could cook."

"Didn't need to with you here," Mr. Red told him without looking back.

Moments later we sat in a wreck of a kitchen. Towers of plates teetered by the sink. A pot lolled on its side on the stove. Mr. Red placed two saucers on the table: one in front of his chair; one in front of Grandmother Miss Lacy's. She didn't flinch.

"Thank you, but I don't believe I care for pie," she said. "We'd like to return something to you. And to show you something we think you'll want to see."

Harm dropped the blueprints on the table.

"I knew you three stole them," Mr. Red said, his eyes glinting.

"Not us three," Harm said. "Me. I took them."

"Red, I hope you'll hear him out," Grandmother Miss Lacy said. "We're probably going to lose the inn," she added. "Flick and his girlfriend will grab it up to get your savings. I'll lose every dollar I've sunk into the place—and so will you."

Mr. Red looked like she'd sent a flying sidekick to his head. "Flick double-crossed me?"

Harm nodded. "He can't find your money without the blueprints. I thought it would be better if we dug it up and shared with Miss Thornton, since . . ."

"We?" he said, his voice climbing.

Harm clamped his lips tight. Then: "I'm sorry I took the blueprints. I was trying to help. But I didn't dig up anything. Your money's still there."

Grandmother Miss Lacy nodded, giving me my cue. "We wanted to show you this letter," I said, taking it from my pocket. "We found it in the inn. It's from Nellie's father."

Mr. Red went pale behind his whiskers. "What's that got to do with me?"

Grandmother Miss Lacy reached for his hand. He pulled it away. "Red, I've been haunted by Nellie's death all my life," she said, her voice soft. "Can't you help me lay that to rest? Won't you at least look at the letter?"

Smart, I thought. He'd do it for her before he'd do it for himself.

Mr. Red unfolded the letter and read it out loud, his voice rough as gravel in rain: *"Darling Nellie, Forgive my greed, forgive my temper, forgive my ridiculous disagreement with Truman. How I wish he'd killed me and not you. I'd give my world to hear you laugh again. Father."* Mr. Red's voice stumbled into silence.

"Red," Grandmother Miss Lacy said, "if you do know what happened that night, please tell me. Who could the truth hurt now?"

Mr. Red's eyes glistened. He dropped the letter to the table and stared at it so hard, I thought it might levitate. Behind me, tap water dripped into the sink. Plunk. Plunk. Plunk.

Mr. Red drew a shallow breath. "Papa was angry with Norton Blake that night," he said, his voice small and flat. "Papa's distillery helped put that inn on the map. You know it did." His voice gained strength. "But when Prohibition hit, Blake turned him out just like that." He snapped his fingers. "One day we were one of the finest families of Tupelo Landing. The next day—outlaws," he said, his voice bitter.

"Father told me," she said.

"When Prohibition ended, Papa thought Blake would take him back," he said. "He didn't. Without Blake we couldn't afford the rigmarole to go legal. Where did that leave Papa?" he demanded.

"It left him hurt, I imagine," she said. "And very angry."

He looked at her, his eyes blazing. "Did Papa and Blake argue that night? They did. Nellie and I heard every ugly word of it. Blake shoved Papa and stomped into the store, dragging Nellie behind him."

His face flushed. "You want to know the truth? I'll tell you. Papa cut Blake's brake line quick as cutting a man's throat. God help me, I stood in the shadows and didn't lift a hand to stop him. I've wished every day since I'd stopped Nellie from getting in that car. But I didn't. I stood in the shadows like a coward and watched Old Man Blake drive away."

He curled his hand into a soft, helpless fist. "So Nellie died. I'm sorry, Lacy," he added, his eyes brimming with tears. "I know you loved her."

"We both did. Thank you for telling me," she said, and her voice drifted away like a lost kite.

Dale propped his elbows on the table. It made him look smaller, somehow. "You were probably about twenty when that happened," he said, staring at Mr. Red.

I frowned. Twenty? Dale knew better than that.

"No," Mr. Red said, swiping his tears with the back of his hand. "I was about your age."

"Oh," Dale said. "The way you told that story, I thought you were way older. Because I can't go up against a grown man, especially one in a rage. I've tried."

Mr. Red looked at Dale like he was seeing him for the first time.

Grandmother Miss Lacy took Mr. Red's hand. This time he didn't pull away. "Dale's right," she said. "You were a child. I don't think for one minute you're responsible for Nellie's death. But you listen to me." She waited for him to look into her eyes. "I forgive you."

He gasped like something hard inside him cracked open. His life unwound across his old face, making him young, younger, until for a moment I sat face-to-face with the ghost of the boy he used to be.

"Nellie forgives you too, Gramps," Harm said. "I know she does because she's liked me ever since I walked through that inn door, the spitting image of you."

Mr. Red blinked and just like that, he was back: an old man in a dirty kitchen.

The stove clock ticked. A chicken clucked at the back door.

"You'd best clean up in here, Red Baker," Grandmother Miss Lacy said, picking up her pocketbook and looking around the room. "This is no way for a boy to live. Get in the Buick, children," she said. "I have things to do."

Mr. Red stood up, walked down the hall, and closed the door.

> Dear Upstream Mother,
>
> Today, Mr. Red told the truth of Nellie's death. He's kept it secret all these years, guilt haunting his life like Spanish moss haunting a swamp.
>
> Now that Red feels forgiven and Grandmother Miss Lacy knows who killed Nellie, do you think Nellie will move on?
>
> I wish you could answer.
>
> Miss Lana says telling a secret changes the heart of the teller and the listener, both. She could be right. Mr. Red called Harm after supper, and asked him to come home. Harm had already packed. He was back home before sundown.
>
> Mo
>
> PS: Skeeter's looking for a buyer for the Duesenberg, so keep your fingers crossed. And Fishbowl Friday's coming up fast. Without Nellie's fingerprint Dale and me got a C at best, and that's only if Miss Retzyl's in a good mood. If you're saving up to send me to Harvard, aim lower.

Chapter 37
Fishbowl Friday

Three days later—Fishbowl Friday—the sixth grade filed into class loaded down with notebooks, DVDs, and a sense of doom. Nellie still lurked in the inn—she moved Lavender's tape measure twice when he tried to measure a new threshold for the dining room. Cute, but not footnote-worthy.

I'd developed my last photos of Nellie with pitiful results: images so blurry and light-speckled, they could have been anything—including sloppy camerawork. Starr was still AWOL with our fingerprint. "We're doomed," I told Dale as the school door clunked shut behind us.

"Maybe Miss Retzyl won't call on us," Dale muttered, heading down the hall. "If we survive oral reports and get Nellie's fingerprint back, we got a shot at an A on the final paper. We're better off than Harm, anyway. He's only got three pages of notes."

Still, Harm swaggered down the hall like a World War

II pilot in an old movie. "Things must be working out good with Mr. Red," I said.

Attila sailed up to Harm. "Fishbowl Friday. I just know I'm going to flunk," she wailed, clutching his arm as we headed into the classroom. Harm looked at me and rolled his eyes.

"Good morning, class," Miss Retzyl chirped. "Please write your name on a slip of paper and place it on the corner of your desk. I'll take a quick look at your rough drafts and drop your name in the fishbowl."

"Tell us that deal again," Jake Exum said. He and Jimmy, who'd worn their brown Sunday suits, had combed their slicked-down hair clear to the scalp.

"Your name goes into the fishbowl," she said. "I'll draw names to see who presents an oral report. Feel free to use audiovisuals. We'll devote the afternoon to your presentations."

"That's for extra credit, right?" Jimmy asked, and she nodded. "Me and Jake volunteer. We got a talent for public speaking. Plus we brought exciting teaching tools."

"Wonderful," she said, her voice going tight. To me, she looked nervous. "I'll put you in the lineup."

Jimmy and Jake high-fived.

I leaned sideways in my seat and peeked at the Exums'

desks. Among the crumpled paper and bent books I could make out brown paper bags.

After lunch we slunk into the classroom, eyes down like Queen Elizabeth after a squirrel disaster. Miss Retzyl smiled. "Now for history."

I raised my hand. "Miss Retzyl, it's only one o'clock. We're facing two hours of history, which I feel is maybe criminal. I'd hate to see you get in trouble so close to your wedding. By the way, have you and Joe Starr announced a date yet? You'll want to reserve the café for your reception. Mr. Li comes back from vacation soon, and karate classes will start up again. It'd be a shame for your nuptials to get bumped by martial arts."

Sal whipped out her weekly planner.

"We haven't chosen a date, Mo. When we do, I'll let the class know," she said, and Sal put her planner away. Miss Retzyl looked at the Exums. Jimmy stood up and buttoned his suit coat. "We'll save the Exums for our finale," she said. Jimmy sat down and fist-bumped his brother. "The laptop's set up if anyone needs it for PowerPoint."

I pinched my nose to disguise my voice. "Anna Celeste volunteers." Attila's worth a good hour of mindless blather, more if her brain's left to graze on its own.

"Mo?" Miss Retzyl said. "Did you say something?"

"No ma'am," I said, and coughed.

"Hair ball," Dale explained.

Miss Retzyl dipped into the fishbowl. "Let's see what fate has in store." Dale stopped breathing as she pulled out a twist of paper. "Sal," she said, beaming. "You're up."

"Good luck," Dale whispered, and Sal blushed.

Sal took center stage. She inserted a flash drive into the computer, and shook her tight curls. I applauded. "Thank you, everyone," she said. "I interviewed my grandmother, whose mom was the finest seamstress this town's ever known. In fact," she said, walking over and tugging the window shades down, "if your ancestors looked good, it's because of mine. Hit the lights, Dale." Dale darted to the light switch. "PowerPoint," she told us, and I heard him stumble in the dark.

"Image one. Great-Grandmother Amanda heading to the Tupelo Inn to fit dresses for some la-de-da rich ladies. Photo courtesy of Miss Lacy Thornton.

"Image two," she said, perching on the corner of Miss Retzyl's desk and crossing her legs. "A dress designed by Great-Grand Amanda. Notice the mid-calf hemline and elegant sweep. Very classy.

"Image three. Great-Grand at her Singer sewing machine. Note the treadle. No wonder she had great legs." Sal rustled her paper. "Here's a quote from my aunt," she said. "'Tupelo Landing was a fashion mecca in its time, thanks to the Tupelo Inn and Great-Grand Amanda.'

"Lights," she said, and Dale slapped them back on.

Sal smiled. "I sew too. In my family we feel even accountants can dress good. Thank you for your time." She jettisoned off Miss Retzyl's desk and headed for her own, her expression a mix of pride and relief.

"Wonderful," Miss Retzyl said, dipping her fingertips into the bowl. We lucked out: "Anna Celeste."

Reprieve! Public speaking is to Attila as rotting banana is to fruit fly. We smiled, urging her on with our eyes. She didn't disappoint.

Attila's presentation hit me like Novocain between the eyes. Forty-five minutes into it, Miss Retzyl interrupted. "Thank you, Anna Celeste," she said. "I think I have the gist of your report on Miss Lacy Thornton."

"But I have decades to go," Attila said, looking shocked. "I'm only in the 1960s."

Dale's hand shot into the air. "I'd like to hear more."

"Me too," Thes said, lifting his head from his desk. The spiral pattern of his notebook's spine crisscrossed his face.

"Thank you, Anna," Miss Retzyl said. "Let's give someone else a chance before our finale." She reached for the bowl.

"Not another one," I begged. I hate it when I beg.

"Please not me," Hannah prayed, closing her eyes.

"Me neither," Dale prayed.

I closed my eyes, trying to sort the fishbowl entries with my personal chi, willing mine to the bottom of the bowl. "Not Mo not Mo not Mo," I whispered.

She reached in. "Mo," she said. "Mo and Dale. Who's giving the report?"

Dale moaned.

"Are our names in there?" I asked. "Because Dale's our spokesman and as his manager I'm saving his voice for The Bash. We can't let the town down. That would be wrong on a civic level and unless I'm mistaken, civic beats history."

She gave me the Surrender Glare. "Mo . . ."

"Yes ma'am," I said, my heart drooping like last week's roses. "Give me a minute to gather our massive trove of information." Dale rattled papers while I pawed through my desk. "While we do that, I'd like to remind everyone On the Verge performs live at The Bash, just one week from tomorrow. We're inviting you to cheer when Dale and Harm take the stage. This cheering's for sixth grade only. Seventh graders have asked and we've turned them down cold."

Out of the corner of my eye, I saw Jake Exum smile stiff as cardboard.

The Exums. It was a long shot, but I took it.

"It's going to take a few minutes to get my papers in order and I know the Exums put together a fantastic presentation. Nobody wants to miss it, so I'm inviting them to leap-frog in. At this time, Dale and me yield the floor to Jimmy and Jake Exum! Put your hands together! Let's give the Exum boys a big welcome!"

Dale, Sal, Harm, and I clapped like maniacs, our applause drowning out Miss Retzyl's voice as the Exums jumped to their feet. Jake buttoned his coat and they marched to the front of the class, each clasping a crumpled brown paper bag.

"Good afternoon," Jimmy said, bowing stiffly to Miss Retzyl and then smiling at the class. "We're Jimmy and Jake Exum from the back row." He unfolded a paper from his pocket, and read. "Our report is on Miss Delilah's candy store, built in 1902. But when we went to interview her she had changed her mind, which is why we need extra credit. She gave us candy if we would go away," he said, nodding at Jake, who started down the first row, dropping a handful of candy on each kid's desk.

The class stirred as he dumped the leftovers on Miss Retzyl's blotter. "A bribe," Dale whispered. "Brilliant!"

Jimmy smiled. "Time was running out, so we went to our neighbor Hank. Hank fought in a war. He learned munitions."

Jimmy took two small jars from his bag. Miss Retzyl snapped to attention. "What's in those jars?" she demanded.

Jimmy looked at Jake. "I think Hank said mix these up," he said, opening the jars and tipping one over the other. "Or else he said not to."

"I know science," Thes screamed, tearing for the door. "Run!"

A pop. A flash. Black smoke billowed into Jimmy's face. "Everybody out!" Miss Retzyl shouted, covering her face. "Now!"

I slid my candy into my messenger bag and grabbed my camera. *Click.*

A half hour later I opened a lollipop and watched the volunteer firemen hose down our classroom. "There's Lavender. Hey, Lavender!" I shouted, rocking up on my toes. "That's a good look for you!" He tipped his fireman's hat. *Click.*

Mayor Little roared up in his Jeep. "Everybody stay calm," he shrieked. "We'll have this disaster in hand in no time."

The entire school had emptied out. Second graders milled around their teachers. First graders huddled together crying. "The Exums look wilted," Dale said.

Harm, who sat on a picnic table, nodded. "Probably seeing more homeschooling in their future."

"Mama says you should be kind in a disaster," Dale said. "Let's go say something nice."

We oozed over. "Hey Exums," I said. They looked

up from their polished shoes, their eyes guarded. "Your report really held my attention."

Dale nodded. "Good candy."

Harm unwrapped a Tootsie Roll and popped it in his mouth. "I wouldn't worry about those eyebrows," he told them, winking at me. "I hear they grow back fast."

Did Harm Crenshaw wink? At me?

The sixth grade swiveled as a dirt-colored Impala skidded onto the school grounds, blue dash light flashing. "Hey, Detective Starr! Dale and me are still waiting for our fingerprint report!" I called as Starr charged across the yard to Miss Retzyl.

"That's sweet," Attila said as Starr hugged Miss Retzyl.

"Gross," Harm and I replied in unison.

Attila smirked. "I don't think it's gross at all. Who are you going to The Bash with, Mo?" she asked, glancing at Harm. "Or can't you get a date?"

A date?

I looked at Dale. Sal moved a half step closer to him. Harm crossed his arms.

"Mo can go with anybody she wants to, except me," Dale said as Thes wandered by, staring at the clouds.

"Really?" Attila leered.

"That's right, Braces Breath," I said. "I didn't mention it earlier because I didn't want to break any hearts, but

I'm going with Thes," I said, giving him a Back Me Up Or I'll Kill You Look.

Harm turned and sauntered away.

The blood left Thes's freckled face. "Right, Thes?"

Thes worked his mouth like a fish tossed on the creek bank. "Yes, honey bunny," he croaked.

Miss Retzyl stormed toward us as water laced with candy wrappers surged out of the front door and swirled down the steps.

I stepped forward. "On behalf of the sixth grade, I'd like to say that was maybe the most memorable history class ever. Thank you, Miss Retzyl."

"Be quiet, Mo," she replied.

She stared at the Exums. Jake and Jimmy buttoned their suit coats and stepped forward, smiling like nervous jack-o'-lanterns. Her gaze lingered where their eyebrows used to be.

"Class dismissed until further notice," she said. "Your history reports are due October 24, regardless. Double-spaced and footnoted." She spun and walked away.

Perfect! Extra time to get our fingerprint report from Joe Starr.

The Exum twins unbuttoned their coats and high-fived.

"See you at The Bash," I shouted. "Remember: On the Verge, eight p.m.! Don't forget to cheer!"

Chapter 38
Good News

The day of The Bash started nice and exploded into perfection around 10:00 a.m. when Lavender walked through the café door. "Good news," he said, smiling at Miss Lana, the Colonel, and me. "Skeeter thinks she found a buyer for the Duesenberg. The town's problems are practically solved."

Miss Lana shrieked, threw her dishtowel in the air, and hurled herself into Lavender's arms. As Lavender laughed and spun her around, a tsunami of jealousy swept me under.

"Are you sure?" Miss Lana asked as he let her go.

"Almost," he said. "That old Duesenberg not only looks gorgeous, she purrs like she means it. Skeeter's still firming up the details and Sal's working on the math, but it looks like Miss Thornton's financial problems are in her rearview mirror and fading fast."

I looked at the Colonel. "So we can keep the inn?" I asked.

He untied his apron. "Maybe," he said. "Let's see what happens."

I smiled at Lavender. "I guess you'll be looking for a racecar soon," I told him.

"Already looking. When I find a good prospect, I want you and Dale to take a look. I always value the opinions of my official advisors."

An official advisor? Me?

"You're on," I said.

We closed the café and carted refreshments to the inn one carload at a time. Lavender's news put a snap in Grandmother Miss Lacy's step and a crack in her whip. Noon found her directing her troops around the pavilion like a blue-haired Napoleon.

"Set these tables for refreshments," she ordered, checking her clipboard. "And we'll want chairs and small tables around the dance floor. We'll set up the buffet here," she said, pointing. "White tablecloths, please. And candles. Everyone looks better in candlelight."

"It's good to have her back," Dale whispered, struggling by with a couple of folding chairs. "I just hope she doesn't work us to death."

She almost did.

Around four o'clock she put her clipboard down and beamed. "Excellent job," she told us. "As Lana would say, we've set the stage. Go home. Rest. I look forward to seeing each of you tonight. Job well done!"

We scattered before she could find something else to decorate.

"Miss Lana says I got to move Cleo away from the inn's porch," Dale said. "You want to come?"

I shook my head. "I got to get ready," I said, grabbing my bike. "I want to look good for Miss Lana. And Dale, don't worry about tonight. You and Harm sound great."

Minutes later I charged through our front door. "Hey Colonel," I said, blasting into the living room. He sat on Miss Lana's Victorian sofa, his hands on his knees, his back stiff. "Is Miss Lana here? I want to ask her about a cure for stage fright, in case Harm needs one."

"Lana's in her suite, finger-curling Jean Harlow," he said, his voice dull. "I'm sure she'd be delighted to see you."

I stared at his scraggly bow tie. "Is that your Skeeter-Bay tux, sir?"

He sighed. "It is. Lana has many wonderful talents. Estimating isn't one of them." He stood up. His coat billowed on his lean frame. The trousers showed two inches of ankle.

The clock on the mantel ticked. "Sal's mama does alterations," I told him.

"Thank you, Soldier, but it's too late." He sighed again. The Colonel's spit and polish. He likes us to look good in a crowd.

Poor Colonel. Adjusting to memories of a lost life is hard. Adjusting in a bad-fitting tux seemed cruel and unusual. "At least you won't be alone, sir," I said. "I'm opting for a vintage costume too. It's hideous, but if anybody gives me grief, I got my karate skills to fall back on. Mary Janes can be formidable weapons on the right feet."

"That reminds me." He crossed to his duffel bag and slid out a shoe box. "I saw these in Winston-Salem, and thought you might like them."

I opened the box.

A pair of red-and-yellow plaid Mary Janes peeked out of orange tissue.

"They're perfect," I said, kicking off my plaid sneakers and slipping them on. I hugged him long and hard. He felt like angle iron, and smelled like somebody else's mothballs. "I just want to mention, sir, you look better in dress blues than anybody I ever seen. And since it turns out you never were actually in the military, your old uniform is costuming. Sort of." His brown eyes snapped to attention. "Excuse me, I got to get dressed," I said, and headed for my flat.

Miss Lana had laid the vintage outfit across my bed.

At least I have my signature plaid shoes, I thought. I picked up a note stilettoed to the jacket with Miss Lana's hat pin:

> *Never forget Bill's advice, sugar: "To thine own*
> *self be true." Wear what you like best. I'll love*
> *you in whatever you choose.*
> *Lana.*

To thine own self be true? That's the Shakespeare quote she meant?

I looked again. Suddenly the outfit didn't look so bad.

White polka dots on soft navy fabric. A skirt whose shirred waist somehow created the illusion of a waistline. A neat white blouse and ultra-cool navy bolero, something a matador might wear. Nellie would like these clothes, I thought.

I dressed, and knocked on Miss Lana's door. "Come in," she called, and turned to look at me. "You're as beautiful as I knew you'd be," she told me, her eyes glistening. She looked at my shoes and laughed. "One hundred percent Mo."

On my way out I detoured by my desk, snagged Volume 6, and dashed off a letter to leave on Nellie's piano.

Nellie Blake, Ghost
The Tupelo Inn
Tupelo Landing, NC

Dear Nellie,

Are you still here? If so, you are cordially invited to a dance tonight, at the Tupelo Inn pavilion. I'm going 1938 cool.

Dale and Harm will sing. Your friends Lacy Thornton and Red Baker will be there. So will Myrt Little—enough said.

The honor of your presence is requested.

Yours truly,

Miss Moses LoBeau, Esquire

PS: Sometimes you have to leave home to find home. I did.

Chapter 39
The Bash

"Wow, Mo," Dale said as I crossed the pavilion a couple hours later. "You look great." It was true: Even my hair had tamed down good.

"Thanks," I said. "You too." Dale's bash ensemble looked suspiciously like his funeral ensemble: black pants, black shirt, black tie. He'd styled his blond hair up in front, like Lavender. "What's that?" I asked, glancing at the suit bag slung over his shoulder.

"A surprise. We'll need about fifteen minutes before we go on," he said, hanging the bag on a corner post as Queen Elizabeth wandered by in a sequined collar.

"What surprise?" I demanded. "As your manager, I got to know."

"You'll see," he said, opening his guitar case and grabbing his guitar. Photos stared up at me from the bottom of the case. My old school photo, a snapshot of Queen Elizabeth, the family photo from Miss Rose's piano—him, Miss Rose, and Mr. Macon. Only he'd taped the photo of Lavender and the Colonel over Mr. Macon.

"I brought them for good luck," he explained, following my gaze. He placed his guitar in the case as Lavender walked up with a bag of ice. Lavender cleans up better than anybody I know. I grabbed my camera. *Click.*

"You two look great," he said. "Where's Mama?"

"She's not coming," Dale said.

Not coming? Lavender looked surprised as I felt. "Is she sick?"

"No. It's okay," he lied, adjusting Queen Elizabeth's collar. "She's heard us sing plenty at home." Dale don't lie good. "I think she wishes she had a date," he added.

Lavender winced. "Yeah, she probably does," he said, dropping the ice to loosen it up. I rushed to hold the cooler steady. "Thanks Mo. Mama's proud of you, Dale, whether she's here or not. I am too."

"I know," Dale said.

Lavender dumped the ice, and spanked the wet off his hands. "Listen Dale, I want you to dance with everybody you can tonight. Ask any girl old enough to walk, any lady who can get out on the floor without a walker, and every female in between—except Anna Celeste."

"But Sal and me are meeting up in a few minutes."

"Dance the first dance with Sal and dance with her most of the night. She'll understand if you explain it to her. Ladies love gentlemen, little brother. Trust me."

"Okay," Dale said, looking doubtful. "But if Sal kills me, it's on you."

"Deal," he said, and winked at me. "Don't forget our dance, Mo."

Forget our dance? Is he mad?

"I wore my dancing shoes," I said, and he hurried away.

The cars started grumbling up the inn's drive just after sunset. Tinks and Sam handled parking. Miss Lana, in her Jean Harlow wig and shimmering party dress, met the guests at the door while Dale and me kept the pavilion punch flowing. The Colonel strode up handsome and confident in his dress blues, his hat tucked smartly beneath his arm.

"My goodness," Mayor Little said, taking a cup of punch and smoothing his ruffled shirt. "I've never seen us looking so elegant. Did you bring your camera?" he asked, straightening his ice-blue bow tie. He held out his glass, turned his head, and fake laughed. *Click.*

He waggled his fingers at Attila's mom. "I'm sure the media will want copies," he said as she minced over in her beige dress.

"Good evening, Mr. Mayor," Mrs. Simpson said. Her gaze swept me head to toe, lingering on my plaid Mary Janes. "And Mo, don't you look . . . comfortable. Have you seen Anna Celeste? She said she was coming with Sal."

I looked at the archway. There stood Attila—with Harm Crenshaw!

"No," Dale whispered. "Harm's gone over to the other side."

Mrs. Simpson's hand went to her pearls. "But isn't that . . . Red Baker's grandson?"

"Spittin' image," I said. *Click.*

Harm and Attila rolled toward us. Harm looked sharp in his usual black pants, plus Mr. Red's crisp white auction shirt and red bow tie. Attila looked frilly. "Mother," she said, "this is my friend Harmond Crenshaw. Harm? My mother, Betsy Simpson."

Harm grinned wide as Texas.

Mrs. Simpson stared a long, chilly moment. "Harm," she said. If her voice went any colder, the punch bowl would freeze solid. *Click.*

"There's Daddy," Attila said, leading Harm away.

I smiled at Mrs. Simpson. "They look nice together, don't they?" I said, cranking my film forward. "I hope they name their first child after me. Mo's a name that works for a boy or a girl. Refreshment?" I asked as Dale ladled a cup of punch.

Mrs. Simpson spun and walked away.

"How did that train wreck happen?" Dale muttered, staring after Harm and Attila.

"No clue," I said, unfocusing my eyes to scan the crowd. No sign of Nellie. Not yet.

The crowd seemed to breathe as townsfolk flowed in and out. "Wow," Dale whispered as Miss Retsyl walked up. "Why's she wasting time on us?" I could see his point. With her hair up and her long dress sparkling, she could have been going to the Country Music Awards.

"There's Myrt Little," I said, peering through a flock of preening Azalea Women.

Mrs. Little perched at the edge of the crowd like a vulture with a new perm. I unfocused my eyes and scanned. Still no Nellie.

Dale and me waved as Hannah Greene and her sister paused in the archway with the Exums. "Don't stare at the Exums' eyebrows," I added as the boys plowed toward us like a couple of tugboats in brown suits.

"Four cups of punch," Jake said. "We came with girls." I filled their cups, trying to ignore the wobbly black arcs sketched high on their foreheads.

"Nice face art," Dale said, very smooth. "Did you use Magic Markers?"

"Sharpies," Jimmy said.

Jake spun to look at Hannah. "The girls are getting away," he said, and they grabbed their punch and dove back into the crowd.

"Salamander's here," Dale said, dropping his ladle. I

waved at Sal, who'd gone Extreme Strategic Ruffles. She looked like a glittery bottle brush.

"Hey, Thes, your turn!" Dale shouted, pointing to the punch bowl. Thes, who stood at the pavilion's edge watching clouds drift across the moon, smoothed his orange hair and trotted toward me as Lavender walked by with a pretty auburn-haired woman. I did a double take. "Hey, that's not a big-haired twin."

"No," Thes said. "That's Miss Retzyl's little sister, from Winston-Salem."

My heart folded its wings and plunged into a screaming nosedive.

Imported competition? Is that fair?

As I struggled to regain my legendary poise, the evening's next Catastrophe Couple stepped into the archway. "Rat Face," I said as broad-shouldered Flick Crenshaw stepped up beside her. "What's she doing here?"

She scurried to the refreshment table.

"You again," Rat Face said, glaring at me. "Where's Lacy Thornton?"

The Colonel stepped from the crowd. If Rat Face had been a Chihuahua, she would have growled. "Thes," he said, "Skeeter's having trouble with the sound system. Could you give her a hand?" he asked, and Thes hurried away. "Miss Filch," he continued, his voice a velvet-draped dagger. "To what do we owe the . . . honor?"

"Where's Lacy?" she demanded, her beady eyes roving the crowd. Across the way, Harm and Lavender started toward us. "I want to make sure she hasn't forgotten our little agreement. And we want to admire our property."

"Admire it now because you'll never see it again," the Colonel said, tugging an envelope from his inside pocket. "A certified check for the inn's mortgage. Paid in full."

She stamped her foot. "What? But that's not possible."

He slipped the envelope in his pocket. "The possible shocks me every day, Miss Filch. We'll see you November first, as agreed," he said as Lavender and Harm stepped up beside him. "I believe that concludes our business."

Dale rocketed up. "What's going on?" he asked. "What's she doing here?"

"Still hanging with these losers, Harm?" Flick asked. "I'd move up if I were you."

Harm stared back steady and cool. "You never did have good taste in friends, Flick." Harm didn't look scared anymore. Or angry. In fact, he looked sure as the wind setting Miss Lana's lanterns swaying.

Flick grabbed Harm's shirt and dragged Harm toward him. "You little . . ."

"Leave Harm alone, Flick," I said, "or you got me and Dale to deal with."

"And me," Lavender said.

"And most of Tupelo Landing," the Colonel added, "including me."

Flick opened his hand finger by finger, and patted Harm's shirt back into place, a trace of sneer haunting his lips. "Good riddance, then." He turned to Lavender. "As for you, we'll settle things on the racetrack."

"I don't settle things on a racetrack," Lavender said. True. There's not a revenge bone in Lavender's body. Dale's neither. Fortunately I got enough for all of us.

"That's right, carrion breath," I said. "But Lavender will be back—soon. We'll blow you off the track. Dale and me are working honorary pit crew," I added. The last was more of a pre-truth than a lie. We've timed laps before.

Flick grabbed Rat Face's bony elbow. "Let's dump these low-lifes."

"One more thing," the Colonel said, his dark eyes glinting. "Miss Filch, you might like to know I've recommended you to your boss."

A recommendation? For her?

"Sir," I whispered, "is your amnesia back?"

He ignored me. "I'm sure your boss will be impressed with your creative use of bank records, Miss Filch, not to mention your stalking and badgering a customer." Her eyes flew wide. "I've never seen a bank employee so skilled at taking property for her own," he said. "I'm sure your actions matched bank policy, didn't they?"

Dale frowned. "It sounds bad when you say it out loud, Colonel." He looked at Rat Face. "She could get fired."

She kept her eyes on the Colonel, quivering like a field mouse staring down a wolf. For a minute I almost felt sorry for her. Almost. I showed her my tongue.

She hissed, and burrowed into the night.

As Flick took off behind her, Lavender glanced at Harm. "Don't worry, you'll see him again," he said. "Life has a way of circling back around until things get finished."

"Spoken like a true racecar driver," the Colonel murmured.

Harm jammed his hands in his pockets and watched his brother walk away.

Moments later, Skeeter tapped the mic. "Testing, testing. Almost ready, Colonel."

"Nice move bringing that check, sir," I said. "Are you really back to being an attorney? I only ask because I hate change unless it's my idea. I need time to over-prepare."

"That wasn't a check, Soldier, it was our utility bill. I scribbled my opening remarks on it last night. But we'll have the check in time and yes, I'm back to being an attorney, of sorts."

He sighed. "I'd better get this show on the road. I don't know how I let Lana talk me into these things," he said, glancing her way.

Miss Lana stood in a group of friends, her head thrown back as she laughed. The lanterns' soft light played against her face. "She looks beautiful," I said. "Maybe it's the dress. Or the wig."

"No," he said, his eyes going soft. "It's one hundred percent Lana."

"Colonel," Skeeter called, putting her headset on. "It's time."

He nodded. "I'd hoped Miss Thornton would show up before I . . ." He chuckled. "Ah-ha!" he boomed, looking toward the trail.

The crowd turned to follow his gaze and fell silent. The frogs' song spiraled around us, and water lapped against the pilings. "What's wrong?" Dale said, looking around. "Are the police here already?"

Two figures made their way through the shadows at the pavilion's edge, to the archway. "It's Grandmother Miss Lacy," I said as she stepped into the light in a midnight-blue dress, dark blue sequins flowing across her shoulders like a stole of stars.

The figure behind her stepped into the light and the crowd gasped. The Colonel grinned. "And Red Baker. In a tux—one that fits."

Mr. Red adjusted his bow tie and held out his arm. Grandmother Miss Lacy hooked her hand in his elbow. An Azalea Woman dropped her cup.

"Red, you've managed to arrive with the most beautiful woman in town," the Colonel said. "Miss Thornton, will you join me onstage?"

Contrary to popular belief, the Colonel can be charming. And kind.

She smiled and shook her head. A small spotlight tracked the Colonel to the microphone. "Cut that light," he ordered, squinting. "You're blinding me."

"So much for Prince Charming," Thes said, taking his place at the punch bowl.

"Ladies and gentlemen," the Colonel said. "I welcome you to Tupelo Landing's 250th Anniversary Bash. And now, the man who promised to save my life by emceeing this event: Mayor Clayburn Little."

Mayor Little bounded onstage. "Hello, fellow citizens," he said. "Eat hearty, dance much, stay long. Before we get started, Reverend Thompson will offer a prayer."

"Brace yourself for the Shy Stampede," I whispered as he started his prayer.

"The what?" Thes whispered.

"Amen," Reverend Thompson said.

"Dance!" the mayor commanded, jumping onto the

dance floor as Skeeter revved up the sound system. As Mayor Little began his electric slide, every shy person within earshot charged the refreshments table, filling plates like they were filling lifeboats on a sinking ship.

Thes cleared his throat. "Want to dance?" he asked. "I'm not very good."

"Me either," I said as Dale and Sal spun by. "We need cover." After a few songs the dance floor filled, and we stepped onto its edge. Thes's hand felt like a feverish fish. "Here goes nothing," he mumbled.

We started out jerky, but when nobody laughed I relaxed. "We look good," Thes said, snigging my foot. "Get ready to twirl."

Before long, we all got good. Lavender looked like a movie star, dancing with Miss Retzyl's sister, and then with every woman and pre-woman there—including me. "You look beautiful, Mo," he said, holding out his hand. "Dance with me?"

Even the stars smiled.

Dale danced with everybody too, just like Lavender told him. Once he even struggled by with Mrs. Little. I was watching Sal wiggle past with Jake Exum when someone tapped my shoulder. Harm Crenshaw. "Oh. It's you," I said.

"Yeah, it's me." He held out his hand. "Dance?"

Me? Dance with Harm? I grinned. "Where's Attila?"

"Who knows? I didn't mean to come with her, really. It's just that you asked Thes, and Sal asked Dale. And I hated to be the only one coming alone. Attila asked me and I thought it would be fun to terrify her mom . . . Anyway, she's not with me now," he said as Grandmother Miss Lacy and Mr. Red tangoed past. "I thought Mrs. Simpson would cough up her pedicure when she saw me. So?" he said, jerking his head toward the dance floor. "How about it?"

Somebody shoved me from behind. "Hey!" I shouted, stumbling forward. Out of the corner of my eye I saw Grandmother Miss Lacy dance away, laughing. Harm grabbed my hand. "Come on, Ghost Girl. Give me a chance."

It's hard to dance and glare at Grandmother Miss Lacy at the same time, but it can be done. Not long, though. "Wow," I said as we skimmed along, "you're good."

"You're not bad yourself, once you escape Thes," he said. "Here's an analogy for you. Thes is to dance as fish is to ski."

I laughed as the song ended and Skeeter pulled the microphone close to her lips. "And now, our last number before special guest stars On the Verge."

Already?

Harm dropped my hand. His face went green. "Where's Dale?"

"Over there," I said, pointing to the stage. Dale grabbed his suit bag and shot out of sight. "Get ready. I'll introduce you slow. And Harm? You guys sound good," I said. "Really good."

Chapter 40
On the Verge

As the last strains of "Thriller" died away, I stepped up to the mic. Skeeter darted forward to lower it.

"Thanks, Skeeter," I said, stalling. "Great music selection. Let's hear it for Skeeter!" The crowd clapped. "Ladies and gentlemen," I said, "I know the sixth grade's excited about what's coming up next, and I feel sure the rest of you will be too."

"Psssst," Sal said from the side of the stage. She put the tips of her fingers together and pulled her hands apart like pulling taffy. "Talk slow," she whispered.

I nodded as Skeeter set up a second mic. "I'm sure we're all dying to hear On the Verge."

"Don't say dying," Dale stage-whispered from somewhere behind me.

"But before they get out here, I'd like to congratulate Detective Joe Starr for landing Miss Retzyl. Where's Detective Starr?" I peered out over the crowd. Starr waved. He has dimples when embarrassed. Interesting. "Way to reel her in, Joe," I said. "The entire sixth grade wishes you luck. Feel free to come to us for advice. And thanks for that fingerprint report. Dale and me appreciate it."

Sal waved her arms over her head. This time she gave me two thumbs-up.

I cued Buddha to spin the lights around the stage and went into my Prepared Remarks, spreading my voice out like a roller derby announcer. "Tonight's duo promises to shock and thrill. They got voices smooth as butter and moves sweet as Miss Lana's blackberry jam. Ladies and gentlemen, the pride of the sixth grade . . ." I pointed side stage. "ON . . . THE . . . VERGE!"

The sixth grade roared.

I backed into the shadows as Dale and Harm rushed onstage and skidded up to their mics, both of them sleek in tuck-wasted, broad-shouldered 1930s suits. They tilted their fedoras low over their eyes and the spotlight skinnied in on Harm as he stepped up to his mic. "Helloooo Tupelo Landing," he crooned.

"Wow," I told Sal. "Looks like he got over his nerves."

She beamed. "Mama's suits look just right on them."

"I'm Harm and he's Dale, and we're On the Verge of . . . well, something good, we hope. Our first number's our three-chord version of the 1938 hit 'Boogie Woogie.' If you can't dance to this, you won't ever dance. Everybody get up," he said, clapping his hands as Dale started slapping out a boogie on his guitar. "That includes you, Gramps and Miss Thornton. Everybody dance."

The sixth grade careened onto the dance floor—dancing alone, dancing in pairs, dancing in clusters. The rest of Tupelo Landing swept around them, jostling and swinging. Thes hopped through the crowd like a berserk robot, twisting and turning nearly in time to the music. Hannah, whose sister had gone AWOL, danced with both Exums until Sal skidded onto the dance floor to take up the slack.

The Colonel and Miss Lana swayed by, the Colonel stiff and self-conscious, Miss Lana practically floating. Queen Elizabeth flew from dancer to dancer—a tornado of sequins and fur.

Dale and Harm sang and played and danced like the music had moved in and set up housekeeping in their souls, their voices clear and strong, their rhythm wild and true. They bridged into another song, and another, and another.

Twice I caught a glimpse of pink. The first turned out to be a scarf. The second, a sweater.

At the end of their set, Dale and Harm bowed and Tupelo Landing went nuts.

I rushed onstage. "On the Verge," I shouted above the hubbub.

"Encore," Miss Retzyl shouted, clapping her hands

over her head. "Encore!" The crowd took up the chant.

"Play an old-fashioned neon cha-cha," the mayor shouted, trying to herd the Azalea Women into a line. Dale grinned at Harm and stepped up to the microphone.

"Thank you all for clapping," Dale said, breathing heavy. "We were afraid you might not." He froze, his eyes on the archway. His first-grade smile broke across his flushed face. "Hey, Mama," he said, his voice soft. "You look wonderful."

We all turned.

Miss Rose stood in the archway, strong and elegant, and every inch herself. I ran to her as the crowd turned back to Dale. "Miss Rose," I said. "I'm glad you came."

She hugged me so strong, I almost didn't feel her tremble. "Thanks, Mo. It's never too late to make a better decision."

I took her hand. No ring.

Onstage, Dale looked at Harm. "This one's slower," he said, "so we can all catch our breath." He took a minute to tune his guitar while the crowd settled down. He hesitated. "I wrote this song for Nellie Blake. Nellie, I hope you like it," he said, looking into the night. He gave the rest of us a shy smile. "I hope you all like it too. Especially you, Mama. And you, Mr. Red. It's called 'Nellie's Waltz.'"

He played a sweet, simple intro and he and Harm stepped to their mics, their voices twining like wood smoke over the Colonel's campfire.

> *Waltz across lifetimes with me*
> *Spin through the stars in my arms*
> *When I look in your eyes*
> *I know love never dies*
> *Please waltz through these lifetimes with me.*

> *Drift down life's river with me*
> *Inhale the moon's secret charms*
> *We know love never dies*
> *as we say our good-byes*
> *Please waltz beyond heartbreak with me.*

The town whirled through "Nellie's Waltz," feet whispering, hearts floating until finally the night stood balanced on the last clear sound of Dale's voice. For a moment I heard only the slap of endless river and the sigh of wandering wind.

Then I smelled rosemary.

Queen Elizabeth sneezed.

Dale and Harm bowed, and the town burst into applause. "Bravo," Mayor Little called. "Bravo, boys!"

The crowd took up the chant, pressing close. I jumped onto the stage and grabbed the mic. "On the Verge," I shouted, and Harm and Dale bowed. "Tupelo Landing's finest!"

They took another bow, and a woman screamed. Then another.

"Is it Nellie? Is she here?" Dale whispered.

The crowd flapped and scattered like terrified chickens as Dale's mule Cleo staggered onto the dance floor, flattened her ears, and trumpeted a ragged bray. She wobbled into a patch of grass at river's edge, sat on her haunches like a dog, and keeled over in the grass.

"Cleo!" Dale tore across the pavilion and leaped the rail. I sprinted after him.

"Is she dead?" I asked.

He looked at me, his face ashen. "Dead drunk. But how?"

Good question.

"Mr. Red's still," I whispered, and he nodded. "We got our chance to pay Harm back for being Ghost Bait. But we better find that still before Starr does."

I looked up. The entire town lined the pavilion's rail, staring. "Skeeter, can you get the music going?" Starr asked, leaping nimbly from the dance floor. "Everybody go back to your business."

"Don't sign anything, Dale," Skeeter called as Michael Jackson's "Thriller" hit the air again. "Let's see that moonwalk, Mayor Little," she sang out over the sound system.

My plaid Mary Janes squished. How could we explain Cleo without tipping Starr off to Mr. Red's still? I stalled. "I accept full responsibility for Cleo's condition unless there's a penalty for contributing to the delinquency of a mule, in which case I had nothing to do with this," I said.

"Good," Dale whispered.

Starr clicked his pen. "Go ahead."

I took a moment. Miss Lana, who possesses world-class ad-lib skills, says the word *if* skirts the truth graceful as an ice skater skirts thin ice. I went for it. "*If* I recall, Anita Filch spiked the punch bowl early this evening."

"Really? When?" Dale asked. Dale ad-libs like a box turtle pole vaults.

"Also, *if* memory serves, I set the spiked punch aside and got a new bowl. It looks like Cleo got into the bad punch. I hope you'll go easy on her. We can get her into rehab *if* necessary. *If* I'm not mistaken, this is her first offense."

Dale nodded. "She's too sensitive to do time."

Starr jammed his pen in his pocket. "Keep her off the dance floor," he said. "I'll figure out how she got plastered myself—if I get over that load of *if*s you just served up."

Crud. He didn't buy it.

He climbed onto the dance floor and strode away.

I grabbed Dale's arm. "Dale, you moved Cleo today," I said, talking quiet and fast. "Where'd you put her?"

"In the meadow near Mr. Red's house."

The still must be close by. In the house? Ridiculous. The shed? No. The dog pen? Of course. "The brambles in the center of his stinking dog pen," I said. "His still was under our noses the whole time. Those dogs would keep anybody out."

I squinted across the pavilion, to Mr. Red's table. "We got to get to him before Starr figures it out."

Harm joined us as we threaded our way through the dancers. "We've found Mr. Red's still," I whispered. "But we got to hurry."

"You're busted, Mr. Red," Dale said, pulling a chair up beside Grandmother Miss Lacy. "A mule won't drink moonshine, but she'll eat corn mash dumped from a still. And you dumped yours in the meadow today, didn't you?" he asked, his voice accusing. "You were in too much of a hurry to haul it down to your pigs."

Mr. Red swallowed, bobbing his bow tie. "No idea what he's talking about, Lacy."

"We'll prove it," I said, pulling up a chair. "We'll follow Cleo's tracks to the mash, and your tracks to the still in your dog pen."

"The dog pen?" Harm said. "No wonder you didn't want me to mess with those dogs. Gramps, if Starr finds that still, you're really busted. And where does that leave us?"

Mr. Red looked away from him. Not a good sign.

"Dale and me been thinking," I continued.

"I haven't," Dale said quickly, "unless what she says next sounds good."

I ignored him. "A faux still would be a good draw for the inn. A local history angle."

Grandmother Miss Lacy draped her arm across my shoulders. She smelled like powder and lemons. "A non-working still," she said, staring hat pins at Mr. Red. She placed a dollar on the table. "I'll buy that display, Red Baker, if it will keep you out of jail."

Red Baker looked at Harm, and then at the dollar bill. Then he locked eyes with Joe Starr. Starr sat watching us like a hawk watches a ditch bank at suppertime.

"Take the dollar," Harm said. I could almost feel the wind whistle through his heart.

"You can't pull the fur over Joe Starr's eyes," Dale warned.

"Wool," Harm and I said together as Detective Joe Starr headed for us.

"Mr. Baker," Starr said. "I'll start following Cleo's tracks tomorrow morning. If I find a still on your property, I'll turn you over to the Feds." He looked at Grandmother Miss Lacy. "I apologize in advance, Miss Thornton," he said, and walked away.

Chapter 41
We Say Our Good-byes

The party wound down hours later.

As the last guests straggled up the path with Mayor Little, Miss Lana yawned and surveyed the landslide of dirty cups and dishes. "Let's leave this happy mess for later," she said, hooking her arm in Miss Rose's. "Come on, Rose, I'll walk up with you."

"And I'll turn out the lights and walk with you," I told Grandmother Miss Lacy as Dale packed up his guitar.

Sal and Dale caught up with us halfway to the inn. "Did you dance with everybody?" Sal asked Dale, slipping her hand into his.

"Yes," he said, and then hesitated. "Well," he said, turning to look at the deserted pavilion. "Almost everybody. I'll catch up with you at the inn," he told her.

Sal shrugged. Dale handed me his guitar and trotted back down the path. "What on earth?" Grandmother Miss Lacy murmured.

"I think I know," I said. I led her to a bench in the crook of the path.

Harm stepped from the shadows. "Hey, Miss Thornton," he said. "Where's Gramps?"

"Red?" she asked, settling onto the bench. "Didn't he tell you?" Harm shook his head, his dark hair falling across his forehead. "He's helping the Colonel dismantle my new still," she replied, stifling a yawn.

"He went for it?"

"Hook, line, and sinker," she said. She looked at Harm. "You're the reason he agreed, Harm Crenshaw. Red could do the time, but he can't stand to think of you without a home."

"Son of a gun," Harm muttered.

Below us, Dale strolled to the center of the moonlit dance floor, bowed, and opened his arms. He tilted his head back and sang to the stars.

"Waltz across lifetimes with me.

Spin through the stars in my arms . . ."

"'Nellie's Waltz,'" Grandmother Miss Lacy said. "Nellie would have given the world to dance that dance with Red. Can you see her, Mo?"

"No," I said, my heart tumbling. "I'm sorry. I can't."

"There," Harm said, pointing. "Across the floor from Dale." He was right. A delicate pink mist floated up from the river, onto the dance floor.

"I still don't see her," Grandmother Miss Lacy said.

Harm smoothed his hair. "Maybe Lavender's right.

Maybe life does have a way of circling back around," he murmured. He drew a give-me-courage breath, and jogged down the path onto the dance floor. *Click.*

Dale stepped aside, still singing, as Harm looked at Nellie and opened his arms.

Maybe it was Harm's 1930s suit, or the moonlight, or the rhythm of the waltz. But time folded back on itself soft and easy as Miss Lana's silk scarf, and a dark-haired girl swept across the dance floor in his arms.

"I do see her," Grandmother Miss Lacy said, her voice full of tears.

Harm and Nellie danced until the music floated away on Dale's last crystal note. Harm bowed. Nellie smiled and looked up at us.

Grandmother Miss Lacy held out her hand and opened it, letting go. "Good-bye, dear friend," she whispered.

"I love you," Nellie mouthed, lowering her hand to her heart. Nellie's eyes met mine and she stood there, waiting.

I smiled. "That's what she wanted Mr. Red to tell you the night she died," I told Grandmother Miss Lacy. "I love you."

Nellie smiled like a blaze of sunshine, and she was gone. Truly gone.

I knew it to my bones.

Harm and Dale strolled from the pavilion, side by side. "Case closed," I whispered, and squeezed Grandmother Miss Lacy's hand.

> Dear Upstream Mother,
> Grandmother Miss Lacy's right. There's all kinds of ghosts in this world.
> There's Nellie Blake, who waited for her friends to understand and forgive, and say their good-byes. Ghosts of guilt and ghosts of sorrow.
> The ghost of romance between Miss Lana and the Colonel. The ghost of Dale's daddy fading away detail-by-detail—out of the living room, out of Dale's room, out of the house.
> Last but not least, there's a ghost of a chance. Which is exactly what Dale and me got of passing history if I can't get our history paper footnoted right for Monday morning.
> Wish me luck.
> Mo

Acknowledgments

So many people had a hand in the creation of this book!

Thank you, Rodney L. Beasley—my first reader and intrepid fellow traveler in life—for your love, your support, and your unfailing sense of direction.

My gratitude goes to everyone who offered input on the early drafts of this book, especially Allison Turnage, Claire Pittman, Mamie Dixon, Eileen LaGreca, Miriam Taylor Bailey, and Patsy Baker O'Leary and her creative writing class.

Thank you, Eileen LaGreca, for the fantastic map!

Thanks to my agent, Melissa Jeglinski of The Knight Agency.

Thanks, Alisha Niehaus, for first welcoming Mo and Dale to Penguin. Thanks, Mary Jo Floyd, for everything. And thanks, Gilbert Ford, for the knock-out covers.

Hats off to the scores of wonderful people at Penguin Books for Young Readers who poured time and talent into this book. In particular, thank you, Lauri